RESURGENCE

Other titles by S. Usher Evans

THE RAZIA SERIES
Double Life
Alliances
Conviction
Fusion

Empath

THE MADION WAR TRILOGY
The Island
The Chasm
The Union

THE LEXIE CARRIGAN CHRONICLES
Spells and Sorcery
Magic and Mayhem
Dawn and Devilry
Illusion and Indemnity

RESURGENCE

DEMON SPRING TRILOGY
Book One

S. USHER EVANS

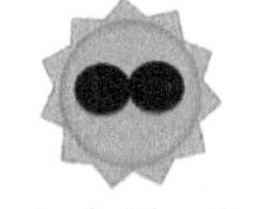

Sun's Golden Ray
Publishing
Pensacola, FL

DEMON SPRING TRILOGY
Resurgence
Revival
Redemption

DEMON FALL TRILOGY
Reawakening
Resurrection
Reclamation

Demon Art by Ashley Gonzales, Zeefa Studio
Line Editing by Danielle Fine, By Definition Editing

Sun's Golden Ray Publishing
Pensacola, FL
www.sgr-pub.com

For ordering information, please visit
www.sgr-pub.com/orders

DEDICATION

To Nicole
A warrior woman
Who can slay any demon

CONTENTS

DEMONOLOGY

The following is a brief introduction to the five kinds of demons found in the human world. The International Coalition for Demon Management (ICDM) is charged with protecting humans from unwanted demonic transformation, but we can't do it alone.

Learn the signs of demonic coercion and don't become a victim.

ATHTAR

First Seen: 1500 BC, Syria
Magical Element: Void
Original Sin: Pride
Original Demon: Bael

The oldest and rarest demons, Athtars live in the Underworld and appear during Demon Spring. They have the ability to manipulate time and space. If you encounter an athtar demon, seek shelter as quickly as possible, and alert your local US Division office.

ELOKO

First Seen: 400 AD, Democratic Republic of the Congo
Magical Element: Earth
Original Sin: Envy
Original Demon: Biloko

Eloko demons use the sound of a bell to hypnotize their victims into a false sense of security. If you think an eloko is trying to coerce you, stomp your feet or clap your hands to disrupt the magic, then run away.

KAPPA

First Seen: 600 BC, Japan
Magical Element: Water
Original Sin: Greed
Original Demon: Mizuchi

Kappas mostly live near water, and will create an illusion of a house or structure. When the victim enters the illusion, it will break and the human will be drawn underwater, given the option to transform or drown. When near bodies of water, familiarize yourself with existing structures, and watch for others coming in and out.

LILIN

First Seen: 200 AD, Germany
Magical Element: Air
Original Sin: Lust
Original Demon: Freyja

Lilins use a mixture of pheromones and glamour (illusion) to lure humans into sexual intercourse, then transformation. If you think a lilin is trying to coerce you, pinch yourself or think of something unsettling, then run away.

NOX

First Seen: 1400 AD, Mexico
Magical Element: Fire
Original Sin: Anger
Original Demon: Mot and Xo

Nox demons use the human's innate fear of demons to construct terrifying nightmares, and the human agrees to transform to cease them. To combat a nox demon, take a deep breath and remind yourself it's only a vision.

PROTECT YOURSELF

If you encounter any demon or supposed demon, contact your local US Division of the International Coalition for Demon Management right away to report the incident.

UNITED STATES DIVISION
INTERNATIONAL COALITION FOR DEMON MANAGEMENT

#demonspring

PROLOGUE

The night was still, except for a lone shadow with two swords strapped to her back. Blood marked a crimson trail behind her, the nick in her leg taking much longer than usual to heal. Overall, it had been a successful night, but she wasn't sure she moved as fast as she used to.

She stopped in front of a large metal door, lifted it just enough to slip underneath, then let it clang behind her. The small room contained an air mattress, some overturned boxes doubling as tables, and two cartons of half-eaten Chinese food. Off to the side was a utility sink with a few dirty dishes and a black duffel bag underneath.

After unstrapping her weapons, she set them against the sink, then peeled off her bloodstained clothes down to her white bra and underwear. Her fingertips brushed her bony ribcage, careful not to mess the ten dark marks along her left arm.

Stark naked, she crossed the room to a wall covered in the same black marks. Retrieving a marker from the floor, she carefully ticked off ten of them. Ten innocent lives saved that night. Too many to count remained.

She returned to the sink, turning the water on to begin the process of hand-laundering her clothes. A flash of silver in the mirror caught her attention.

A gray hair.

Mortality was a bitch. As was this stark reminder her time was running out.

CHAPTER ONE

Jack Grenard set a box of his office supplies down. The small, glass-enclosed office seemed cramped with two desks facing each other, but it would do. He wasn't sure what he'd been expecting on his first day back after a three-year hiatus from the Division, but so far, the slow pull of grief hadn't come. It would eventually, but for now he was too preoccupied with learning where the break room was and how the Atlanta office differed from the one in Washington, D.C. For one, there was only a tenth of the staff. For another, there were no memories here.

Except, of course, for the photo of their wedding day, found at the bottom of his personal effects. He cradled the frame in his hand, memories of how happy they'd been tainted by how their story would end.

A knock on the door drew his attention from the photo. Cam Macarro, Jack's partner of almost a decade—and best friend for even longer—stood in the doorway with a soft smile on her face. "Came to check on you."

Jack held up the framed photo. "Found this."

"Look at you two," she said, placing a hand on the small of his back and pointing to the figure of herself in the photo next to her sister. "And look at how skinny I was."

"You're still skinny," Jack said after a too-long pause. He put the photo down, ready to not look at it for a while.

The rest of the box contained his professional accolades—awards, photos of him with presidents and congressmen, and the photo with his father and grandfather on the day he'd graduated from the Academy for Demon Management in Denver. Mementos from a life that seemed a thousand years in the past.

"It was weird working cases without you," Cam said after a moment. "But I'm glad you're here. I think it'll be good for you to get back to work."

Jack had to chuckle at that. "Accounting wasn't real work?"

"You're not an accountant, Jack. You're a demon-killer. It's in your blood, same as mine."

That was an understatement. Jack's family had been involved in demon hunting since the first lilin arrived in Germany around 100 AD. Cam's family, too, could trace their lineage back to the Aztecs who'd battled the original nox demons in Mexico in the fifteenth century.

Jack smiled. "So, what are the cases like down here?"

She chuckled and took a seat at her desk across from his. "To be honest, there really isn't a lot to do. The demons are very…

southern," she said, dipping into the Charleston drawl favored by Jack's mother. "Most everyone in Atlanta has sworn fealty to the same lilin demon, so it's a pretty easy job."

"And you like that? What happened to All-Action-Cam?"

A smile curled onto her face. "Action doesn't get you promoted anymore. Now it's all about which demons vouch for your fairness and which Division leaders are gonna retire. I hear the bureau chief in Pensacola is getting up there in age."

"You're going to drag me down to Pensacola next?" Jack snorted. "Good thing I like the beach."

"As if I could ever think of getting promoted without my partner by my side. I'll make you deputy, at least. Deputy Director Jack Grenard."

"Director Cam Macarro," Jack replied, knowing full well Cam would be a director someday. "As much as I'd love to be your deputy, that means I'd have to implement all your crazy efficiency ideas. And you know as well as I do those never go the way you want them to."

"That was D.C. This is different."

"So you say."

They stared at each other for a moment, knowing full well how different it was going to be.

"Well, Jackie, are you ready to head to your first staff meeting?" Cam asked, breaking the awkward tension in the room. "I know how much you missed those."

Jack chuckled and grabbed a pen and pad from the drawers in his desk. "We had staff meetings in accounting."

"But they didn't involve how many heads got cut off, did they?"

"Sometimes they did."

She threaded her arm through Jack's. "I'm glad you're back."

———⬥———

Truth be told, Jack was itching to get back to helping people. After Sara's death, it had been an easy choice to walk away from demon-hunting. He'd thought a boring job would help dull the guilt and quell the nightmares. But all the lack of action had done was make things worse.

Cam had been asking him to join her in Atlanta ever since she'd transferred two years ago. She seemed to think they both would get "back to normal" as soon as they were up to their old tricks. For his sake, Jack hoped she was right, because he was starting to forget what normal felt like.

Cam led him into a Division-standard meeting room. Like everything in Atlanta so far, it was familiar, right down to the paintings on the wall. The logo for the International Coalition for Demon Management (ICDM), the overarching world governing body, hung prominently at the front of the room. The crest bore fifteen swords, representing the fifteen Council seats.

Jack tried to sit in one of the chairs lining the room, but Cam grabbed him by the wrist and forcibly sat him down next to her.

"I haven't earned a spot at the table," he whispered.

"Never stopped you before," Cam retorted

"All right, all right." A short Korean woman walked into the room—Deputy Director Patti Kim, if Jack had to guess. "Everyone take your seats. We've got a lot to cover today."

Cam cleared her throat and nodded at Jack.

"Yes, Macarro, I see him," Kim said. "Team, the world-renowned Jack Grenard has graced us with his presence after a three-year hiatus from active duty." The look she gave him was frosty. "We all hope your reputation is as sterling as Agent Macarro says."

Before Jack could answer, Cam did for him. "It is."

"Yes, well," Kim muttered. Cam had always walked a fine line between teacher's pet and teacher's thorn, and based on the way Kim was avoiding her gaze, Jack wagered that hadn't changed. "Demon activity in the southeast has been steady, although we've seen lilin spikes in Mobile and New Orleans as of late—"

"Mardi Gras?" Cam said.

The corner of Kim's mouth twitched. "Yes. That's our guess. We've dispatched a few agents down there to keep an eye on things."

Cam made a noise, and Jack nudged her gently. They were both thinking the same thing: less a spate of demon activity and more a paid vacation for a couple of demon-hunters.

"Sadly, the word from the higher-ups is that we'll have to keep our resources close to home this month. Seismologists are predicting Demon Spring will happen sometime in the next two to three months, and we've got to start our preparations."

Demon Spring. Jack had almost forgotten all about it.

Although hundreds of thousands of demons lived amongst the humans, there were still thousands more in the demonic realm. Once every four years, the barrier between two worlds grew thinner in areas with heavy earthquake activity. One lucky city then became ground zero for the influx of demons.

Jack and Cam had been sent to Los Angeles four years before, during the last event. While most demons who lived amongst humans still resembled them, Underworld demons were disfigured and grotesque after spending years in their own magic—and less inclined to spare human life. For Division resources, it was a feat to keep the human casualties at a minimum.

"I should've waited a few months to come back," Jack noted dryly under his breath.

"It's not Demon Spring without you, Jackie," Cam replied with a smirk.

"Headquarters has already started preparing. They've put together a task force to monitor the traditional breach sites." Kim turned to the PowerPoint behind her and zipped through the slides, landing on a map of the US. The map was sectioned into five pieces, with the southeast division skimming the bottom of Virginia and cutting Texas in half. Within the southeast, there were three red zones, areas where schisms had occurred in the past. Memphis was highlighted, as was the border between Tennessee and North Carolina and the entire state of South Carolina.

"My money's on Asia this year," Cam said. "We've never

been there. Could make a fun vacation."

"Might sit this one out," Jack said quietly.

"Like hell you are. I didn't drag you down to Atlanta to be my partner for us to sit things out."

"Macarro." Kim's sharp voice cut through their conversation. With a warning look, Kim went back to the presentation. "We have unconfirmed reports this year… Bael might make an appearance."

A shudder rippled through the room, and even Cam grew somber, although she said, "They say that every time."

"It's more than the usual chatter, I'm afraid. Headquarters wants us to be on our toes. I don't have to remind you what happened the last time Bael came to this world."

Jack had heard stories from his great-grandfather. The so-called King of the Demons had last appeared in Charleston during the summer of 1886. Thousands of humans dead, chaos across the southern half of the United States. It made the carnage he'd witnessed in Los Angeles look like a day at the park.

"I'm not saying we should panic," Kim said after nervous murmuring erupted in the room. "Just remain vigilant until the chaos dies down." She paused, flipping to the next slide with more information on what to do if Bael should show up. "We're hoping this will be a routine Demon Spring, so no need to worry about all this." Even so, the tension around her eyes was an unmistakable omen. "That's it for today. Please make sure to submit your timesheets on Thursday."

"We're all going to die. Don't forget to submit your

timesheet," Jack whispered to Cam, who chuckled.

"You know they hype us up every time," she said, although it sounded more for her own benefit than Jack's. "So, partner, what are your plans for the day?"

"Paperwork, then presumably unburying myself from emails. I haven't checked in over two weeks."

"Actually, Grenard, HR wants you to retake orientation this morning," Kim said. "You've been out of the field for a few years and they want to make sure you remember protocols."

"Or learn them in the first place," Cam muttered.

CHAPTER TWO

Jack felt like the oldest man in the room when he walked into the large meeting space. The attendees—new recruits probably fresh off the streets—couldn't have been older than nineteen or twenty. Most probably hadn't *seen* a demon, let alone fought one. Although most humans knew about demons and magic, the majority pretended it didn't exist—until a friend or family member was targeted. Then, they'd join the ranks of the demon hunters in whatever capacity they could with wide-eyed optimism.

The kids at orientation reminded Jack of the person he'd been. They were excited about all the good work they could do. It had been a long time since Jack had felt anything; even being back in this room was like seeing the ghost of the man who'd died on the living room floor with Sara.

A middle-aged black man walked into the room, carrying a

leather briefcase and a tired smile that told Jack he was growing weary of giving the same speech every week. But after a sip of coffee, the man perked up. He introduced himself as Agent Jones, and breezed through several slides about what the orientation would be covering, from administrative details like forms and timesheet submission deadlines to the history of the Division and demons themselves.

"Any Academy graduates in here today?" he asked, glancing at Jack when he raised his hand. "Ah, Grenard, right?"

Jack nodded as heads swiveled in his direction.

"Excellent, and a few others, too. I apologize. Some of this information will be rehashing what you already know. We'll begin, as always, with the origin of demons." He flipped to a slide with photos of cave drawings.

"How the first demons were created is subject to much anthropological and spiritual debate. Generally, though, we know that at least five early humans were trapped in what we call the demonic Underworld. There, it's said the humans corrupted the world with an evil miasma—a magical atmosphere of sorts— that both gave them supernatural powers and turned them into the monstrous creatures we know as demons."

Jones then displayed photos of a rather disturbing-looking nox demon with a muzzle, razor-sharp teeth, and blood-red eyes. A boy in the front row shivered as a girl raised her hand.

"Excuse me, Agent Jones, but every demon I've seen looks human."

"Yes, yes, I'm getting to that," Jones replied with a tight

smile. "Around 1400 BC, the first demon, known as Bael, emerged in ancient Syria. In that first Demon Spring, thousands of humans were slaughtered, most in a single village. Every four years, Bael would reappear and slaughter more humans. Sometime around 600 BC, the first kappa demon, Mizuchi, arrived in Japan. But unlike Bael, who simply killed humans, Mizuchi began transforming humans into kappa demons like him."

He flipped the slide to an old canvas painting from Japan, showing men, women, and children drowning in a lake and a froggish-looking creature standing above them.

"When the Spring ended, some demons remained amongst the humans. Many of those early demons died from the lack of demonic magic. Others, however, realized they could live amongst the humans if they spawned—or created more demons. When a demon transforms a human, that neophyte becomes a source of miasma and power for the maker. The more demons created from a single maker, the more powerful that maker becomes. And if their spawn create spawn, who then create more spawn..." He chuckled. "That's how you get a lilin demon like Nunzia, our local demon lord in Atlanta.

"There are five types of demons," Jones continued. "Bael is an athtar, or a void demon. Kappas, water demons, emerged in Japan in the sixth century BC, as I've said. There are also lilins, lust demons who appeared in Germany in 200 AD, and the eloko demons who arrived in the Congo in 400 AD. They use bells to hypnotize. The last demon type to appear is the noxes, the shapeshifting fear demons, around 1500 AD in Mexico.

"Although demon hunters had been in existence since the dawn of civilization, the first attempt to form a coalition happened in 820 AD at the House of Wisdom, the premier cultural and education center in the ancient Muslim world. The next such coalition happened in 1556, after a major earthquake in Shaanxi that released over ten thousand demons into China. The Chinese were the first to perfect a blade for severing the head of a demon, the descendant of which is used today."

He changed slides to a photo of an ancient curved knife, molded to a red hilt. Jack had actually seen that exact sword before, as a boy, when he'd accompanied his grandfather on a council trip to the International Weapons Institute in Shanghai.

"Our US Division, as it stands today, was established in 1890, after the great Charleston earthquake that ushered in the last major demon rampage in 1886. ICDM, the larger international organization, was formally chartered in 1920 and has agents in every major city and country in the world. It is governed by a Council of Fifteen." Jones' gaze landed on Jack, who knew what was coming next. "Grenard, isn't your grandfather the US representative?"

"Uh, yeah," Jack said, as heat crept up his neck.

"Excellent," Jones said, turning back to his slides. "Our goal here, ladies and gentlemen, is to prevent demonic transformation. First and foremost, it's our job to educate the population on the dangers of demonic coercion. For many humans drawn to the idea of immortality and power, they find out too late that it's a lot harder to get out of than get into."

A girl up front raised her hand. "Do demons ever turn back into humans?"

"Only if the maker is killed, and the only way to kill a demon is to behead them," Jones replied. "And even then, killing the maker doesn't always result in reversion, especially if the spawn have become powerful in their own right. To keep unwilling participants at a minimum, we work with our local demon lords to make sure every new spawn created is strictly legal with a binding contract. Some of you assigned to the field will be responsible for monthly audits and the like."

Jack glanced around the room, spotting a few confused faces in the crowd. It was counterintuitive, on some level, to work with the very creatures who were hunting them. But it was how the Division exerted their (albeit limited) pressure on local demon lords and prevented an all-out buffet on humanity. Jack had never quite made peace with the part of his job that required him to kiss ass or work in moral gray areas.

He hadn't had to kiss anyone's ass in accounting, but he also hadn't saved many either. And that, he supposed, was why he was sitting through the banal orientation so he could get back out there.

By lunch break, Jack had nearly nodded off more times than he could count. But he perked up when he saw Cam waiting for him outside the orientation room, and even more so when she offered to take him to the best sushi place in town.

"Have you unpacked yet?" Cam asked, grabbing one of the edamame and popping the seeds into her mouth.

"Nearly there," Jack lied. All the boxes in his apartment were exactly where the moving company had left them. "So what are we working on right now?"

Cam smirked, reaching into her briefcase. "I like the sound of that 'we.' Kim's been assigning me to a lot of politically delicate cases recently."

"You?" Jack said with a snort.

"Fuck off, Grenard. I'm damned polite when I want to be," Cam said with a glare. "Most of the agents down here don't know the first thing about strategic planning or earning favors. So I've been greasing the wheels, making friends, getting a roster of helpful demons when I need help."

Jack chewed on an edamame. "Helpful demons? Isn't that an oxymoron?"

She glared at him. "*Anyway,* about six weeks ago, there was a little dust-up between one of Nunzia's lesser demons and a trespasser from Montgomery. The Montgomery lord is an eloko, and he's testing the waters, seeing if Nunzia is willing to give up some of her domain."

"And Nunzia is…?"

"The demon lord of Atlanta—lilin." Cam glanced around the sushi place and lowered her voice. "I've heard rumors that she's a second to the original lilin herself. 'Course, that could just be her demons trying to play up her power. But I do know she's been ruling Atlanta since Sherman burned it to the ground."

Jack nodded. Lilin demons were lust personified, using pheromones and glamour to trick their victims into sleeping with them—and then the victims would become so obsessed, they'd beg the lilin to transform them. Lilins also used this magic on Division resources whenever it suited them.

"And she's *southern*, which means she'll bless your heart while tearing you apart. She doesn't destroy her opponents through nightmarish visions like a nox, but bankruptcy and character assassination. She found out that one of the best chefs in Atlanta had a cousin who'd been turned by a kappa lord in Chicago. So, she had her newspaper reporters slam his new opening and the health department shut him down before he even served one customer. Last I heard, he'd taken a job as a chef on a cruise liner in Norway."

Jack whistled. "I'd take the nightmares from a nox demon."

"But the good news is, as long as you play her game, you can get her to...well, do what you want." Cam glanced around again.

Jack followed her gaze and saw nothing out of the ordinary. "Does she own this place too?"

"Yes," Cam said. "But it's the best in town, so I don't mind eating here."

Their sushi arrived, arranged spectacularly atop a wooden boat serving platter and the waiter placed it on the center of the table. Chopsticks in hand, they dug in, fighting over pieces of the spicy tuna and the volcano rolls. Cam was right; it was damned good sushi.

"So this dust-up between demon lords, what happened?" Jack asked between bites.

"The eloko, named Parras, poached the daughter of one of Nunzia's politicians," Cam said, snapping her chopsticks together as she considered her next morsel from the array before them. "The girl was barely eighteen, and although Nunzia claims the transformation was coerced, I'm not completely convinced."

"Eighteen, daughter of a crooked politician?" Jack sat back, already full. "Prep school?"

Cam nodded, swallowing another bite. "Sounds like good old-fashioned teenaged rebellion to me. Although kind of like getting a tattoo, this one's permanent."

Jack took another roll, too tempted by the delicious food to stop when his stomach said to. Rebellious teenagers comprised about half of all demon transformations, which was why the Division had an extensive program set up to combat it in schools.

"And not only is it permanent, but it pissed Nunzia off, big-time. She sees her spawn as her family, and their human families are her property, too. She's been rattling cages all up and down I-85, searching for the best way to destroy Parras. I've been trying to stem the tide, working between them to make peace before both cities go up in flames."

"What do you have so far?" Jack asked.

"Not a whole lot. And Parras seems to think that if he waits until Demon Spring, he'll be rewarded." Cam put down her chopsticks. "Which worries me a little."

"Demons are always thinking Bael will come back. Most are proven wrong."

"Yeah, *but*," Cam said, leaning forward, "Nunzia is an old, *old* demon. Most of her inner circle are pushing eight hundred. She's got thousands of demons in Atlanta under her command. What kind of moron would want to go up against her unless he was damned sure he wasn't going to get his ass beat for it?"

"Has Parras shown a penchant for reckless land grabbing?" Jack asked. "Who's his maker?"

"Xerxes, the lord in Dallas."

"Could it be a proxy thing? Maybe Xerxes wants to cause trouble with Nunzia?"

Cam shook her head. "I called in the Dallas office. Xerxes made him, but there's barely a connection between them anymore. Parras built himself an empire in the wilds of central Alabama when no one was looking, and now he's practically his own demon lord."

"So if Parras thinks Nunzia is on the outs with Bael, and also thinks Bael is returning, then by pissing off Nunzia, he'll have established his loyalties?"

"That's what I'm working with," Cam said, tapping her chopsticks against the table.

Jack chuckled. They'd started investigations on less. "What's our next move, partner?"

"Your next move is to get your butt back to orientation," Cam said with a devilish grin. "I get the joyous task of spending the afternoon with Mommy Dearest and her rebel teenager. I'll let you read my report after I finish it."

"Or you could go to orientation and I'll go interview them?" Jack pulled out his wallet. "I'll even pay for lunch."

"And have Kim on my ass? Not a chance." Cam snatched the bill from the table. "And don't even *think* about paying for lunch."

CHAPTER THREE

Jack's first week back as an active demon hunter was mostly uneventful. Once he got settled, he'd be working a combination of night and day shifts—usually two days for paperwork then two nights for hunting, then three days off. Cam had arranged it with Kim to give them four day shifts in a row so she could bring Jack up to speed on her current cases. Besides the Nunzia-Parras spat, she was trying to settle a few human-demon disputes.

"Almost every demon in this city is a lilin, so most of them belong to Nunzia," Cam said, handing Jack a file. "Although most cases I have don't rise to her level, so I rarely deal with her. Thankfully. I don't think I want to get on her bad side."

Jack nodded, reviewing the case report of a county inspector who'd turned up dead after dinging a lilin's bar for faulty electrical. The cause of death was blunt force trauma, but there weren't any witnesses.

"So…what's the request form to set up a demon meeting?" Jack asked.

"1050," Cam said with a smile, handing it over. "See? You're back at it like nothing's changed."

That was a bit of a stretch, but Jack didn't correct her. This particular document was a formality, an official notice that Jack and Cam would be headed to a demon establishment. A copy would go to the local demon point of contact to be signed, so there would be an official record of demonic approval.

"Our main suspect is Nevsa, right?" Jack said, reading the original case file. "Where does he fit in the pecking order?"

"Something like fifteenth from Nunzia. Twenty years old, if that. He owned the bar before he was turned. From what I've heard, he was getting too old to manage it so he decided to become a demon to do it indefinitely."

He'd heard stranger reasons. "Do you think we have a case against him?"

"The better question is whether Nunzia would let us bring charges," Cam said, plucking her iced coffee off the desk and taking a long sip. "Have I mentioned how much I missed you? Missed this?"

"Me too," he said with a forced grin. He'd fallen back into their easy pattern of work and conversation quicker than he'd expected. Despite the different office setup and faces walking by, it was almost as if they were back in D.C. But that also made him think Sara would be waiting for him at home, reopening the painful wound he was trying hard to heal.

Cam stood after a long silence and stretched, then walked out of the office. Jack continued working, typing up a few notes on the bar owner-inspector case. As demons went, twenty years old was still pretty new. Demon lords tended to have less attachment to younger spawn, so with some sweet talking, they might be able to convince this Nunzia to let the Division have her spawn.

Or, as usual, the demon lord would work some deal with the Division to get off scot-free—

Clack-clack-clack.

The doorway darkened and Jack leaned back in his chair, his gaze dancing up the length (or lack thereof) of Cam's outfit. The black skirt barely covered her ample rear, showing off muscular legs encased in four-inch stiletto boots. Her crimson top left little to the imagination, fitting snugly against her flat stomach and round breasts.

He frowned. "No way."

Cam flicked a curled lock behind her ear. "Yes way. Jack, you haven't even looked at a woman in years."

"I'm looking at one right now, and she's gorgeous."

Cam curled her red-tipped fingers around her hip—when had she had time to paint her nails? "This isn't up for debate. Both our mothers told me to look after you, and I'm looking after you. We have a very rare Friday night off."

"Probably by your doing." He shook his head. "Look, I appreciate the gesture, but I'm not really looking to get into anything for a while. Maybe ever."

"Sara would've wanted you to move on."

Jack heaved a breath and swallowed the lump in his throat. "Even if I wanted to, if I walk into any bar with you looking like that, no woman will even come near me."

"And that's why I'm going as your wingman!" she announced proudly. "I'll butter 'em up, give them the sob story about how you're a widower—"

"No," Jack said firmly. "Don't mention her."

Cam sighed. "Fine. No widower. But you're going out with me."

"I'm not going to a club."

"No, I picked a nice, *quiet* place with seats, old man," Cam said, grabbing Jack by the hand and pulling him to stand. "Just like old times."

True to her word, Cam had found a place to Jack's liking. The lighting was low, the music bearable, and the crowds still thin.

Jack had thought he'd put this lifestyle behind him when he'd married Sara, and to be back at a bar, sizing up women, seemed like starting all over. He'd known that, eventually, he'd have to try again. Eventually, he'd have to smile and flirt and talk about himself. But now that eventually had arrived, he wasn't sure he was ready for it.

Cam was flirting enough for both of them, though. The tough, no-nonsense partner was gone and in her place was a boisterous woman who drew the attention of everyone around her. When Jack had been Jack, they'd made quite a pair, getting into trouble and charming their way out of it.

Now he was a ghost watching some memory of a past life.

His gaze landed on the couples, scanning them for signs of danger. He'd never quite lost the habit, even when he was approving expense reports in the accounting department. In most cases, there were no visible differences between demons and humans. In the Academy, they'd been trained to look for behavioral cues. Demons were predators, and they tended to latch onto humans who seemed lost, drunk, or otherwise vulnerable. Cam used to say look for the wasted white girls, and a demon might not be too far behind. It was unsurprising that demon hunters often prevented a number of sexual assaults as well.

But Jack doubted he'd find either of the two in a place like this. It was small, cozy. The bartender chatted with those at the bar as if they were old friends. Couples on the couches kept their hands to themselves as they sipped on cocktails.

"Here's your beer," Cam said, reappearing beside him and shoving the cold bottle in his hand. "I've scouted the area. That group over there looks to be a bit out of your range—maybe forties." She pointed to some older women at another table clearly enjoying their happy hour. "The second group, over there, might be closer in age, although I'm not sure if you'd be down for someone in her early twenties."

She paused for a breath, which Jack took as an invitation to interrupt. "Cam, I appreciate this, but I'm not ready to be down for anyone right now."

"Talk to someone," Cam said. "That's all I'm asking you to do. That girl over there, she's cute."

The girl was cute, but young. "Nah."

"What about her? The older woman?"

"Nah."

"Jackson."

Jack took a long drink. "Camilla."

"You've got to start talking to someone," Cam said.

"Did you find yourself another sister?" Jack snapped, anger warming his ears. "Because you're asking me to replace Sara and I don't think I can do that."

Her face went slack and, for once, she didn't come back with a smart remark. After a moment, she softened and placed her empty glass on the table.

"I'm sorry. You're right. I shouldn't be pushing you."

Jack's anger deflated as well. "I'm sorry, too. That was out of line."

"Yeah, it was." She lightly punched his shoulder. "Finish your beer and we'll get out of here."

"Really?"

"Yeah." She smirked and threaded her arm through his. "As your punishment for yelling at me, you're buying dinner."

At a burger place nearby, their small argument was forgotten over greasy fries and dripping burgers. Jack ate to his contentment, especially after Cam swore she'd stop pushing him to move on.

"For now, anyway," she said, licking her fingers. "I'll give you three months."

It was as good as he'd get from his meddling partner, and he'd take it. Jack sat back, patting his full stomach and watching the crowd out the window. It was still relatively early, but the streets were filling with evening activity-seekers. In his post-dinner stupor, he casually studied each face as it passed by, looking for the signs of demonic activity.

"Right behind you, Grenard," Cam said.

"Huh?"

"You're looking for a demon? Check out the couple behind you. Lilin demon and a brand-new boy toy."

At first glance, they seemed like a human couple. But the blond with pale skin was a little too interested in his date, and the young hispanic man was already tipsy. It was small signals, the flare of the nostril, the movement of the blond's hand on the back of the plastic seat that was almost too fluid. Enough to raise the hair on the back of Jack's neck as the demon and his date stood and walked toward the backdoor, looking ready to get into something personal.

"What do you want to do?" Cam said when he turned back. "Care to tangle with them?"

"We should call for backup. I don't have my weapons."

Cam pointedly sipped her drink and stood up. "We don't need backup. It's *one person.* We say we're Division, and he'll scamper. I mean, for crying out loud, he's a lilin."

"You sure you can run after a demon in those shoes?"

"Are you seriously asking me that question?" She raised an eyebrow. "Did you forget Los Angeles?"

"I remember a lot of complaining," Jack said, cracking what felt like his first smile all night. "Fine. But I'm not carrying you —"

"Don't say things you don't mean," Cam replied, tossing her bag of uneaten food in the trash. "Let's go."

With Cam flashing her Division badge at the cooks, they headed through the kitchen. Standing on either side of the backdoor, they cracked it open, listening.

"...I can't take this any more. I'm dying. I need this." The human was on his knees, gripping the shirt of the lilin with tears in his eyes. "Just once more. Please, that's all I need."

"I told you," came the drawling response of the lilin. "Once is all I give for free. If you want more, you'll have to pay for it."

"I'll pay anything! Please! I've been thinking about you for days now—"

The lilin grabbed the man and pulled him to his feet. "I'll take my payment now, then."

"I think that's confirmation enough," Cam said, pulling a small knife from somewhere between her breasts. "Will you do the honors?"

Jack bowed and kicked the door all the way open, and they rushed into the dark alley behind the restaurant.

"Division, stop what—Ah, *shit*!"

Where they'd expected a single demon, there were *five*—four who appeared to be bodyguards. Thick, beefy, muscular bodyguards with arms the size of Jack's torso, along with their lilin demon boss and intended human victim.

"What's this?" the blond hissed, his eyes an eerie red. "Division creeps?"

"Y-yeah. Stop what you're doing or you're under arrest," Cam said.

"Cam, we should let it go," Jack said with a nervous pounding in his chest. It wasn't that he wanted to leave a defenseless human in an alley to be transformed, but he also knew there wasn't much they could do for him.

Besides that, if this demon had brought backup and was performing the act himself, he was somebody important. So not only were Jack and Cam picking a fight with four demonic body-building bodyguards, but also a demon powerful in his own right.

"I'm almost finished," the head demon said, turning back to his human.

"You can't just..." Cam began with a frustrated growl as the guards ambled toward her and Jack.

The lilin's eyes glowed once more, and his mouth widened revealing sharp, black teeth. He clamped his open mouth on that of his victim's, who jerked under his grip. The lilin gripped the other man's head and exhaled loudly, sending a rush of wind out from the couple. Jack got a whiff of sex and flowers, which sent its own line of pleasure straight into his groin.

The demon released his new spawn, who looked no different except for his glowing white eyes that faded back to green. For a moment, the man laid on the ground, dazed and blinking at nothing. Then he sat up and smiled, grinning at his new master.

"That was amazing…"

"I know," the lilin said, brushing the man's cheek. "Are you ready to go home and meet the rest of the family?"

The human nodded, grinning like he'd just received the best blow job of his life.

"Son of a *bitch*," Cam swore.

"Take care of this Division problem," said the head demon, looking to Jack and Cam. "Then return to the apartment."

Jack was sure this looked incredibly silly to the lilins—two underprepared Division agents, one in a mini-skirt and the other in dress pants, trying to order them around.

"We shoulda called for backup," Jack said with a sigh.

"What, do you think I'm an amateur? Of course I called for backup," Cam replied with a defiant toss of her hair. "But we have to buy ourselves some time. You still know how to throw a punch, don't you?"

"I hate you."

"I told you not to say things you don't mean."

Cam darted forward, but was caught mid-stride by the center demon. She broke his grip with a well-placed slice to his arm, a stomp on his foot, and an elbow to the stomach. The demon was stunned for a second then came right back with fists bared.

Jack, on the other hand, took a more cautious approach,

hoping he could avoid going toe-to-toe until the Division backup Cam had sent for arrived. On average, a team would scramble in thirty minutes. Based on the size of the demons, they might be too late.

"I don't suppose we could maybe avoid all this and—" The first punch landed hard against his jaw, sending him stumbling back until he smacked his head against the brick. Dazed, he got only a moment's respite before the second fist hit, clocking him on the other side. He recalled enough of his training to duck, just in time for the flesh and bone of the demon's knuckles to slam against the wall with a sickening *smack*.

Jack took the opportunity to dart around the demon so he wouldn't be trapped. But his escape was short-lived, as the other demon grabbed Jack by the neck and tossed him back into the fray. Coughing, Jack got to his feet and rubbed his jaw.

"You guys are a little different than the demons I'm used to," Jack replied. "Aren't lilins supposed to be lovers, not fighters?"

The answer came in the form of another fist to the face. Dazed, his knees gave out, but before he could fall to the ground, the demon hoisted him back up by the shirtsleeve. He blinked as lights flashed in front of his eyes, and heard the telltale sign of someone cracking their knuckles.

"Let them go," said a female voice.

There was a new figure in the alley, holding a sword glinting in the moonlight, and wearing a ski mask to cover her face. She couldn't have been more than a hundred pounds, a tiny wisp of a thing.

"And who do you think you are, precious?" asked the demon holding Jack against the wall. "Don't you see this is lilin business?"

She reached behind her and drew the second sword from her back with deadly calm. "Let them go, and you'll be allowed to live."

They burst into laughter.

"I think you'd break a nail," the demon holding Cam said.

"Oi," Cam growled, kicking helplessly against her captor. "Sexist."

"Let's just deal with these two and get back. I wanna get a turn with the new spawn." The two demons turned to Jack and he held his breath, wondering how much time had passed since they'd called for backup.

Jack opened his mouth to try to plead his case, but the demon no longer had a head.

"What the...?"

The body fell to the ground. All Jack could do was stare at it. Had he been hit harder than he'd thought?

Then the head of the other demon slid off its body. The grip on Jack's shirt released as the second decapitated corpse fell on top of the first.

"*Jack!*" Cam called. "Jack, are you okay?"

"Yeah, I—" The words died on his tongue. The new figure's sword was covered in blood—Jack hadn't even seen her *move*. And now she was pointing her bloody sword at the final demon, who pressed Cam against him like a human shield.

"Let her go," the figure ordered again.

"Who the hell are you?" asked the demon. "Don't come near me!"

"I will tell you again," said the figure, swinging her sword around with ease. "Let the girl go and you may live."

"N-Not until you—"

One second she was there, and the next the lilin's head was detached from his body. The figure hadn't seemed to move; but her blood was bloodier than it had been.

"Are there more?" she asked Cam. "More victims?"

"And who the actual fuck do you think you are?" came Cam's biting retort. "We had this covered."

A derisive snort erupted from the woman. "I don't expect gratitude, but you most assuredly did not have this covered. Your friend was about to be killed."

"Ignore him. He's rusty," Cam said with a wave of her hand. "We're with the Division."

"D-Division?"

In one movement, she spun on her heel and dashed out of the alley.

"Hey…hey, wait!" Cam called, running three steps before stopping. "This is not a running bra. She's lucky this isn't a running bra."

Jack coughed and nodded to Cam's breast, which had popped out. Cam snorted and shoved it back inside her shirt. It wasn't the first time he'd seen them, and it probably wouldn't be the last. He also knew that even with a running bra, Cam couldn't have caught up with her. There was something superhuman about that woman, and Jack was just glad she was on their side. For now.

"So, is there a vigilante demon-killer here in Atlanta no one told me about?" Jack asked, rubbing the knot on the back of his head.

"Not that I'm aware of," Cam replied, her gaze still on where the mystery woman had gone. "We'd better call this in. This is…"

"Oh," Jack said, checking his hand for blood. "Really? I mean, she did help us…"

Cam's eyes narrowed. "I take you to a club full of willing young things and you get the hots for this…*colibrí?*"

"What the hell is a colibrí?"

"Hummingbird," Cam said with a small laugh. "Cause she flitted around and she weighs nothing."

Jack half-smiled. "Apt. But I don't have the hots for her. I just want to know more before we elevate it."

"Uh-huh," Cam said. "And how do you plan on doing that? She's gone."

"I—"

A scream pierced the night. Jack and Cam shared a tense look, and then took off running toward the sound of it.

The screeching came from a woman, who was pointing at the fourth and fifth headless body Jack had seen that day. Even more surprising, the lilin victim was laying in the middle of them, blinking wildly and most assuredly back to human. He lifted his head and looked at Cam.

"W-what happened?"

"I honestly have no fucking clue," she replied with a look at Jack.

CHAPTER FOUR

"So what you're telling me is that you have nothing," Kim said, a tense look on her face. "And why couldn't this wait until morning?"

It had been a little over an hour since Cam and Jack had requested backup, and thirty minutes since they'd amended that for a cleanup crew. Atlanta PD had roped off the scene in the back alley and were now assisting with crowd control. An ambulance came to take the recently-reverted human to the hospital, and Cam sent a couple lower-level agents along to make sure he didn't bolt before giving a statement.

Kim had arrived shortly after that. Apparently, five demons being beheaded by a single actor wasn't newsworthy to her.

"I thought you might want to know there's an unknown element roaming the streets of Atlanta with demon strength and demon speed, who, surprisingly, is killing demons," Cam replied with no small amount of heat. She'd donned her Division windbreaker, an odd contrast to her high-heeled boots and short skirt.

"Sounds like intrademonic political beef," Kim replied.

"Yeah, except this demon seemed different," Cam said, tossing a 'please-help-me' look to Jack.

"Uh, yeah," Jack said, clearing his throat. "She seemed to want to interfere on behalf of the human. That doesn't seem normal to me, either."

"Perhaps the human was just in the right place at the right time," Kim said. "This could've been for any number of routine reasons. I'm still not seeing why you felt the need to call me out here—"

"Because she sliced their heads off like it was nothing," Cam insisted. "And with Demon Spring approaching, this could be a portent for other bad things—especially if Bael might be making an appearance."

Kim bristled and zipped up her jacket. "I think that's just a rumor circulated by the higher-ups to get more funding from Congress. But you didn't hear that from me. In the meantime, this is your investigation, but your top priority is getting ready for Demon Spring and solving the Nunzia issue with Parras. I'll elevate your report when I get it tomorrow first thing." She glowered at Cam. "First. Thing."

"Yes ma'am," Cam ground out through clenched teeth.

"I'm going home. Do me a favor and don't call me after nine again unless Bael himself appears."

"Pardon me." An older black man with short-cropped hair and thick glasses approached the group. "Agent Kim, evening. This is something you might want to see."

"What do you have?" Kim asked.

"Damndest thing. These demons, they all belong to Nunzia." He scratched his nose. "And, er…one of these corpses is Pueyo."

Kim's eyes widened. "Are you certain?"

"Who's that?" Jack asked Cam.

"One of Nunzia's thirds," Cam whispered. "A five-hundred-year-old demon."

Much like demon lords themselves, the older a demon was, the more spawn they had, and the more powerful they were. Someone like Pueyo should've been able to use his magic to sway the mystery woman into putting down her sword. Unless, of course, she was more powerful than he was.

"And if that ain't enough," the agent said, "these kills are the cleanest I've ever seen. Normally, when you're decapitating a demon, it takes a few hacks. This was…well, like a knife through butter."

"Do you think she's athtar?" Cam asked Jack. "She certainly fought like one."

"Have *you* heard of an athtar demon living above ground?" Kim asked, pointedly, although she sounded a little shaken. "Nobody's seen one since the nineteenth century."

"You didn't see her, Kim," Jack replied. "She moved faster than any demon I've ever seen."

"Say she is. Do you know what kind of panic that would

cause?" Kim replied. "We'd be overrun with ICDM agents before we could say 'Demon Spring.'" She shook her head. "We don't need that kind of crap when we're trying to get ready."

Cam opened her mouth to argue, but Jack gave her a look. In the first place, Kim didn't seem in the mood to entertain dissenting thoughts. In the second, he partially agreed with her. The last thing they needed was to divert time and resources away from Demon Spring prep.

"I've got to call Navarro," Kim said after a long pause. "This is way above my pay grade. May be above hers, too. Nunzia will want a meeting in the morning, I'm sure." She looked at Cam. "I want you two to find me whatever you can to offer as leverage. She's going to want someone to pay, and since we don't have any leads on who did this..."

Cam swallowed, looking shaken but not deterred. "We'll start tonight."

Kim nodded. "Tomorrow is going to be unpleasant. Whoever did this has no idea the shitstorm she just unleashed."

"Here you go, partner," Jack said, placing the third coffee of the night (or morning) on Cam's desk before taking his seat. He would've asked if she'd had any luck, but the crease in her brow was the same as when he'd left. Dawn was breaking over the city, and he was feeling the sleepless night.

Jack had spent the evening sifting through data in the Division online archives, but it was proving difficult to impossible to find anything of value. He had no name, no telling physical features. And Kim had been right—the last time an athtar had been seen above ground was in 1886. Searching for demon-killers had netted a million results of spats between kappas and lilins and elokos, but nothing about athtars.

Which meant it was up to Cam to placate Nunzia before their meeting.

"We're fucked," Cam announced. "Nunzia's never let a favor go unanswered. She's going to want us to bring her someone to pay for this, and we have nothing."

"What d'ya think she'll do? Are we talking nox-type fury or...?"

Cam shook her head. "No, Nunzia's not going to fly off the handle. But she's having me run back and forth to Montgomery because the *daughter* of a *recent transition* was turned by someone else..." She chewed her lip. "I told you, her spawn are her family, and she's extra protective of them. She's going to hold this over us for decades, probably. Every single forced transition from here on out is gonna be swept under the table."

"Maybe not," Jack said, trying to be helpful.

She sighed and rubbed her face. "What I can't get over was how damned easily Colibrí decapitated them all. It's like David said last night: a knife through butter. Maybe Xerxes *is* using Parras as a proxy. Maybe he wants to take Nunzia out. Maybe he sent this woman to—"

"Or maybe she's a lone actor," Jack said. "She seemed pretty freaked out about the Division."

"That's another thing, I've *never* seen a demon shake in their boots when they hear the word 'Division.' It was like she couldn't get away fast enough."

"Why do you think she intervened then? To save our lives? The other guy's?"

"That seems like the logical answer, and at the same time, it makes no sense. What kind of demon is afraid of the Division, saves humans, and can kill a third of a powerful demon lord like she's swatting flies?" Cam asked.

"An athtar?" Jack said quietly. "Are we still working with that theory?"

"Yes…based on watching her fight. No, because athtar demons don't normally stick their necks out for people. As if *any* demon would do anything for a human."

"Maybe she's some sort of weird cross-breed," Jack replied, returning to his computer to search more. "Maybe a human and a demon got together and got busy."

"Yeah, find me an example of that, Jackie-boy," Cam said. "Now you're just throwing out nonsense."

"There are no bad ideas in brainstorming," Jack said with a half-smile. "But I'm starting to think we aren't going to find anything on this woman by the morning. Want some help sifting through Nunzia's files?"

At 9:45, Kim appeared on the other side of the glass, then turned and walked away. It was time to face the music.

Dread and uncertainty mixed with stale coffee and vending machine food as Jack followed Cam down the hall to the conference rooms. The office was now abuzz with activity, with a few more security guards mixed with the regular agents. The higher-ups were obviously taking the threat of a demon war seriously.

Unlike the staff rooms, which boasted glass windows and bright lights, this room was completely void of windows, even on the door. Jack knew from his time at the Academy that demon meeting room walls were loaded to the gills with miasma sensors and other technology to combat demonic lures, but they didn't do much good.

Cam sat at the center of the table, and Jack took the seat next to her. She adjusted her padfolio on the table, tapping her pen against her talking points, as if they'd give up more answers if she stared at them long enough. Kim was already at the head of the table, staring at her phone with a grim expression. She didn't say a word to either of them, presumably knowing they'd found nothing.

The air in the room changed as voices echoed in from the hallway.

The demon who strode in wore a designer suit, and her white hair feathered around her face. She carried extra weight on her hips and midsection, and coupled with the blood red lips and fake eyelashes, she could've fit in at any Georgia country club— or good ol' southern kitchen. But the power radiating off her was palpable; this was an incredibly strong demon.

Walking in with her was a thin, pale, older woman with blond hair, matching Nunzia's charm and then some. Agent

Navarro was the director of the Atlanta office—Jack had met her personally when he'd interviewed for the job. Then, as now, she'd been gracious and welcoming, although now her graciousness seemed forced as she walked with the demon.

"Well, I say, Ay-gent Nay-varro," said the demon with one of the thickest Georgian accents Jack had ever heard, "I just don't know what we're going to do. I thought the Division was here to keep the peace, and now I find someone's slaughtering my children. I may have to put in a call to my friends on the Council."

Jack felt the gaze of Agent Navarro on him, but he said nothing.

"Please, Lord Nunzia, have a seat and we'll get to the bottom of this," Navarro said, offering the seat.

Nunzia's gaze swept the room, taking a moment on each person, before settling on Cam. "Ay-gent Macarro. You keep popping up, don't you, sugar?"

Cam offered a tense smile. "This was unintentional, I promise you."

"Hm." Nunzia glanced to Jack, sizing him up with a bit of lust that made him uncomfortable. She barely acknowledged Kim before settling down at the head of the table.

"So, Ay-gent Macarro," Nunzia began, "please tell me how you happened upon this tragedy."

"Agent Grenard and I were eating dinner," she began.

"Oh, are you two…?"

"He's my partner. And my brother-in-law," Cam said with a

steely glare.

Nunzia's gaze passed between the two of them, as if cataloguing their relationship into her long list of potential weaknesses.

"We saw a potential demon attack in progress and decided to intervene," Cam continued after a brisk nod from Navarro. "There were five demons in total."

"My third and his four bodyguards," Nunzia said. "And I'll remind you, Mr. Hernandez was on his way to sign a transition agreement."

"Yes, I'm sure he was," Cam said with a tight smile. From Jack's recollection, the human had already been transformed, but he didn't want to bring that up. "While we were assessing the situation, an unknown third party appeared and...well...took out the five demons."

Nunzia twittered with laughter. "One person, against five demons? A *third*?"

"That's what we saw," Jack replied.

"Pardon me if I don't believe you," Nunzia said. "There's obviously a relationship here. It seems to me like your Agent Macarro has gone rogue and her partner here is—"

"Her partner is the grandson of Frank Grenard," Jack replied coolly. "Perhaps you can call him to vouch for our character."

"I do declare, a real Grenard? In my city? My, my..." She smiled, although there was challenge in it. "Bless your heart, I thought all the Grenards were in Charleston."

"I decided on another career path," Jack said. "Prefer to get my hands dirty in the field. Help innocents, like the man your third was attacking."

"Attacking?" She laughed, and Jack got a whiff of perfume and flowers. "That's a bit of an accusation. I'm sure you know, Agent Grey-naard," she drew out his name as if it were delicious on her tongue, "that in this country, we are innocent until proven guilty. You can't be doling out vigilante justice—"

"And *we* didn't," Cam said, tossing a warning look to Jack.

"And who might this *mystery* third party be?"

"We don't know," Jack replied. "But she—"

"She?"

"She," Jack continued, "is most assuredly not human."

"I see," Nunzia said, her slow, Georgia drawl all but gone. She ran a fingernail along the edge of her blood red lips, clearly deep in thought. "So Agent Navarro, how do you plan to resolve this…new issue."

"Agents Macarro and Grenard are looking into it," Navarro said. "It might be a demon from another city. If so, we'd like to avoid a fight."

"As would I, sugar, as would I. And I doubt it's someone *knowingly* encroaching on my territory, as *most* demons in the southeast and I are on good terms." Her gaze swept to Cam, and Jack could practically read the subtext about Parras.

"Yes, well," Cam said after another long pause. "We will keep you informed. And please accept our apologies for the loss of your demons."

Jack stopped himself before he made a face. They should be

apologizing to the family of the human who was attacked, not placating the demon who let her spawn run loose. This was the sort of political maneuvering his grandfather did on the Council, and it had been a big reason why Jack had chosen fieldwork over the bureaucracy.

Nunzia left shortly after that, her chipper facade back as she charmed everyone who passed her in the hall. Jack got the feeling that the southern accent was part of her magic, because the room became cold and uncomfortable in the long silence after she left. Kim stood up, clearly feeling the aftereffects, and glared at them.

"You two had better find me something on that mystery woman," she said. "Before the end of the week."

CHAPTER FIVE

Without any strong leads on the mystery woman, Cam redoubled her efforts on the Parras case, figuring that if they couldn't solve the former, they could buy themselves some time with the latter. So for the next few days, she assigned herself to Montgomery, calling Jack on the ride over to complain about how little progress she was making.

"Hey, I have an idea," she said, her voice muffled from the car Bluetooth. "Why don't we offer your ass up to Nunzia and see if Colibrí comes to rescue you again?"

"Very funny," Jack said, pressing the phone headset into his shoulder. 'Set a hostage trap' was on his list of possible ways to find the mystery woman scribbled on his dry erase board. He'd also made a list of all possible places he might find information about the mystery woman, and he'd spent the past two days exhausting every one.

"Well, good news," Cam said. "I'm getting close to securing a meeting with Parras. Sometimes being obnoxious wins the day. Now whether I can make him give up something Nunzia finds valuable, that's another story."

"For my sake, I hope you can. I haven't been able to get anything out of anyone. I checked with all your contacts, too."

"Yeah, Kim said Nunzia's already started to tell her demons not to talk with Division agents unless approved personally by her."

"Fantastic," Jack said, walking over to his board and erasing all the options for Nunzia's demons.

"We're not popular, what can I say?" Cam sighed. "I think she's conducting her own private investigation for La Colibrí and wants us to stay out of it. While I'm all for finding this chick, somehow I think Nunzia's methods might be a little less restrained. I can just see her now." She cleared her throat. "Wey-ell, Ay-gent Ma-cay-ro, y'all weren't doing what I said, so I just did it. If y'all did y'all's jobs, I wouldn't have had to kill a hundred humans. Bless your heart, shrimp and grits, biscuits and gravy—"

"Oh come on, we aren't that bad," Jack replied with a hearty chuckle.

"Okay, I'm at the Montgomery office. Another day of being obnoxious awaits."

"Go get 'em, tiger," Jack replied, then added, "Shrimp and grits, biscuits and gravy, bless your heart, and all that, too."

He hung up the phone to Cam's laughter. Feeling a little

lighter about his list, he grabbed his black marker and walked to the white board. Maybe if he understood *why* she'd intervened, it would help lead him to her. He'd written everything from "confused demon" to "government-created superhuman" to "magical" on the board. The only thing left to do now was to walk down to the Atlanta archives and start reading.

But first, he needed coffee.

The sun beat down on him as he crossed the street to the small cafe opposite the Division headquarters. The shop was bustling with mid-morning coffee-seekers, and Jack waited in line, skimming faces and behaviors for signs of trouble. He didn't expect to see a demon so close to Division offices, but he looked anyway.

Two young professionals were engaged in conversation, and there was a somewhat familiar man at the counter—he was probably a Division agent as well. Three businessmen in the middle table were innocuous, and the two college kids with earphones reading books didn't look too suspicious either.

But the woman in the corner hunched over her laptop did.

Jack had no idea why she struck him as odd. She couldn't have been more than twenty-five, but there was something old about her. She wore no discernible jewelry except a small charm at her neck, and her clothes—black shirt and dark pants—were as plain as any he'd seen. They hung off her thin, lithe frame which was almost too skinny to be healthy. She certainly didn't look like anyone capable of causing trouble, but Jack's gut hadn't steered him wrong before.

And it was waving a big red flag about this woman. Could she be the mystery savior?

"Can I help you?" the barista asked, dragging Jack's attention away.

"Y-yeah," he replied, forcing himself to smile. "Medium caramel macchiato."

She wrote down his order on the cup and he paid, keeping the odd woman in his periphery. She hadn't moved or noticed that he'd noticed her, and he wanted to keep it that way. Jack loitered at the pick-up counter, focusing his attention on the two professionals near the woman, hoping he'd come off as checking them out instead.

He took his coffee and sat down on the opposite side of the shop. Keeping his head down, he chanced another look over to her, just to make sure he'd seen correctly the first time. There was no mistaking it; she was staking out the Division.

Whipping out his phone, Jack pretended to text as he snapped a quick photo. He emailed it to himself, just in case, then stood and sauntered over to the sugar packets, taking his time to select one, even though his macchiato was already sweet enough. Out of the corner of his eye, he saw her gaze draw to him, so he turned and offered his most disarming smile. She returned it with an icy glare.

It was hard to believe *she* of all people would be capable of slicing a demon's head off. Her sallow skin should've been four shades darker than it was, giving her a sickly appearance accentuated by purple bags under her dull green eyes. He even saw a few gray hairs poking out from under the mess of black.

Chuckling to himself, he crossed the cafe and helped himself to the seat across from her.

"I'm sorry, seat's taken," she said, her voice low and dangerous. Her laptop was high quality, almost a little too nice for someone who looked so ill. The hairs on Jack's arm stood up, as if he were in the presence of someone with demonic magic.

"By who? Your charming personality?" Jack replied, ignoring the warning sirens going off in his head.

"I'd tell you, but I'd have to kill you."

"I think you'd find me hardier than most men." That earned a breathy chuckle, but her fingers stopped clacking when he added, "But I think you already knew that."

"Are you done drooling?" she asked, her tone laced with a surprising amount of energy. "Go back to your hovel and leave me be."

"You know the demons you killed last night?" Jack asked. "They were Nunzia's."

The woman leaned back in her chair, a sly expression on her face. "That old bat is still alive?"

So, she'd had no idea. "You killed one of her thirds. She's pissed."

"And why are you, Agent Altar Boy, aiding a powerful demon like her? Don't you work for the Division?"

Jack didn't have a good answer for that, so he went with the truth. "The Division likes to keep her placated so we can utilize her network of spies and take out the bad demons. Common practice for demon lords."

She quirked a brow and folded her arms across her chest. "Nunzia *is* a bad demon."

"I'm just following orders," Jack said with a half-hearted shrug. "Whose orders are you following?"

"Here's an order for you: Beat it."

"I'm sorry, I can't," he said. "You've broken a few laws—"

She snorted. "Are you going to take me in?"

Knowing she was the creature who'd decapitated a third made him a little hesitant, but she really looked more like a finch than a hawk.

So, he smiled at her. "I was going to ask nicely. You seem like a reasonable monster."

To his surprise, she closed her laptop and put it in her bag, then sat back with her hands clasped on the table. "Well? Take me in."

Jack hesitated for just a moment, and that was all she needed. She was nothing but a dark blur, but he sure felt the fist in his stomach. The next thing he knew, he was sailing through the air and slamming head-first into a table. He stared at the ceiling, panting and letting his brain catch up with his body, although as soon as he registered pain, he wished his brain had stayed behind.

"Are you okay, mister?" asked the barista, peering over him with wide, fearful eyes.

"What the hell just happened?" Jack coughed. "Where is she?"

"She's…gone."

"One more time, Grenard," Kim said from the other side of her desk.

Jack calmly explained what had transpired at the coffee shop, right down to when she flipped him over with her bare hands. A few Division operatives had been in the coffee shop, and they'd helped him across the street while calling for backup to question the witnesses in the shop. He just hoped they had a better description of what had happened than he did. "It was all a blur" wasn't very helpful.

"She was so little, though. I can't believe she just tossed me like that," Jack said, pressing the ice pack to his bruised stomach.

"I can flip you over. Doesn't make me a demon," Cam replied with a frown on her face. Jack wasn't sure who'd called her, but she'd arrived almost as soon as the medic had cleared him to go back to work. She'd spent the whole walk to their office yelling at him for being a reckless idiot, and he was sure he'd hear more when they left.

"This is different, Cam. She didn't even…it was like I weighed nothing."

"And you say she was doing what, exactly?" Kim said.

"Staking out the Division," Jack said, tapping his finger against the cut on his forehead to see if it was still bleeding. "Typing on a computer. Didn't get a good look."

"Hm," Kim said. "And why did you engage instead of asking for backup? If she was able to take out a demon lord's third—"

"Uh…" Jack coughed, withering under the gaze of two very pissed off women. "Thought I could talk her into coming back?"

"That was unbelievably idiotic of you," Kim snapped. "Not only did you jeopardize your own life, but the lives of the people in that coffee shop with you. And you let our best lead get away because you thought you could talk her into coming in?"

"In my defense," Jack said, wincing as his head throbbed, "I wasn't completely sure she was our mystery woman until we started talking. And I didn't just engage her—I took a photo."

"Well?" Kim said, annoyed. "Where is it?"

"Ah…well, she took my phone," Jack said, blushing a little as Cam made a dismissive noise. "But I did email it to myself. If you'll let me get back to my desk, I can share it."

That seemed to placate Kim. "Fine. Send the photo and we'll put out an APB."

Jack nodded, grateful he'd gotten out of that meeting relatively unscathed. Cam followed, her lips pursed in her "I-told-you-so" face, but waited until Jack was sitting at his desk before she unleashed again.

"For real, Jack. You could've lost your job just now."

Jack's head began to hurt. "I know."

"You got your ass beat by Pueyo's guards, and you thought, you *thought* you could take on Colibrí? Who killed them without breaking a sweat? I know you've been out of the field, but that's freshman-level stuff."

"You had no problem engaging with her the first night we saw her."

"Yeah, because we didn't know better," Cam replied, her tone only growing angrier with his deflections. "She showed up out of the blue. This? You knew better."

"I know, Cam," Jack said. "I made a mistake, all right?"

"Yeah, and you could have died."

Her anger was gone, replaced by a wide-eyed fear that Jack had very rarely seen from his partner.

"Cam, we could've died that first night, too," he reminded her gently.

"Yeah, but *I* was there. *I* wasn't there to back you up today." Cam turned away from him. "All I know was I got a call and the first thing they said was, 'Your partner's been injured' and all I could think about was…"

She didn't have to finish, and Jack knew this wasn't about the mystery woman or Jack doing something stupid. Maybe Cam hadn't recovered from Sara's death as much as she let on.

Instead of arguing, Jack held up his hands in surrender. "I won't do it again."

"Good," she said, reverting to her annoyed pinched face. "I swear, Grenard. Going after an athtar by yourself. What's wrong with you?"

"You think she's athtar then?" Jack said. "Confirmed?"

"If you saw a blur, that's consistent with descriptions of athtars in the past," Cam said. "Which, again, *why* did you—"

Jack's heart dropped from his chest. "It's gone."

"What's gone?"

"That bitch," Jack said, searching through every file folder on his machine. "I know I emailed it to myself. I saw it come in. She must've hacked into my phone and erased the email. Who does that?"

Cam jumped up and leaned over his shoulder. "Maybe it's in your sent items? Archive? Trash?"

But it wasn't anywhere, and it also wasn't in the list of online photos automatically backed up from his phone. It was completely and utterly erased.

"I don't understand," Jack said, clicking the refresh button over and over. "She couldn't get into my phone without my fingerprint, unless she's some sort of…techno-wizard demon hacker, too."

"Colibrí keeps getting more and more interesting," Cam said.

"Well shit, now I'm going to get it," Jack replied. "At least I've got my…"

But he didn't have his research either—not in his email, or his desktop. "She hacked into Division resources."

"W-what?"

As if on cue, a mousy black girl poked her head into the room. "Excuse me, Agents Macarro, Grenard. Agent Kim wanted me to let you know you're wanted in her office. Something about a massive security breach and files missing? And it's stemming from your account."

CHAPTER SIX

Cam looked more worried than Jack as they followed the assistant back down the hall to the directors' offices. Only this time, they bypassed Kim's and went straight into Director Navarro's. There were already five other people inside, including Kim and the security lead Jack recognized from his first day on the job.

"Ah, Agent Grenard, Macarro," Navarro said.

"What's going on?" Cam asked. "Jack didn't—"

"Don't worry, we don't think this stemmed from Grenard's stolen phone," Kim said.

Jack actually sighed in relief.

"And really, we should be thanking you," Navarro said. "This breach has been going on for hours. We only found it because of the incident across the street. Luckily, we've been able to isolate the vulnerability so we don't lose any more data. Agent

Rubinski was explaining it to us. Please, have a seat."

The IT lead described a cyber attack on Division headquarters that exploited a vulnerability... Jack lost what they were saying until they asked him if he'd noticed anything of value missing.

"She wiped all my files related to my research," Jack said. "Apparently, she doesn't want us to know who she is."

"Surprise, surprise," Cam said. "But you said you hadn't found anything important about her, right? What could she have been interested in?"

Jack shrugged.

"So we're dealing with a demon who can not only throw a full-sized man across the room, but also has the skills of a hacker?" Navarro said. "And who says this job isn't fun? Can you tell us anything about her, Grenard?"

"She looked sick?" Jack tried. Navarro raised a brow at him and Jack shrugged. "I mean...when have you ever seen a demon who didn't look healthy? I wouldn't have believed she was our mystery woman if she hadn't...well, you know." He gestured to his forehead.

"Maybe she's got demon cancer," Cam muttered under her breath.

"We've got our resident sketcher on his way to debrief you, so maybe we can at least have an idea who we're looking for," Navarro said. "As much as I don't like that you went in rogue, I'm grateful you did. This could've been much worse."

Jack nodded and rose with Cam, hoping to find some pain

reliever and maybe take a half day so he could relax after the excitement. But Kim caught him before he was three steps out of Navarro's office.

"A word," she said, then to Cam, added, "alone."

Jack braced himself for the fourth lecture of the day, and tried to remember why he enjoyed his job as he settled in the same seat. But Kim didn't look nearly as angry as she had before. In fact, she looked more pensive.

"The D.C. office warned me you and Macarro would be trouble if you paired up again," she said. "I have to say, they were right. You're already attracting the weird ones."

Jack had to laugh at that. "I can't say I was looking for trouble this time."

"Yes, well." Kim flipped open the manila file on her desk. "Trouble seems to find you."

Jack spotted a familiar picture that sent electric panic down his spine. He tried to avoid the images, and forced his mind not to replay that horrific night.

"Macarro told me about your wife—demons, right?"

His throat tightened. "Yes."

"Tough," Kim said, as if she understood what it was to lose someone the way Jack had. Jack highly doubted that. "Macarro speaks of her often, and of you. I know she's pleased to have you back at work with her, even if it means more headaches for me."

"I'm glad to be back, too," he said, if only to move the conversation along. "Was there something you needed?"

"You've been here less than two weeks, and you've already

had two infractions. I would be well within guidelines to write you up for both of them. By all accounts, going up against a demon solo is grounds for suspension at best."

"But you aren't going to do that because…?"

"You have something I need," she replied. "I'm headed to a budget meeting at the end of the week, and word on the street is that they're cutting our funding. I've got a few projects in the works now that I'd hate to see cancelled. Any chance you could put in a good word for us with the Council?"

"You mean with my grandfather?" Jack sighed. He'd rather take the suspension than have Frank's name giving him a pass. "I'm notoriously unlucky with convincing him of anything. He's never forgiven me for choosing field work over the Council."

"I see. Well, do your best. We could use some of that money. You might want to mention that our IT systems need an upgrade since we've had a security breach."

That you'd like me to say was my fault too, I bet. "I'll see what I can do."

"What did Kim want to talk about?" Cam asked when Jack walked back in.

Cam would've thrown a fit if Jack told her what Kim had asked, so he shrugged and told a half-truth. "What else? Wants me to get money from Frank. Same ol' shit."

She narrowed her eyes, as if sensing his lie, but let it go. "You know, I wish someone would ask me to use my connections. Maybe I should change my last name to García so they'll know

I've got a family member on the Council too."

"Your dad would flip," Jack replied, staring at the wall. His headache was verging on a migraine now, and he was tired of this whole place. Perhaps agreeing to come back to the field had been a bad idea after all. But where else could he go? Back to D.C. and the memories of Sara? Or to Charleston, where even more pain and what-ifs remained?

"Kim seems to like you, though. She gave you a pass."

"Kim likes my connections, that's all." He rubbed the front of his head.

"She hates me," Cam said. "I don't know if you noticed. She can't stand being in my presence for more than five seconds."

"You know you don't have to stay here, right?" Jack said. "With your experience, you could go to any city in the world."

"I like it here. The city, I mean. And I know Kim is looking to retire in the next five years, so if I play my cards right, I could take her place."

"Is that what you want?" Jack asked. "Really?"

"We're not getting any younger, Jack. We're not demon. We age."

Jack couldn't argue with that. His body still ached from the beating it had taken recently. "Did Rubinski say anything else about the breach?"

"No, but she says given enough time, she might be able to find your phone, or a backup on the server. Right now, she and her team are trying to plug the holes. We've sent a group over to check the coffee shop, so it's probably going to be out of commission for a few days."

Jack shook his head. "Something she said bugged me. About Nunzia being a bad demon—"

"Don't let her get to you. She was just trying to distract you."

"But she's right."

"I know she's right. I also know she was trying to distract you."

Jack nodded. "Hey, do you think you could go get me some pain meds from the medic? I forgot to ask for some."

Cam tutted at the abrupt subject change, but stood and walked to the door. Before she got too far, she turned around and pecked his forehead in a motherly way.

"This is God's way of telling you that you're a fucking moron."

Then she walked out.

Jack didn't get the half-day like he wanted. Instead, he spent the entire afternoon being debriefed by several different divisions and an hour with the forensic artist. The drawing that came out didn't look exactly like her, but at least they had something to work with.

Luckily, Cam had stopped commenting on Jack's idiocy, but Kim and Navarro had continued to make veiled references for the rest of the day. Their gratitude at being alerted to the cyber-attack was soon forgotten in favor of reminding him that he'd let the primary suspect in Nunzia's third's death walk away.

So, it was with no small amount of relief when Jack finally arrived at his apartment. His back still ached from where the demon-woman had flipped him. He was looking forward to a glass of whiskey to dull the pain and put him to sleep.

His place might look good one day, if he ever got around to unpacking the boxes. He wasn't even sure what was in them anymore. Cam had done all the packing and arranged the movers. But he had a sneaking suspicion that only half his things had arrived in Atlanta. Cam had probably taken it upon herself to get rid of all Sara's things.

But even with Sara's clothes and mementos gone (or, more likely, in a storage facility), Jack couldn't bring himself to open any of the boxes. He was still using paper plates and cups instead of unpacking the dishes and silverware. Perhaps he thought if he never unpacked, there could be a chance he could one day move back to D.C., and to Sara.

Evenings seemed to be the hardest. He missed coming home to the smell of something cooking, and the bright smile on her face when he walked in the door. He missed being able to tell her every detail of his day, and listening as she complained about how Congress was screwing up her well-thought-out policy suggestions at the environmental think tank where she worked. They'd bitch, have a glass of wine, and then cuddle on the couch watching something stupid on Netflix. He could still feel her curled up against him, hear her laughter at the same joke they'd seen fifteen hundred times before.

But like mist burning off the lake, the memory was gone,

and Jack was left alone in his apartment once again.

He loosed a shaky breath and placed his wallet on the counter. Those were the kinds of thoughts that had kept him stuck for three years. Some day, he would have to let go of the hope that things would ever return to normal.

Some day, he mused. But not tonight.

He grabbed a red plastic cup from the stack and poured himself a large drink, which he gulped half of in one swig. Cup in hand, he was on his way to the fridge to figure out what was still edible when he stopped short.

His cellphone sat on the kitchen counter.

He heard movement behind him and spun around, ready to fight.

"I just *love* what you've done with the place."

The mystery woman strolled through the boxes containing Jack's life, a satisfied smirk on her face. She was still pale and sickly, although she carried herself like a powerful demon with her two long, thin swords strapped to her back.

She flipped open the lid of one of the boxes and tutted, "Looks like you need to take a few days off and unpack."

"What do you want?"

"To return your stolen property," she said.

"Why did you take it?"

"That's my business," she replied with a dangerous glint in her eye. "As is my identity, so stop digging."

"I wish I could, but I have a job to do," Jack said, wishing he'd had the foresight to unpack more of his weapons. All he had was a glass of whiskey to defend himself.

"I didn't realize the Division was taking orders from demons," she replied lazily, peeking into another box.

Jack finally marched forward and slammed the box shut. "We're just trying to prevent war between factions. So, if your intent is to—"

"I'm here to save lives," she said. "Something you should be doing too."

"Why? You're a…well, I think you're a demon."

She cracked a smile. "I was."

"But if your maker was killed, you should have—"

"My maker is very much alive." She shook her head, as if she'd decided she'd said too much already. "The point is: I'm not here to cause a demon war, and I'm not going to hurt anyone. So put away your sleuthing hat and leave it be."

"You know that's not an option."

She turned to him, pleading in her eyes. "I'm asking you *nicely* to please stop."

"Why?" Jack asked, taken aback by the sincerity in her voice. "If you mean us no harm, why not tell us who you are?"

"Because others…might harm me." Again, she screwed up her face, as if she'd divulged too much. "Just take my word on this. I'll leave town. Nunzia's already on his shitlist—"

"Who?"

"None of your business," she replied. "If I promise to go, will you put the investigation aside?"

"Who's trying to hurt you?" Jack shook his head. "Who

could hurt you? You're a powerhouse—the Division would be glad to have someone like you on our side."

"The Division is full of demon spies," she replied quietly, running her fingertips along his kitchen counter. "Whatever you know about me, they'll know too."

"Are you joking?" Jack actually laughed. "We have wards and detectors to make sure no demons get inside—"

"Your pathetic human technology is no match for Bael." Her gaze met his, and her eyes shimmered in the darkness.

A shiver of fear dripped down Jack's spine. "*Bael* is after you?"

She swallowed once, indecision on her face again. "In a matter of speaking. It's better if he doesn't find me."

"I think you're safe. He hasn't been seen topside in over a hundred years." At least, Jack hoped they were safe.

Her lip curled in anger. "And if you think the barrier between that world and this one is enough to contain him, you're an even bigger idiot than I thought. We exist in this world because *he* allows it—"

"Or he can't find you?" Jack suggested.

"Or he can't find me," she said, calmer. "And trust me, it's better for everyone if it remains that way."

"Fine, I'll lay off," he said, picking up his phone. "But tell me one thing: Why is a demon killing demons?"

She snorted. "I used to be a demon. I...I was cursed. I'm simply trying to undo it so I can get back to normal."

And then, as quickly as she'd arrived, she was gone.

CHAPTER SEVEN

"You're shitting me."

"I wish I was, Cam," Jack said, looking out the window. He wasn't confident his apartment was secure, and he was completely confident that his phone had been compromised, so he'd had to find a phone. After sweeping the neighborhood for signs of the mystery woman, he'd made his way to a nearby Waffle House.

He'd had to sweet talk the late-night waitress, flashing his Division badge and promising her it was a true emergency, but she'd finally relented and let him use the phone.

"Why didn't she just toss the phone?" Cam asked.

"I think the visit was more her asking me—us—to lay off. She just really doesn't want to be found," Jack said, glancing around the diner for the fifth time. He and the waitress were the only ones in there, but he was still on edge.

Cam muttered something in Spanish. "Listen, she stole government property. She's interfered with Division business. And now she's telling you to drop the investigation? Seems fishy."

"I agree...to an extent. I don't think we should stop the investigation, but I think we should cover our tracks a little better."

"Uh-huh. So what? Is she pretty?"

Jack chuckled and shook his head. "Cam, seriously. Don't even go there."

"It's a legitimate question."

"I mean, she's..." Jack ran a hand through his hair. "She's not awful. But she's the one taking an interest in me, not the other way around."

"Bullshit," Cam said. "You've got some kind of weird fascination with her. It's why you engaged her instead of getting backup. It's why you aren't *completely* freaked out that she showed up at your apartment."

"Oh, come on, Cam, that's ridiculous."

"Jack, she could've killed you. Twice! And you're acting like you got a visit from the tooth fairy. She's picked up on your wounded male scent and she's giving you the puppy dog eyes so you'll do what she wants."

Jack glared at his reflection in the window. "That's not fair, Cam."

"It's more than fair." She paused. "Maybe you don't have the hots for her, but you aren't thinking rationally. And not to state the obvious, but you do remember that your wife was killed by demons, right?"

Jack felt those words in his gut, but shook his head. "It's not the same. She's on the run from Bael. And she thinks if I continue investigating her, it's going to get back to him and he'll find her."

Cam made a few noises on the other end of the line. "You're telling me that the King of the Underworld is looking for Colibrí?"

"That's what she insinuated."

She sighed loudly. "Jackson, if Bael, or *anyone* close to him is after this chick, you're better off leaving her to fight her own battles. She's a big girl. She can take care of herself. And you, puny human man, would be fondly remembered as a bug on a windshield. I say you let the bitch alone and tell Kim it's a dead end."

"You can't tell me you aren't a little interested in figuring out who she is. Especially now that I know there's a curse involved." He grinned to himself, knowing he was about to lower the boom. "I mean, have you ever heard of something so strange? Demon curses?"

A pause. "Don't you do this to me, Grenard."

"Do what?" Jack asked innocently.

"Try to tempt me with a research project. It's the Seattle kappa demon all over again."

"I have no idea what you're talking about. I simply asked an innocent question: have you ever heard of demonic curses?"

"I will answer that question if you admit you're interested in Colibrí for reasons not totally career-related."

Silence descended on the line between them, but Jack gave in first. "Fine. I'm a little curious for non-career-related reasons. Happy?"

"First step's admitting it. And you're right, the more we learn about Colibrí, the less she makes sense. Of course, she could've been lying her tail off to you, so let's keep that as an option."

Jack's smile grew when he heard the *clack-clack* of a keyboard. "So you're in?"

"Don't make me regret this. Okay, a cursory search—pun intended—shows that curses are legend, but there's been no documented cases."

"Can you—?"

"Already emailed you," Cam said. "But what kind of curse would cause her to save humans?"

"She said she was trying to undo it," Jack said. "Whatever that means."

"You know, maybe all this is a red herring. Maybe she's actually trying to take over Bael's spot, and that's why she doesn't want to draw his attention."

"I highly doubt that. Who'd want to take on the king of the demons? And an athtar at that?" He paused. "Wouldn't that mean he made her?"

"Yeah, but listen, I've been thinking about this since you got tossed today. This chick is obviously powerful, and the only demon she fears is apparently Bael. So maybe she's angling to take him on during Demon Spring? But she's got to keep her plan a secret for a sneak attack."

"If she kills Bael, all the demons he turned would return to their human state, right? Including her?"

"On *rare* occasions, a powerful demon will remain a demon if their maker is killed. But we're talking a Nunzia-level demon. Who knows what would happen if someone took down the King of the Underworld?" She released a breath. "Part of what makes our job easy is that the demons topside live in fear of Bael returning. So they keep their aspirations low, which prevents a lot of the infighting. Without him around as the Big, Bad Wolf..."

He tapped his fingertips against the counter and nodded at the waitress, who was giving him the death glare for using their phone for so long. "Look, I'll keep researching curses, and maybe during rounds tomorrow we can start asking around and see if anyone else has seen her. But Cam...can we please keep our findings between us for a while? *Not* because I'm doing it to protect her, but I also don't want a bunch of ICDM agents from Charleston taking it away from us. And I'd rather she doesn't find out I lied to her about stopping the investigation."

"I guess. But only until Demon Spring is over. Then we'll come clean and hand it off. I doubt anyone would care until then anyway."

"You're the best, Cam."

"Yes, I'm aware."

Jack returned to his apartment and tried to go to sleep, but he found himself too preoccupied with demon curses and the silence that came with being all alone. Instead, he retrieved his personal laptop to get some work done, since his Division computer was still being scrubbed. It meant he had to use the virtual private network, which was slow and buggy, but it was something to do until he fell asleep.

Unsurprisingly, Cam hadn't just sent him one email, but ten.

She'd found small mentions of curses, but no indication of who cast the curse, or who *could* cast one, or if they were simply the same superstition about witches and wizards that had permeated human mythology. Pre-ICDM, the Europeans had had a very medieval view of demon hunting. Anything that wasn't sanctioned by the church was considered demonic, and anything demonic was burned at the stake. But since the woman was already a demon (presumably), that was a dead end.

Taking his cue from Cam, Jack searched the internet for information on curses and hexes. He found more than a few shops in New Orleans offering to cast anti-demon spells for a nominal fee. New Orleans, being the devilish city it was, had a reputation for drawing demons and humans alike. But Jack wasn't sure if these so-called "witches" providing spells were real, or as fake as the plastic charms they sold in the tourist traps.

Of course, he and Cam could always take a quick trip down to Louisiana to investigate in person. Cam wouldn't say no to an offer of fresh beignets.

But before he put in any travel vouchers, he accessed the Division's online archive and inputted the same search terms. He wasn't surprised when the results weren't substantial. The few books he did find were located in the Charleston archives, but that option was less tempting than New Orleans. Jack's parents and grandfather lived there, and while he had no issue with them in particular, the city held a lot of memories he would rather forget. The last time he'd visited, Sara's ghost had hung over every toast and conversation from Christmas to New Year's. Reminders of the life they'd planned and the one he was slowly trying to piece back together.

He grabbed his glass and took another sip to burn away those thoughts and get back to the matter at hand.

For the Charleston books, he could request an inter-archival loan, or even ask his grandfather to put in a call to have them ship it. He was, after all, the US representative on the ICDM council, and had the authority to do pretty much whatever he wanted.

Which reminded Jack of Kim's request.

He groaned and rubbed his face. It wouldn't be the first time he'd sent this type of email, but he hoped, in vain, it would be the last. He took another sip of his whiskey and typed:

Grandfather,

Hope you're well.

Jack paused, every inch of him screaming not to finish the note. He hated this part, hated using his connections to cover his ass. But he'd hate it even more if he got suspended and Frank or Jack's father George got word of it, and *they* interfered.

Wondering if you could locate a funding request by Patti Kim, here in Atlanta. She submitted a few weeks ago, and hasn't heard anything.

Would that be enough detail? He never wanted to come outright and say, "Hi, Grandfather, send money." There were still nepotism and ethics laws to be concerned with.

Let me know if you make it out this way. We'll grab a steak.

- Jackie

Jack decided that was enough of that unpleasantness, and sent the email. He returned to the curse information Cam had sent, but it wasn't two minutes before he got a new email in his inbox.

Jackie,

Glad to know I'm not the only one up late working.

I looked into your request. Hasn't made it across my desk yet, but I'll check with my counterparts over in the Division. Doubtful

Atlanta will get any extra money, but I wouldn't rule it out. We're expecting the fissure to happen on the west coast this year. Good news for us, though.

Hope to see you at this year's prep meeting. I know your parents miss you.

All the best,
Frank

P.S. - Tell Cam I said hi.

Before every Demon Spring, Frank hosted the US Division agents in Charleston for a two-day seminar to coordinate efforts across the country. The purpose of the event was twofold: to learn some new anti-demon techniques and to establish plans with the city most likely to be affected.

Jack and Cam had attended twice—once as Academy students and once as field agents. Both times, they'd been bored to tears as the agents discussed everything from triage techniques to how to request military support.

Of course, in the thick of Demon Spring, with thousands of Underworld demons springing from the fissure, all the carefully coordinated strategies went out the window. He and Cam just fought off as many as they could in the initial flood and then spent the rest of the Spring saving humans who hadn't heeded the evacuation warnings.

Despite what Cam might think, Jack wasn't eager to jump

back in the front lines again. Before Sara's death, blood and gore had been a game to him. He and Cam had kept score of how many demons they'd killed in a single day—winner bought the loser a lobster dinner. But that had been before he'd understood the true meaning of death, before the sightless gaze had been on his own wife's face instead of some random demon's.

Now, death was something to be avoided at all costs.

Jack typed an email to Kim, paraphrasing his grandfather about the status of her request, and hoped it would be enough to keep him out of the dog house.

CHAPTER EIGHT

When Jack arrived at the Division office that next morning, he found it abuzz with activity about the demonic breach from the day before, but, luckily, no mention of his late night visitor. He trusted Cam not to say anything to hurt him intentionally, but sometimes she got a little overzealous.

Still, he felt it his duty to turn in his phone. He told the security officer that it had appeared on his doorstep, which had resulted in a slew of morning meetings with Navarro, Kim, and others. Cam's gaze burned a hole in the side of his head as he lied about talking to the mystery woman, but she didn't say anything against him.

Jack was able to convince both Navarro and Kim that the mystery woman was quickly becoming a cold case, and that Nunzia would be more interested in the resolution of the Parras case. Luckily for Jack, Nunzia had conveyed the same to

Navarro.

"So we'll put this to the side for now," the director said. "If you hear anything else from her…"

"I'll be sure to let you know," Jack replied.

Back in their small office, Cam's face was pressed in almost permanent disapproval. Jack did his best to ignore it as he hand wrote the forms and reports for reporting an unannounced demonic visit, as his computer was still being scrubbed.

"Serves you right," Cam said, typing loudly on her computer for effect. "Don't understand why you're covering for Colibrí."

"If I told Kim she'd been in my house, do you think I'd ever be able to go home?" Jack replied, glancing up from his forms.

"That's your reasoning?"

"Yep."

She pursed her lips.

"Seriously," Jack said.

Cam held out her hand. "Give me half."

Jack handed over a stack of forms, and Cam got to work, muttering about saving his ass, stupid boys, and hormones.

There was a knock at the door, and Kim popped her head in.

"Got your email," she said. "Thanks for elevating it. Let me know if you hear anything more."

Jack nodded, grateful that was the end of it.

"In the meantime, Navarro has asked me to recertify you in weapons," Kim said. "You'll need to report down to the armory at noon for your test."

"That's not a lot of notice," Cam replied with a frown.

"Well, it's clear Agent Grenard is eager to get back out into the field. It's best to get this out of the way." She glanced at Cam with no small amount of annoyance. "Perhaps you might want to brush up on protocols yourself, Agent Macarro."

With that, she left, Cam seethed, and Jack was now a little worried.

"Teflon Grenard strikes again," she said. "So what's that email she was talking about?"

"Kim wanted me to get her money," Jack said. "It was either send an email to Frank or get written up for engaging a demon without certification."

"Kim is such an asshole," Cam said. "You know you didn't have to send that email. Navarro wasn't going to suspend you."

"Yeah, I know," Jack said. "But I figured I might as well grease the wheels and keep her from complaining too much."

Cam rolled her eyes, muttering something in Spanish. Jack had picked up a lot from Sara, so he caught 'idiot' and 'pushover' and 'moron.'

Right before noon, Jack and Cam made their way upstairs to the armory with their weapons. As Academy graduates, they were trained in a wide assortment of weapons, but upon graduation and entry into field work, they were allowed to carry a single weapon of choice. Cam carried a macuahuitl, a traditional Aztec weapon that looked like a large wooden bat with sharp teeth. The Mexican Division had updated their weaponry over the years; Cam's version was made of strong, black plastic with teeth that could retract with the push of a button. She carried it on her back, attached by a magnetic connector. It had been a gift from her Great Aunt María, the Mexican Councilwoman who sat opposite Frank.

Jack had also received a weapon from his Council-sitting relative. His knives were made of the same military-grade plastic, with sharp, curved blades almost the length of his forearm. For years, they'd been his pride and joy. But after Sara's death, he couldn't even look at them, let alone train with them. He could make do in the field, but under the scrutiny of a trained expert, he wasn't sure his skills would measure up.

"What's up?" Cam asked. "You're quiet."

"Just wondering how badly I'm going to fuck this up," Jack said, twisting the handles in his hand. "It's been a while since I've used these."

"It's like riding a bike," Cam said. "Only with pointy objects."

The elevator doors opened into the armory, where several agents were engaged in hand-to-hand combat. The trainers, dressed in gray tank tops, stood to the side, watching them in stony silence. Every so often, one would bark an order or critique, then return to silence.

Jack prayed he wouldn't have an audience.

"Agent Grenard here for recertification," Cam said, walking up to the main check-in window.

"Grenard?" A woman with thick, beefy shoulders and arms approached them. She was obviously Russian, and a good head above even Jack. "I'm Alyonna. I will do certification."

Jack reached for the woman's hand and was a little unnerved by the strength of it. "H-hi."

"I will review weapons first."

Jack unsheathed his curved knives and handed them over. Alyonna wielded them with ease, swinging them in front as she tested their weight and balance.

"These are excellent quality. Made in Shanghai?" She tossed the blade in the air and caught it one-handed. "You've got connections."

Heat crept up Jack's neck. "Yeah. You could say that."

"So what does he have to do?" Cam asked as Alyonna used his knives to slice through a piece of paper.

"He'll need to demonstrate mastery of aim, technique, ability." She turned to examine Cam. "Are you partner?"

She nodded.

"Then you test him. I watch."

Cam shrugged and started marching forward, but Alyonna grabbed her by the shoulder.

"Need weapon for testing, too." Cam handed it over. "This club is…Mexican?" she asked, holding it up as she had Jack's knives. With a flick of her wrist, the sharp teeth sprung out from the sides of the weapon. "This is fine instrument."

"My great aunt got it for me," Cam announced proudly to everyone within hearing distance. "She's the Mexican Councilwoman."

Alyonna examined each tooth closely. "Mm…needs some sharpening. Do you care for your weapon regularly?"

Cam bristled while Jack chanced a snort of laughter. She snatched the club from the inspector's hand.

"Have you done a test like this before?" Alyonna asked Jack. She handed him a pair of wooden sticks that would stand in for his knives, and Cam took the long wooden broadsword.

"It's been a few years," he admitted.

Alyonna smiled, but there was little comfort in it. "Partner will take it easy. No blood."

"Oh, that's no fun," Cam replied, turning the stick in her hand a few times to warm up.

"Are you ready? Yes? Begin!"

Cam swung first, and he crossed his sticks to block, although she got a little closer than usual. She knew it too, as she quirked a brow in amusement before removing her sword from his grip. Jack parried it and attempted to fight with his other sword, but she twisted out of the way, smacking her sword against the back of his knee.

"And you're immobile," she said with a smirk.

"Continue," Alyonna said. "He is not dead yet."

Jack lunged again, but his attack was easily blocked. An attempt at a side swipe ghosted by her side—if he'd had real knives, she would've had a nasty cut. But not a fatal wound on a demon by any stretch.

In his moment of distraction, Cam's wooden sword came down on his shoulder, knocking the knife from his hand. She quirked a brow then glanced at Alyonna, who didn't look pleased.

"C'mon, Jack," Cam whispered. "This is easy shit."

"I know," he said, wiping the sweat from his brow. "I can do this."

"Yeah, you can," she said, turning the weapon in her hand. "So do it."

They engaged again, once, twice, three times. Then Jack saw an opening on Cam's right and pressed the tip of his knife to her side.

"Good," Alyonna called.

Cam stepped back, an unreadable look on her face. Again, Jack swung for her, and again, he caught her shoulder.

That was when he realized what the look meant—Cam was letting him win.

"Pay attention," she whispered, glancing to her right hip, which was presented to him without defense. He batted away her sword and pushed both wooden tips against her neck.

"End," Alyonna called. "I let you pass. Barely."

Cam grinned and punched Jack in the shoulder. "Way to go."

"Yeah, go me," Jack replied weakly.

"But you will join me once a week to train," Alyonna said. "You have technique but it is sloppy. Practice, practice, practice."

"Sloppy, Jack. *Sloppy.*"

"Yes, I heard her."

After a quick shower, Jack and Cam left work early and

headed to the nearest bar for happy hour to celebrate Jack passing. Or, more specifically, Cam gloating about how she was much better at it than he was.

"I'm just saying, maybe you should give back that medal you won in our third year," she said.

"What, give it to you?" Jack barked a laugh. "It should go to Sharon Michaels then. She came in second in the match."

"That little bitch cheated," Cam snarled.

"Yeah, yeah, I remember."

Cam took a swig of her drink. "You slept with her, didn't you?"

Jack squinted at the wall, trying to remember what the girl looked like. "I did, didn't I?"

"So many girls you can't keep them all straight, huh?"

"Well, you know, they all pale in comparison to..." Jack swallowed and looked at his beer, shocked at how easily he'd forgotten. Happiness melted away like ice cream on a hot sidewalk, and he was left with the odd numbness of remembering that his wife was dead.

"So, um... How are you settling in?" Cam asked after a few awkward moments. "Feels like it's been ages since we've talked about anything other than work."

"Besides the demon vigilante who shows up at night?" He smiled, but there was little happiness in it. "I'm totally loving Atlanta."

"Really?" Cam asked. "I mean, are you really happy here?"

"I...guess I haven't thought about it enough. I'm glad work

has been busy though." Jack's first night shift was the following evening, and he wasn't really looking forward to having the day to himself.

"And you're seriously okay to go on rounds tomorrow night, right?" Cam asked. "I mean, after everything. You're—"

"Cam, we're just checking in on Nunzia's people, I don't expect to be picking any fights. As long as you promise not to get me involved in any."

"Oh, speaking of promises." She pulled a small envelope from her pocket and placed it on the bar. "Thought you might want these back."

Jack quirked a brow and unwrapped the present. The bag fell to the table, revealing a set of coins, connected by a leather cord. Each coin was rimmed with a rubber border and had a design etched on it.

"Thanks," Jack said, taking the coins by the leather bracelet. They were a traditional set of anti-demonic wards the Garcías had been using since the first demons arrived in ancient Mexico. Many saw it as an old tradition that was pure superstition, but the charms had saved his and Cam's asses more times than not.

Cam's mother had given them to him when he and Cam had graduated the Academy, telling him that he was an honorary García and deserved the same protections Cam had. But after Sara died, he'd given them to Cam for safekeeping. He didn't feel he deserved to carry the talisman of her family.

"I knew I wasn't going to keep it," Cam said after a moment. She flashed her bracelet, jangling the metal coins she wore attached to a metal bracelet around her wrist. "Besides, mine work better."

"In your dreams." Jack chuckled, carefully moving the coins around. "Lilin magic is…?"

"Blue."

Jack pulled the talisman from the set and ran his finger along the etching. "Still don't know how these work, do you?" Jack asked, turning them over in his hands.

"Haven't been able to secure the funding to research it. Tía María thinks it's stupid, so she won't push it on the Council. But I'd like to propose a study to your grandfather to see if we could turn these things into weapons," Cam replied, playing with the talismans around her wrist. "Assuming we *could* find a willing demon to study the effects on, or maybe just kidnap one and pretend like we killed it so the local lord doesn't retaliate."

"You could slip a talisman onto a lilin next time we're out," Jack offered.

"Nah, that's a little too risky. Besides, they could just throw it off. And I'm not willing to piss Nunzia off more than I already have." She took a long drink. "To think, I was getting somewhere with her until Colibrí came along and fucked everything up."

"It's a little ridiculous, isn't it? That we have to kiss ass and make nice with the demons." Jack peeled the sticker off his beer bottle.

"Don't let Colibrí get in your head. We only make nice because we don't want war to break out between demons and humans."

"But it does, every four years. Demon Spring happens and we're fighting back the Underworld creatures. And the topside demons don't do a damned thing to help us. They join in." Jack sat back. "So I can't help but wonder why we don't just annihilate them?"

"Because we're human, and they're immortal. And although there's a hell of a lot more of us than them, they also can do a lot of damage to us." She sighed. "I think the deep, dark secret your grandfather is keeping from us is that we really aren't in power. We're just the fingers in the dykes, plugging holes before the entire damned wall collapses."

"If they have all the power, why don't they use it?" Jack asked.

"Maybe the same reason the Division doesn't really press too hard against demons like Nunzia. There's a weird, permanent truce between the two sides. And maybe as long as neither side blinks, they won't know who really has the upper hand."

Jack chuckled and drank his beer.

"What's with these introspective questions?" Cam asked. "Are you rethinking coming back to field work?"

"Maybe. I don't know. I haven't been back long enough to have an opinion. Maybe I'm just trying to figure out what I believe again." He picked up the talisman, considering it for a moment. "Every time I take something like this, I feel like I'm finding little bits of myself again. But the weird thing is, they don't feel the same. It's almost like I'm trying to glue pieces of shattered glass together and getting crap all over the edges." He slipped the talismans around his wrists. "I'm not a poet. But that's what it feels like."

"Then maybe you should stop piecing your life back together and start making a new one." Cam played with the little straw. "I mean, I know it's easier said than done. I was lucky that I had work to throw myself into after everything. Made it less about losing my little sister and more about just another case."

Jack glanced to her. "Don't you miss her?"

"Every damned day," Cam replied quietly. "But I guess I forced myself to separate the two. To put aside my grief while I was working. I told myself that if I stopped, some other poor girl would get murdered. Some other sister would have to bury her Sara. That's what kept me going."

"You're stronger than I am," Jack said softly.

"Well, no shit," Cam replied with a sad smile. "But I'm glad you decided to come down here. Even with the vigilante, Kim, and Demon Spring, it really didn't feel right to do this stuff without you. As much as I love work, it's easier to feel normal with you around."

Jack gripped her hand and kissed it. "Felt weird not having you boss me around all the time, too."

CHAPTER NINE

Jack spent most of the day watching Netflix and trying to sleep. As an accountant, he was never asked to stay after business hours, so his body had grown accustomed to working during the day and sleeping at night. But back in field work, he was expected to pull at least two all-nighters every week. It was going to take some time to get readjusted.

As dusk fell outside, he peeled himself off the couch, showered, and put on a pair of loose-fitting pants and a shirt he could move in. He didn't expect to get into any trouble tonight, but there was always the possibility. Especially when working with Cam.

He retrieved his knives from their case and swung them around for a moment, testing their weight in his hands. Alyonna had been right—he needed to practice.

"I love watching you put on your knives, Jackie."

A chill skittered down his spine, and bittersweet memories crept into his mind. Sara standing in the doorway of the living room, her arms folded across her chest and that sparkle in her eye that usually meant a late arrival for him. She hated everything demon-related, but she *loved* watching him practice with his knives. It made her feel safe to know he could protect her.

That she'd died on the very floor he'd trained on was the cruelest of ironies.

He fought against remembering what had been seared into his mind, but it came anyway. Her body on the floor, her throat ripped out in the style typical of nox demons. The Division agents he worked with forcing him out of his house before he melted down completely.

The worst memories weren't even real. He could only imagine her fear when the nox broke in. Her screams of terror, begging someone—begging Jack—to save her. She must've believed until the very end that he would protect her with those knives she'd loved so much.

He hadn't even gotten a chance to say goodbye.

Before he could stop them, the tears had begun to fall down his face as his heart throbbed in pain, like it was physically shattering. This was the grief that had haunted him since that day. It no longer followed him like a shadow; now, it was a surprise tidal wave, a tornado that hit without warning and pulled him back to the darkest period of his life.

His phone vibrated, reminding him that it was time to leave.

He forced himself to take deep breaths, needing to feel normal—to be normal—on his shift. He'd left his grief behind in D.C. and wasn't going to let this brief relapse ruin what had been excellent progress.

His breath shaky, he straightened and finished fastening his knives to his hips, grateful he wasn't going to be alone that night.

By the time Jack picked up coffee and pulled up in front of Cam's house, he was nursing a numb feeling in the back of his mind. But for Cam, he would pretend he wasn't drowning.

"Just like old times, huh?" Jack said, rolling down the window of his car. Cam flashed him a smile as she slowly walked down the steps of her row house, looking half-asleep still. Her wild hair was balled behind her head, and her Division jacket hung from her arm as she opened the car door and sat down. She took the second cup of coffee in the cupholder.

"You sure know how to win a girl's heart, Jackie," she said, sipping the drink. "For both our sakes, I hope tonight's easy."

"What's on the menu?" Jack asked.

"We've got to stop by Nunzia's headquarters for the monthly audit," Cam said, scrolling through her phone. "Do some random inspections at a couple smaller bars."

While that sounded like normal business for two Division agents, Jack was in need of some deeper distraction. "Want to see what we can rustle up about the mystery woman?"

"Colibrí?" Cam's eyes narrowed. "Did she show up again?"

"No, but I thought it might be a good opportunity to ask around while we're out in the city. See if anyone's seen or heard of her."

"The problem with that is most of the demons in this town are Nunzia's. And since she's freezing us out, I doubt any of them will talk to us."

"It's possible," Jack replied. "But we could still try. Sometimes demons are willing to spill even when the boss says no."

Cam sighed. "Promise me if we don't find anything, if this is a big dead-end, you'll put this one on the back burner? Kim's going to ride us hard until this Demon Spring is over, and I just have a gut feeling we're in for it this time."

"I promise," Jack said with a nod. "Where to first, partner?"

"Belly of the Beast. Nunzia's favorite bar."

"What's it called?"

"…Belly of the Beast."

"Well, she's not unobvious, is she?"

Belly of the Beast turned out to be a swanky restaurant with a giant pig for a mascot which served, unsurprisingly, pork meals. That was the front, anyway, and from what Jack could tell walking by the restaurant, it was busy with happy, *human* patrons. But one moment inside and he felt the other reason for the crowd—lilin magic.

"W…what's going on in here?" Jack asked.

Cam clicked her tongue. "Nunzia and the Division have an agreement. She's allowed to use a little magic to keep her customers happy. We do periodic audits to make sure she isn't over the allowable limits."

"And... nobody becomes obsessed?" Jack asked.

"It's not a lot of miasma, and it's coming from a lot of different demons, so no," Cam said. "In my view, it's skirting the line between what should be allowed, but what can you do? Navarro allows it to keep the peace. But this isn't even the worst of it."

Cam led him past the main restaurant to a back door marked "Employees Only." She cracked open the door and sweet-smelling miasma rushed into Jack's nose. The power seeped into the air and settled uncomfortably in his stomach. Cam, similarly uncomfortable, pressed her own blue-covered talisman against her skin and looked a little less green.

His eyes adjusted to the darker room, which was much quieter than the restaurant. Couples sat at small booths holding hands and talking in hushed voices with doe-eyed expressions. For a lilin place, it was incredibly G-rated.

"This is the other half of her business," Cam said. "Twenty bucks gets you an hour in this muck to jumpstart your romance."

"*This* can't possibly be legal," Jack said. "There's enough miasma to lure the entire city."

"As long as it comes from six or more lilins, it's legal." She led him over to a booth where they sat down. "And there aren't any lilins in here making transformations. So they say, anyway."

"Don't know why any human would willingly seek this out.

Marital problems or not."

"Probably the same reason people drink," Cam replied. Given enough time, they'd adjust to the sensation, but both would have a wicked headache if they stayed more than a few hours in such a powerful place.

"What can I get you two?" asked a waiter. He eyed them. "Human or demon?"

"Division," Cam said. "Just here to do your monthly check. Can you send over your manager?"

He bristled, as if the very idea of Division operatives in his section would result in his suspension. But he went to the bartender, who glanced over at their table and rolled his eyes before disappearing into the back room. A few breaths later, a young blonde woman appeared, flashing a bright white smile.

"Agent Macarro, pleasure to see you again," she said, offering her hand. She glanced at Jack approvingly. "Who's your friend?"

"Partner," Cam said. "Jack, this is Angela, one of Nunzia's seconds."

"Pleasure to meet you," Jack said, holding out his hand. When the demon took it, he got a buzz of pleasurable energy. But thanks to the talisman, the effect was dulled.

"Can you make this quick, Angela? The demon juice is thick tonight," Cam said.

"Sure, sure. Come back to my office. We've had a few transitions tonight, but it's all within allowable limits."

"Uh-huh," Jack said, folding his arms.

"Completely legitimate." Angela flashed another smile. "I'd

be happy to show you two the contracts."

"Cam, why don't you take this? I'm gonna ask around for our other project," Jack said. He wasn't sure if he wanted to advertise to Nunzia's second that he was leading the investigation, although he got the distinct impression she knew more about him than she let on.

"Sure," Cam said, earning a frown from Angela. But the demon left with Cam anyway.

Jack made sure to press the talisman into his hand as he walked up to the bar where the demonic smoke was pretty thick. The bartender gave him a once over and then went back to cleaning glasses.

"What are you drinking?" he asked.

"I have a question."

"Can't answer nothing without the boss's approval," he grunted.

"Well, it's not about an investigation," Jack said. "Just a professional curiosity. Something I heard about in passing."

The bartender put down one glass and grabbed another. But he didn't tell Jack to get lost, so Jack assumed that was good news.

"Do you know anything about demon curses?"

"Curses?" He snorted and spat on the bar, then cleaned it with the rag. "Who cares about curses?"

"I do, and I'm asking." Jack slid a hundred-dollar bill across the table. "What about cursing a demon to…repent? Or make amends, or—"

The demon tilted his head back and howled with laughter. Jack winced, knowing the conversation was at an end. No one else would speak to him now.

"Oh, that's rich. You hear that in a church somewhere? Someone promising to bless a demon to make 'em repent for all the lives they took?"

"So, you've never heard of it," Jack said, standing. He tossed down another twenty. "Thanks for your time."

"I will say," the bartender said as Jack walked away, "if there were such a curse, it'd be the worst thing imaginable."

Jack stopped. "Why's that?"

"Demons gotta make more demons if we wanna live in the human world between Demon Springs. It's how God made us, you know?" He chewed on a toothpick, as if there was a bad taste in his mouth. "So we use our magic and trick 'em into turning. But we can do it because we don't feel nothin' for them, only survival. If someone were to curse a demon with feelin' guilty? I doubt that demon would be able to transition another human ever again. And that's the worst way to die—of starvation."

"H-how long would it take?"

"Depends on the demon, o'course. Me? A year. Maybe two. Someone like Nunzia?" He shook his head. "Centuries of feeling like your insides are gonna eat your outsides. Can't imagine a worse torture."

A pair of dull green eyes and ashy skin popped into his mind's eye. She certainly looked famished. "Thank you." He tossed down another twenty as Cam was walking out of the back room. Her cheeks were flushed, but her gaze determined.

"How'd it go?" Jack asked.

"Angela's been trying to get me to sleep with her since I started," Cam said, rubbing her face. "I'd be flattered if I didn't know it was to keep me from bringing charges against her boss."

"I've been 'flirting' with the bartender to no avail," Jack said with a small laugh. He filled Cam in on what he'd just learned. "Trying to figure out what she meant by 'undo' it. I think maybe she's done something horrible, or a whole lot of somethings, and she's been cursed to make amends for it. At least that's the theory that makes the most sense to me."

"Other than usurping Bael," Cam said.

"Yeah and…well, *that* theory is so far-fetched," Jack said. "He's an original demon. No one's even come close to taking him out."

"That we know of," she replied. "We don't exactly have a demon news network to tell us what's going on underground. Maybe he's up to his eyeballs in constant rebellion. Maybe *that's* why no one's seen him."

"Fine, fine," Jack said, waving his hand around. "Let's just get out of here before I puke. This lust magic is getting to me."

"You sure?" Cam asked with a coy expression. "I'm sure one of these ladies would be happy to help you jumpstart your sex life…"

"Let's go, Camilla."

—⟨✶⟩—

For the rest of the night, neither Jack nor Cam brought up Bael, Colibrí, or anything related to subjects other than their primary cases. Cam confirmed that Nunzia's contracts had all been legal (or as legal as she could verify), and so they drove around, looking for trouble and finding little.

As the sun peeked over the tops of the buildings, Jack pulled his car into his parking garage and trudged to the elevator, unbuckling his knives so he could flop into bed and sleep for the rest of the day, just in time to get up for his second night shift.

The elevator dinged, and he got off, already picturing the mattress, the bedsheets, the...

Movement caught his eye, and he stopped in front of one of the hall windows. In the dim light of the early morning, under the streetlight, there she was. The mystery woman. She leaned against the post, staring up at the building. He wasn't sure if she could see him, but he was sure she must've seen him arrive. In her hand was a rather large sword, and the message was clear.

Well, if she wanted to kill him, she could go ahead and get it over with.

He stood at the window for a moment, waiting for his impending death with numb acceptance. But she didn't move, didn't dash across the street. Just stood, staring at his apartment building. From this distance, he couldn't read her face, but he imagined the indecision he'd seen when she'd broken into his apartment.

She sheathed her sword on her back and stepped out of the light, her shadow disappearing down the street.

CHAPTER TEN

The second night of rounds had been much like the first, although instead of hitting Nunzia's bar, Jack and Cam audited some of her spawns' businesses. Yet again, they'd uncovered nothing illegal at any of them. A routine, if slightly boring, set of rounds.

The mystery woman hadn't shown up again as far as Jack could tell, but he had a feeling she'd make herself known if she had a problem with him. He hadn't mentioned it to Cam—after all, what was there to mention? He was certain the woman knew he was continuing the investigation, and he was also certain she could kill him if she wanted to.

After a short weekend where he failed to unpack any boxes, he arrived at work to find his laptop and cellphone returned to him, scrubbed of all traces of hacking. He also found an email from Kim telling him to stop in her office as soon as he was able.

Since Cam hadn't arrived yet, he gathered up his coffee and made the trek.

"You wanted to talk?" Jack asked, poking his head into her office.

"Come in, Grenard," Kim said, turning away from her computer to face him. "How were your first patrols?"

"Uneventful. Nunzia's trying to freeze us out, it seems. Punishment for the mystery woman investigation."

Kim snorted. "And how is that going? Anything new to give me?"

"Nope. Haven't seen her," Jack said, hoping he sounded convincing. "Did you call me in to talk about it?"

"No. I called up to Charleston this morning to see the status of my funding request."

"Did you get it?" Jack asked, hopeful this wouldn't turn into another favor-asking situation.

"Denied," she said with a shake of her head. "However, I was informed that you and Agent Macarro are to represent our office during the Demon Spring preparation meetings."

"Ah." Jack scratched his nose. He had a feeling Frank was behind that. "You could send someone else?"

"It was a direct order from ICDM," Kim said, looking a bit put out. "And as much as I hate to admit it, the two of you have some background with these kinds of meetings. You've been on the front lines of a Demon Spring before. You know what to expect."

"You don't think there's going to be a breach near Atlanta,

do you?" Jack asked.

"No, of course not," Kim said. "But because we've never been at ground zero, we don't get the funding for training, or the agents with experience. You two, while rusty, are some of the best we have." She flipped the paper on her desk and Jack saw his test results from Alyonna. He was still surprised he passed. "We'd like to ask Charleston to increase our training budget, too."

There it is. "You know, I could just call Frank—"

Kim chuckled. "You're that averse to an all-expenses-paid trip back home to Charleston?"

"Not really, I just..." Jack considered his words. He wasn't interested in sharing how he felt about Charleston with Kim. "I don't want anyone around here to think I'm getting preferential treatment because of who I am."

"I'm sure," Kim said, unconvinced. "Well, that's all. Unless there was something else you needed from me?"

"No," Jack said, standing up. "Thanks."

"We've been volun-told to go to the Demon Spring prep meeting in Charleston," Jack said, as he walked into the office. Cam was already there, and a fresh coffee was sitting on his desk along with a breakfast sandwich.

He sat down and dug in, two bites in before he realized Cam hadn't said anything to his announcement. At the very least, he expected a squeal of excitement that they were going to the councilman's office.

"Did you orchestrate this?" Jack asked.

She feigned innocence. "Maybe."

"Camilla…"

"Fine, yes." She sat back and threw her hands behind her head. "Frank emailed me and asked if I wanted to represent Atlanta at the meetings, and I told him you and I would love to —"

"*You* would love to," Jack said, folding his arms over his chest.

Cam shrugged. "You haven't been home since December."

"I just moved here!" Jack said, scrambling for excuses. "I haven't even had time to look around the city, let alone plan big trips to Charleston."

"Your mom thinks you're avoiding her."

And she wasn't completely wrong, Jack *had* been avoiding her. But Christmas had been rough, and every time he spoke with his mother, it just reminded him of that black week.

"It's not going to be a fun trip," Jack said after a moment.

"Everything is fun if you try hard enough." She narrowed her eyes. "What's wrong? Did something happen with your mom?"

"It's not her…" Jack said, lamely, not wanting to lie, but not wanting to tell the whole truth either. "Kim wants me to ask Frank for money again. Something about training." Jack shook his head. "Do you think it's too late to change my last name?"

Cam surveyed him for a moment. "No, I don't think that would work. You've got the Grenard nose. I think it's too late to hide yourself."

"Great."

"Cheer up, Jack," Cam said, standing and grabbing her coat. "I've got to make another trek to Montgomery for the day. Want to come?"

As tempting as that was, Jack was eager to get back to the office to continue his curse research. And today, he was hoping to spend some time in the library downstairs.

The bartender had given Jack some direction, in any case. She was powerful enough to kill a 500 year old demon, but she was also starving to death. Jack also just got the sense that she was *old*, which meant she might be somewhere in the annals of ICDM literature.

Jack made his way down to the Atlanta archives in the basement of the building, his bag of notes in hand. He was greeted by a man who looked surprised to see another human being.

"Hello! Are you lost?"

"Nope," Jack said. "Have a little project I need to do some work on. Can I have a look around?"

"Of course," he said. "My name is Rupert."

"Jack," he said, not offering his last name. He was getting tired of people using it against him.

Unfortunately, there must not have been much to do in the archives but look up new hires. "Grenard?"

Jack sighed. "Yes."

"Oh, excellent!" Rupert said, clapping his hands. "Well,

we've got a lot of good information down here. Not as much as Charleston, of course, but a lot of our texts haven't been digitized. They won't allocate any more resources to it." Rupert frowned, as if he disagreed with that opinion mightily. "It's all fun and games until someone can't find the answer they're looking for in Google."

"Well, that's why I'm here," Jack said, hoping he could get out of the conversation without another favor to take with him to Charleston. "Have you heard anything about demonic curses?"

He furrowed his brow. "I've never heard of demonic curses, no. Other than primitive humans using it to describe the transformation of a demon."

"No, that's not it," Jack said. "What about a demon-killing demon?"

That drew a laugh from the archivist. "Where would you like to start? Demons have been killing other demons for as long as they've been on this realm. They just do it more civilized now."

"What about one who isn't being civilized?" Jack said, running his finger along a nearby book spine. "A female demon."

"Hm. Haven't heard anything about that specifically, other than the gossip."

"Gossip?"

"Yeah, heard one of Nunzia's demons ate it the other night. Big stir up... Oh." He nodded. "That's why you're here."

"Got anything other than water cooler talk?"

"I... You know, I might. Let me see what I have in the

back."

Jack followed him through a row of cardboard boxes marked with different dates and demon names. A few had been marked "Nunzia," but Rupert didn't stop until they reached the back of the archives where he had a stack of old books on a desk.

"Ah, here we are," he said, pulling one from the group. "This is a listing of all the most powerful demons of the past five hundred years. Most of these are fairly well-known, or dead, so we haven't prioritized digitizing it. But if she's as powerful as rumors say, she would definitely be in here."

"Right, thanks. What do I need to fill out to take this with me?"

"T-take it with you?" He chuckled nervously. "I can't let you take that—"

"I'm a Grenard," Jack replied with a half-smile that usually worked better on women than men. "I can put in a good word for you with my grandfather on the Council. Get you some digitization equipment?"

"Oh!" His face lit up. "Well, in that case..."

"Gross..."

The disfigured face of a kappa demon gazed up at Jack from the pages of the book. This particular turtle-faced demon had been found in Australia during a Demon Spring in the 1920s, where it lived for a few years before disappearing back underground. This demon, called Kareu, was over a thousand years old, and created by Mizuchi, the original kappa demon, himself. Kareu had killed scores of people by flooding a village with water, and then took the survivors as his spawn.

Discomfort churned in Jack's stomach. He'd been reading this book for the better part of two days, and every demon he came across horrified him more. It wasn't just the humans they'd turned into spawn, it was the sheer number they'd flat-out killed.

He'd canvassed the book cover-to-cover and hadn't seen anyone who resembled his mystery woman. In fact, the only human-looking creature in the book was Bael, and he got his own chapter. He hoped her absence meant she hadn't committed any atrocities, but even he wasn't that optimistic.

"You look perplexed," Cam said, breaking the silence of their office. She was writing up a report on her latest meeting in Montgomery.

"How many people d'you think she's killed?" Jack asked, after a moment.

"What?"

Jack sat back and folded his hands behind his head. "There's not one demon in this book that isn't a complete monster. Just wondering if that means Colibrí killed humans, too."

"Yeah? That's how it works," Cam said, craning her neck around her monitor. "Makes her a little less appealing, huh?"

"It just...it doesn't make any sense," he replied, flipping through the pages. "It's like this eloko demon in Ghana. Massacred an entire village. Children, even. That demon's probably a cold-blooded killer with no remorse. But this woman? She's..."

"She's what? Pretty?"

"Tortured."

"Hm." Cam sat back. "And why is that confusing you, Jackson? You aren't trying to help her. You're trying to capture her. Those are our orders." She cocked her head. "Isn't that right?"

"Mm," Jack said, returning his attention to the book. There was a particularly gruesome photo of a fully transformed nox, his face wolfish and deranged with a snout and long, dripping teeth. To make the photo complete, he wore the heads of three humans around his neck. Jack swallowed and turned the page.

"I see what's going on," Cam said softly. "You think if you can somehow…*save* this woman, it'll make you feel better about Sara?"

"W-what?" His face warmed. "I didn't—"

"You didn't have to." She sighed and leaned back in her chair. "That's why you're so interested in her. It's not because she's unusual or pretty or the case is odd."

"It's because she's a demon hunting demons—"

"C'mon, Jack. You can't fool me." She tilted her head in a way that was almost too patronizing. "Look, you've been blaming yourself for three years. But Sara's death *wasn't* your fault."

He flinched. They'd had this conversation for days—weeks, really—after Sara died. Cam had been convinced, based on the evidence, that it had been a random murder by a new demon, but Jack couldn't accept that. Not when that new demon had been owned by one of the most feared noxes, who was starting to chafe under the Division's thumb.

"Jack, demons kill humans. That's what they do. And Sara was…" She swallowed, and there was a hint of the sadness that she kept locked away. "Sara was just an innocent victim."

"They were sending a message."

"Okay, so what if they were?" Cam said. "Are you gonna let them win the war? You've got to pull yourself together and get back out there."

Easier said than done.

"La Colibrí is cut from the same cloth as the demons who killed Sara," Cam said quietly. "Maybe you should focus on that so you won't get twitterpated."

He frowned. "I'm not *twitterpated*."

"You're showing interest, which for you is twitterpated," Cam said with a small chuckle. "I know you want someone to save, but she's not the one you need to worry about. Maybe focus on saving *others* from *her*."

"What, like Nunzia's demons?"

"No, like the humans who'll suffer if the Atlanta and Montgomery demon lords go to war with each other," Cam said. "Why don't you go with me to Montgomery tomorrow? We're going to go visit Parras finally. I could use your support."

"So you think you've got a deal Nunzia will like?"

"Hope so." She tapped her pen against the table. "Either he offers up one of his seconds to Nunzia, or I'll let her deliver her own justice to him and the Division stays out of it."

Jack flinched. "Both those choices suck."

"Well, column A means we prevent an all-out demonic war before Demon Spring," Cam said. "So I hope, for his sake, I can convince him to do that instead."

CHAPTER ELEVEN

The next morning, Cam picked Jack up before dawn, offering a cup of coffee and a bright smile. They would spend the morning working with the Montgomery team before heading to Parras in the early afternoon. Due to the heavy uncertainty with this case, Cam had requested backup from the Montgomery team, although she wasn't so sure they were up to the task.

"You know these small offices. They just try to keep the local demons happy and not rock the boat," Cam replied as a highway sign flew by. "This whole Parras thing has them nervous. They aren't prepared to handle it if he goes completely rogue."

Jack nodded. "What's Kim's guidance?"

"Fix it," Cam replied, blowing air between her lips.

"Then it's a good thing she put you in charge," Jack replied.

"She expects me to fail." She chewed on her nail.

He reached across the car and pulled her hand away from her

mouth. "She doesn't expect you to fail."

"She does," Cam said, replacing the finger after swatting his hand away, "because she hates me and she wants me to transfer to another organization."

"Maybe she wants you to succeed and transfer to another organization."

At that, Cam laughed. "Yeah, so it's win-win for her regardless." Then she paused, and said, "Look, I know you're giving me shit, but I really need your support. I need today to go well."

"What's the big deal?" Jack asked. "We've done hundreds of these meetings. We go in, we offer their options, they pick one, we leave."

She drummed her hands on the steering wheel for a moment. "Jack, if I can prevent a firestorm between Nunzia and Parras, that'll be…well, if it won't put me up for promotion, it'll get me a few steps closer to it." She exhaled. "I don't get many of these kinds of opportunities."

Jack glanced at his partner, noticing for the first time how nervous she looked. It was unlike Cam—cool, unflappable Cam—to be so concerned about something that seemed trivial. Connections aside, Cam had an illustrious career that included graduating top of their class and resolving some of the trickiest cases in D.C. Dealing with a low-level demon should've been small potatoes for her.

"What's really bothering you?" Jack said.

She chewed her lip. "I don't know. Part of it is worry that I won't get Parras to do what I say. And while that looks bad for my career…I'm more nervous about what it means, big-picture. Nunzia's powerful. She could squash him like a bug if she chooses to. So whatever he *thinks* is waiting for him is better than the consequences of tangling with Nunzia."

"I don't think that's the case here," Jack said, although he didn't quite believe it. "I doubt Parras is any more connected than any of the other pissant demons we used to deal with. It's a classic case of getting too big for his britches—"

"Good God, Grenard, could you *be* any more southern?"

Jack chuckled. "Point remains. I don't think you should worry about Parras or about what he thinks he knows. How could he know something that Nunzia, who was probably turned by an original demon, doesn't?"

The ghost of a smile appeared on her lips. "I guess you're right."

"Of course I am," he said, sitting back. "I'm Jackson Grenard."

She snorted then chuckled. The chuckles turned into cackles, which drew snickers from Jack, which made Cam laugh even harder. Round and round they went, until they were heaving breaths with wide smiles on their faces.

"All right, all right, I can't breathe. I'm going to kill us," Cam said, wiping the tears from her eyes. "God, Jack. I can't laugh like that when I'm driving."

"Sorry, sorry," Jack said, watching the road sign for Montgomery fly by. "I haven't laughed like that in years."

"I know," she said with a wide grin. "It's good to hear it."

Compared to Atlanta, the Montgomery Division looked like a mom-and-pop shop. The entire workspace comprised half a floor in a large office building downtown. After signing in and getting their visitor badges, Jack and Cam commandeered a small conference room. Jack worked on the stack of release forms and other administrative minutiae while Cam left to meet with the Montgomery agents-in-command. She returned two hours later with a group that filed into the empty seats.

"Pretty impressive for a morning's work," Jack said as Cam joined him at the head of the table.

"I've been glad-handing them for a few weeks, promising a big bonus check for anyone who comes with me," Cam said. When Jack quirked a brow, she blushed slightly. "Kim increased my operations budget."

"Thought you said she wanted you to fail?"

"She does. She just wants me to fail spectacularly." She nodded out to the room. "I mean, look at what I've got to work with."

Looking at the crowd assembled, Jack wasn't inspired with confidence. The Montgomery office seemed not only lax in their physical fitness testing, but most of those assembled might not even be certified to carry weapons. If all went according to plan, though, they wouldn't be needed other than to sit in cars. Sometimes just bringing an army was enough to keep problems at bay.

"Listen up, people," Cam said, commanding the room's attention, "we need to be ready for Lord Parras to throw us a wild card. Most of you have been briefed on the situation, and I'll need those who have to fill in those who haven't. Our goal is to secure a written and verbal agreement from Parras and get out. Agent Grenard and I will be going in first."

A murmur of interest arose in the room. Jack supposed that even in Montgomery, Alabama, his family name was well-known.

Cam cleared her throat, as if annoyed they were more interested in him than her. She called on each of the leads in the room, confirming layout details of Parras' mansion home. Jack sat back and watched his partner command the room as if she were director. Gone was his bombastic partner who was the thorn in every director's side. She spoke with authority, intelligence, and a clear understanding of what she was asking these people to do. She was every bit the future leader that she wanted to be.

Cam caught his eye, and he nodded in support of whatever she was saying. In the past, seeing her take the lead would've rubbed him the wrong way. Now, it was a relief.

He let himself fall back into his thoughts, picturing her getting a promotion to a director in a city about this size. And he wasn't quite sure he'd go with her. After all, his reintroduction into active duty in Atlanta had been tepid at best. He liked the work, but he also just liked being near his best friend. As she grew in her career, their carefree days of laughing in the car would come to an end. He'd have to take on the mantle of more responsibility with her—or figure out a new career.

"Agent Grenard and I will arrive in my car. The rest of you will be split up amongst the vans. Agents Chen and Grant have your assignments." She nodded to the two agents on either side of her, who started naming people to accompany them in the vans. Chen would be Team Alpha, the one Cam would call when things got bad. Grant's team would be there if things got worse.

"Agent Macarro, is this necessary?" asked a young black woman with tightly coiled braids. "I mean, Parras is still a low-level lord…"

Cam bristled, revealing some of the concern she'd shared in the car. She glanced at him for help, so he cleared his throat.

"Agent Macarro knows we're better safe than sorry," Jack said. "We've been through a few of these that seemed routine, but we needed more backup than we had."

"Besides that," Cam said, grinning, "if you don't go, you don't get your bonus check. So let's hit the road."

Parras' compound was situated on a large property on the outskirts of town. Like most older buildings, it had once been a plantation house, with a sweeping entrance lined with live oak trees and large, empty fields that stretched all the way to the main byway. As soon as they turned onto the gravel road, the demonic miasma began to churn at Jack's stomach. He popped two antacid tablets and offered them to Cam, who declined with a silent shake of her head and flashed her talismans.

"Keep these handy."

She parked the car in the front of the large, two-story white mansion. She exited the car and grabbed her briefcase, adjusting her Division jacket with authority. Jack took an extra moment to do the same, knowing they were both being watched by Parras and his people. If they didn't walk into the room with gravitas, the demon would sense their weakness.

"Agent Macarro, here to speak with Lord Parras of Montgomery," Cam announced to the empty porch.

The front door swung open, and a skinny black woman appeared, a curled smile on her face. The eloko magic arrived almost immediately—she was someone high in Parras' organization. Maybe even a second.

"Agent Macarro, such a pleasure," she replied, descending the steps in her blood red heels. She had a faint accent, but Jack couldn't place it. She gestured to the cars that had pulled up behind them. "Was it necessary to bring your entire office?"

"I hope it won't be, Fallonne," Cam said, shaking the woman's hand.

"Who's your friend?" Fallonne asked, eyeing Jack up and down. "And is he single?"

"Jack Grenard, Agent Macarro's partner," Jack replied with a soft sigh. "And no, I'm not available."

"Mm," she said, picking up on the nuance of his words. "Lord Parras is expecting you. I'll walk you up to his office."

Jack had seen his share of old mansions, having grown up in

one. But Jack's house paled in comparison to this place. The tinkling of a bell above put Jack at ease, reminding him of the pleasant days of his childhood. Everything began to look familiar, from the oil paintings on the wall to the oriental rugs on the floor. Even the furniture in the quaint sitting room sent Jack back to summer afternoons climbing on the antiques in his house.

"Air is thick in here," Cam said with a frown.

"Well, it's been a while since we've had humans," Fallonne replied with a casual glance back at Jack. "And it's been so dreadfully rainy, we haven't had the chance to open the windows."

Fallonne slid a single finger along the pane of glass as she ascended a grand staircase. The creak of the stair under his foot took Jack back to sliding down the bannister and getting a talking to by his father.

"You okay?" Cam asked, taking him by the arm.

"Yeah?" Jack replied. "Why wouldn't I be?"

Fallonne led them to a pair of double doors, which she opened with little fanfare.

"Lord Parras," Fallonne said with a deferential nod of her head. "The Division agents are here to see you."

The man who stood seemed familiar, or at the very least, he looked like a cool guy. His ebony skin and white smile put Jack in a fine mood, as did his deep, melodious voice.

"Welcome, Agents," said the man, clapping his hands. "I'm so very glad you could join us."

Why were they even there in the first place? Jack couldn't remember, but the wallpaper looked exactly the same as back home in Charleston. He opened his mouth to speak, but Cam tugged at his hand roughly. He couldn't understand why she looked so upset until something cold and metallic pressed into his palm.

The veil lifted from his eyes and he coughed in the miasma. He blinked once, twice, then reality snapped into focus. The office walls were splattered with stains and yellowed by smoke— the stench now burning Jack's nostrils. The carpet, too, was brown and dirty, the comfortable pattern gone.

But the man at the center had kept his slick smile and perfect suit, as well as the deep baritone voice.

"Did you bring a rookie with you?" he drawled, his voice laced with the same ringing bell that had ensnared Jack at first, but now it just sounded like a mosquito in his ear.

"Rein it in, Parras," Cam replied, taking one of the two seats. "We've come to discuss the violation of Division ordinance 402.13. Unauthorized transformation of a human under a rival demon's purview."

"And I've told you before, Agent Macarro," Parras said, batting his eyes at her. "Miss Beckett came to me of her own free will. I can't help that she was unhappy with Nunzia's offering."

The eloko magic increased, and the skin on Jack's cheek itched. But he didn't trust himself to say anything, not after he'd been so easily ensnared by the magic. He must've been more out of practice than he'd thought.

"Knock it off," Cam said, obviously unconcerned with Parras' magic, or the demons who lined the room. Jack hadn't even noticed them at first, but now they worried him more than the miasma. Was this about to go south? Had they brought enough people? And even if they had, were their backups ready for what was coming?

Instead of succumbing to panic, Jack looked to his partner. If she wasn't worried, then he wouldn't be. But it was sure hard to keep the nervous voices at bay.

"I told you, I don't care what Nunzia says or does," Parras said. "There's about to be a new sheriff in town."

"You're sure about that?" Cam said, quirking a brow. "So sure that you're willing to tempt fate with a lilin as old as Nunzia?"

The demon smiled, and Jack swore he saw a few extra rows of teeth. "I'm not worried about a lilin when I have the belu athtar at my back."

"Since when does Bael, king of the Underworld, care about some demon lord in the backwoods of Alabama?" Cam asked.

A flash of anger crossed his face. "You know so little, human. Bael rewards those who declare their loyalty to him. He doesn't care if you're a thousand year old demon or a measly little neophyte."

"Well, that's all well and good," Cam said. "Except Bael is still down in the Underworld until Demon Spring. Once I give Nunzia the word that you declined Division mediation, she'll bring the wrath of her Georgia goodness down on you faster than you can say 'bless your heart.' Do you think you can last until then, or are you willing to give me one of your seconds to keep her at bay?"

Jack stared at Cam, in awe of her yet again. She really was a force to be reckoned with, able to mask her feelings of insecurity, dig deep, and force the situation into one she could win.

At first, Parras didn't react, and Jack feared he'd reject the deal and they'd have to go back to square one. But as he pressed the anti-demon charm into his palm, he saw cracks in the demon's armor. Sweat had broken out on his forehead, and he clenched his fountain pen a little too tightly.

After a moment, he leaned back in his chair and beckoned Fallonne. They conversed quietly before she nodded and left the room.

"Fine," Parras said. "I will give you a second with assurances that Nunzia will keep her distance from me for the next year. Please inform her people to contact my people and we'll make the trade."

"As long as you keep your mitts off of her people," Cam said, standing and grabbing her briefcase with victory in her eyes. "I'll remind you that you're the one who brought this on yourself."

"And I'll remind Bael which human insect bothered me the most," Parras said with a smile curling onto his face. "I hear he's got special methods for torturing humans. Perhaps he'll let me do it."

"Bael, Bael, Bael, that's all I've heard for three weeks," Cam replied with a triumphant glance at Jack. "But they've been talking about him coming back for over a hundred and thirty years. I'll have to see it to believe it."

Parras chuckled. "You and me both, human."

CHAPTER TWELVE

"Excellent work, Macarro. Here's a new case. Another one of Nunzia's demons causing trouble over in Decatur."

"Thanks," Cam said dryly. "We'll get right on it."

Kim disappeared through their office door and Cam chuckled as she gave Jack the file. "Thanks for staving off demonic war, here's your new assignment, have it done by Friday."

"Life in the field," Jack said with a fake smile.

They'd returned from Montgomery about an hour before, after taking the entire car-sitting squad out for barbecue as thanks for helping out on the case. The group had been a good distraction from all the things Jack had on his mind. Mainly, how completely useless he'd been.

It had been…well, years since he'd let a demon suck him in like that. Since his first year at the Academy, he'd been trained to recognize the signs of demonic coercion and use mental techniques to block it. But Jack had forgotten everything he'd learned. And if Cam hadn't been there to pull his ass out of the fire, he might've found himself dead or a demon.

"So? Spill. What's it about?" Cam asked. "The case."

"Ah, it appears we have a forced transition," Jack said, snapping out of his reverie. "And if we weren't already on Nunzia's shortlist, it's concerning one of her seconds."

"This one's going to have to be on you," Cam said with a grimace. "I've got a ton of work from the Parras agreement, including making sure the bastard completes the transaction in two days." She turned back to her computer with an exaggerated sigh. "After all, I can't take all the glory *all* the time, although I'm sure I'll be doing most of the work for you. Lord knows you can't fill out a form to save your life."

Cam was teasing—Jack used to be *terrible* at form-submission—but it landed a bit harder than she'd meant it to. He stared at the initial case file, suddenly forgetting what he was supposed to do first. Should he call someone? Contact Nunzia?

"Unless you don't think you're ready," Cam said, interrupting his frenzied thoughts.

Was he that transparent? Jack slumped in his chair. "I don't know what's wrong with me. I mean, eloko magic? They use a bell. That should've tipped me off. Maybe I should—"

"That's why we have partners," Cam replied. "I've got your back. You have mine. So you slipped up. You remember in D.C. when my mouth nearly got us killed?"

"Which time?"

"Exactly," she said with a laugh. "You've saved my ass just as many times as I've saved yours. It's not a competition." She paused and her gaze grew a little softer. "And it's going to take you a few months to get back into the swing of things. I probably shouldn't have asked you to come with me on such a high-profile case, but..." She played with her pen. "To be honest, I was really nervous this was all going to go to shit, and I liked having you there with me. Even if you almost got turned into an eloko."

Jack snorted. "Thanks for saving me from such a horrific fate."

"Why don't we do this? There are a few easy cases on the back burner. Like the one with the murdered building inspector," Cam said, digging through her files to find it in her desk. "It's an open and shut case, and you've already gotten all the paperwork approved, right?"

Had he? Jack couldn't remember. But he wasn't about to admit that to Cam. "Sure."

"See? You just need a win. So, let's go get you a win, partner. Then everything will go back to normal."

Despite the front he'd put on for Cam, Jack hadn't shaken the feeling that his own stupidity was going to get them in trouble again. It was a pesky little thought that nestled in the back of Jack's mind, whispering in his ear when he and Cam left headquarters to visit the inspector-murdering bar owner.

"I'm glad we're wrapping up this case," Cam announced to the car as they inched forward in mid-morning traffic. "After all, the inspector's poor widow has been waiting for weeks. And we haven't done anything with that case. Even if we can't bring charges, we should at least provide some closure."

Jack nodded.

"You brought the case file, right?"

He jumped. "Er..."

"Oh Jackson," Cam said with an exasperated sigh. "I told you to grab it."

"Sorry, I was..." Distracted? More like off his game. "Sorry, Cam."

"No big deal," she said, turning on her blinker. "Just hope some of these assholes let me in so I can get to the exit."

Almost half an hour later, Cam pulled up in front of headquarters, and Jack jumped out to run to their office. Except he forgot his badge, so he had to come back out and get that *then* he went to the office, got the file, and came back.

"What took you?" Cam asked when he finally sat back down next to her.

"Just wanted to make sure I didn't forget anything. We have the case file, the approved forms, and evidence, if we need it." He paused. "That's all we need, right?"

Cam clicked her tongue. "You okay, Jack?"

"Yeah." Jack sank into the seat. "Yeah, I'm okay."

"Don't let that Parras thing get to you," she said.

"I won't."

The traffic was horrendous, so it was nearly three when they arrived to the bar. It wasn't much—an older place with one of those soft drink-sponsored placards outside. Next to it was a barber shop and on the other side a boarded-up building with a sign so faded Jack couldn't read it.

"This was worth becoming a demon for?" Cam said, almost reading Jack's mind. She shut the door and winked at him. "Don't forget the file, partner."

Jack, who'd slammed his car door already, opened it and grabbed the file off the dashboard.

"This is an easy one, Jack," Cam said. "Just get his statement. And don't forget to use the talisman, in case he tries anything funny."

"So you want me to do all the talking?" he said with a little bit of trepidation. "Seriously?"

"You've got to jump back in the water some time," Cam said. "Besides that, you've done this a million times. It's like riding a bike. And I'll be here to back you up."

Jack clutched the file against his side and walked up the stairs. On some level, he appreciated what Cam was trying to do. But on another, more realistic level, she was probably giving him too much credit.

"Nevsa?" Jack called into the dark, mostly empty bar. It was a far cry from the Belly of the Beast, and smelled more of smoke and booze than miasma.

"What?" came the gruff reply. The man at the bar looked about seventy, with pale white skin complete with liver spots and a wife beater. Jack guessed he just wanted the lilin immortality without the beauty that came with it.

"I'm here to ask you about the murder of Abel Harcroft," Jack said.

"Yeah, and who're you?"

"Jack Grenard," he said, as Cam gently pressed a hand against his lower back. He walked toward the demon and placed the file on the counter. "US Division."

"Hmph," he said, picking up the file folder.

"Yeah, no," Cam said, stepping forward to yank it out of the demon's hand and hand it back to Jack. "Agent Grenard, why don't you tell him why we're here?"

Instead of giving him the evidence was the unspoken end to that sentence. "Uh, yeah. So Mr. Harwood—"

"Harcroft," Cam correctly gently.

"Harcroft was in here two weeks before his murder, talking to you about a plumbing—"

"Electrical."

Jack bristled. *Get it together.* "Electrical issue. We've got the report from the Fulton County building permit office. They were going to shut you down, looks like."

"Were," Nevsa replied. "Not anymore."

Jack thumbed the manila folder, his mind drawing a blank on what he should say next.

"Obviously, this looks bad," Cam said, stepping forward.

"Not as bad as your amateur partner," Nevsa replied with a snort.

"You're a peon in Nunzia's organization," Cam replied, sliding onto a seat and taking the file from Jack. "A nobody. I doubt she'd even know who you were if I were to take my sword out of the car and slice your head off."

"Yeah? Want to test that theory?" Nevsa said. "I ain't afraid of no Division agents, and I ain't afraid of no building inspector. They leave me alone, they get to live."

"Now see, that's an interesting thing to say," Cam said, glancing at Jack as if to say, *Jump in any time…*

But he had nothing. He couldn't see how they were going to get Nunzia, who already had them over a barrel, to agree to let them arrest and dispatch of this guy.

"*Anyway,*" Cam said, wrenching her gaze away from Jack. "I've got a file here that says I'm allowed to take care of you."

"Yeah? Lemme see it."

Cam pulled the document out of the folder and handed it to the demon. He glanced over it, then chuckled. "Why don't you come back when you've got a signature?"

"What the…?" She closed her eyes, and Jack heard her counting to ten in Spanish. "*¿Por qué no obtuviste la firma de Angela?*"

Jack had picked up enough of the language to understand her, and to know that he'd fucked up royally.

"Fine. I'll get a signature. And I'll be back for your sorry, white-trash ass," Cam said. "Come along, Jackson."

"Do you want to discuss what the actual fuck just happened

in there?"

They were halfway back to the main city center when Cam finally spoke, and her silence had done most of the haranguing for her. Jack could barely stand to be in the same car with her.

"Maybe coming back to the field was a bad idea," he replied quietly.

She clutched the steering wheel. "Jack, this shit is second nature. We've done a thousand forms, a thousand interviews. Are you still spooked from the Parras thing? And tell me honestly."

Jack shrugged, too exhausted to give a straight answer. He was getting tired of this song and dance, of feeling like he was stumbling over his own two feet. Of blaming his own incompetence on losing Sara. At some point, he would have to accept that maybe he was to blame.

Cam was right. He'd interviewed thousands of demons. This was supposed to be second-nature.

So what was his problem?

"I'm sorry, Cam."

"I don't want an apology. I want my partner back," she said.

They arrived at the Belly of the Beast just as the dinner rush was getting started, so they had to wait for someone to fetch Angela. She wore a slinky green dress that brought out the color of her eyes, and looked excited to see the two of them until Cam told her the purpose of their visit.

"Oh, Nevsa," she said with a frown. "That's one we wish we could undo."

"I can make that happen, you know," Cam said.

Angela smirked and took the folder. "This is pretty circumstantial evidence. Why would a demon kill a building inspector when he could just as easily fix the problem?"

"Maybe because he's an ass?" Cam said. "Look, you know it's not my nature to ask for favors, but..." She glanced at Jack and he knew she was about to debase herself for his benefit. "We're sort of in a bind on this case. He's such a young demon, and you said yourself you wished you could undo it. Besides that, I got Parras taken care of."

"That, my dear, is not yet a complete transaction," Angela reminded her.

Cam swore in Spanish. "Can't you do us this solid and sign the paper so we can take care of him?"

Angela clicked her tongue, then smiled. Jack caught a whiff of perfume and flowers, and pressed the lilin talisman against his wrist.

"I wish I could," she replied. "But sadly, I don't think Nunzia would be too pleased with me making any deals with the Division until we discover who's behind Pueyo's death. Unless, of course, you have any information to share on your investigation there?"

"I don't know. Jack, do we have anything to share?" Cam asked.

"No," he said, and that was the truth. "But when we do, we'll share it."

"Well, until then, I don't believe I can help you," Angela

said with a bright, saccharine smile. "Now might I suggest the two of you stick around for dinner? We've got a succulent pork rib on the menu."

"Thank you, but we've got to get back to work," Cam said. "Mr. Harcroft's widow isn't going to accept this as an answer for why her husband's murderer is still walking around."

Angela tutted and actually looked a little sorry. "I wish I could help you but…my hands are as tied as yours."

CHAPTER THIRTEEN

"Fucking fantastic," Cam replied, hanging up the phone. "Just fucking *fantastic*."

Jack winced, almost afraid to ask, but did so anyway.

"That was the Montgomery guys. Parras just dropped off his sacrificial lamb. He promoted a *fifth* to a second. As if Nunzia wouldn't be able to tell." She stood and buried her head in her hands, inhaling and exhaling loudly. "Okay. Maybe I can work with this. Maybe I can get Navarro to drop this new forced transition case against one of Nunzia's seconds, too. Maybe that'll sweeten the deal."

Jack sat back in his chair, unsure how to help.

"Either way, I've got to drive my ass out to the meeting spot," Cam said, grabbing her jacket. "And give Angela a call. Oh, I'm sure this will go over very well."

"Do you…want me to go with you?" Jack asked.

Cam hesitated, chewing on the corner of her lips. "Uh, no. Not really. Maybe you could hang behind and finish the paperwork for the case? We'll need to fill out the closing forms, file an official record of the agreement, that sort of thing."

In other words, Cam was tired of babysitting him. Jack couldn't blame her.

"You got it," Jack replied, sulking back in his chair. "I think I'm due to go down to Alyonna and practice a bit anyway."

"Hey, yeah," Cam said, brightening. "Get some of that nervous energy out. I'm sure that'll make you feel better."

Jack nodded. "I think so, too. Drive safe."

After changing in the locker rooms, Jack made his way down to the training room carrying his leather knife holster in his hands. He could've put them on—after all, he was licensed to carry within the building—but he was a little afraid of what that would do to his psyche.

There wasn't much to help the discomfort, though, which amplified when he walked into the training room. Cam had let him win, but he had a feeling anyone he fought with today wouldn't be as kind. Especially Alyonna.

The Russian was wrapping up a training session with two young agents with brilliant technique and seemingly endless energy. Jack must've looked like that once upon a time, when he was the sparring champion at the Academy. And damn it, he would get back there again.

At least, that was what he told himself as he shook Alyonna's hand.

"So what's first?" Jack asked.

"I want to test physical fitness," she said. "Take a lap around."

That was easy, at least. His fighting ability was one thing, but he'd kept in shape during those three years in accounting. The lap was followed by a series of physical fitness tests, from push-ups to sit-ups to dead weight lifting. Jack performed admirably on every one, surprising even himself with the ease at which he was able to complete each test. By the end of the circuit, he was sweaty and feeling quite good about himself.

"Excellent," Alyonna said, handing him the wooden knives. "Test skill now."

His confidence took a nosedive almost immediately. "All right."

Gripping the wooden knives with sweaty palms, Jack braced himself for the pain that was to come. Alyonna spun a double-sided wooden spear a few times, then lifted the right side toward him. Jack easily deflected it.

"Good."

Then the left.

"Good."

Then the right again, a little faster and harder, then the left. Jack exhaled—this was a simple exercise.

"You're thinking," she said, narrowing her eyes at him. "Don't think. Just do."

Jack nodded. He hadn't even realized he'd *been* thinking.

The spear landed on his shoulder, and he ducked out of the way, cursing and holding onto it.

"Thinking," Alyonna said. "Why are you thinking so much?"

"I have no idea," Jack said, rotating his shoulder and wincing. "I'm not doing it on purpose."

"Hm." She put the spear on the ground and retrieved a pair of knives similar to Jack's. "Get your knives."

"What—you mean my real ones?" Jack said. "Are you crazy?"

She gave him a look that said plainly she'd never been asked such a thing.

"A-all right," Jack said, walking to the edge of the sparring area where he'd left his knives. He slid the leather holster on, and gripped the plastic handles of his knives with sweaty palms. They slid against his skin, so he wiped his hands on his pants and tried gripping again—still slippery.

"I don't have all day."

He returned to the ring and waited. "Don't we need to sign a waiver for this?"

She flashed a smirk before engaging with him. He barely had time to pull his knives to knock away her attacks, and it was purely defensive. Even if he'd wanted to fight back, there was no way he could get a strike in.

"Fight back," she snarled as the wooden instruments easily overpowered his steel. "Are you not Division agent?"

He sure as shit didn't feel like one at the moment. He was a miserable failure, unable to complete even the simplest tasks—

like getting a signature from a demon.

"*Ow*!" The wood slammed against his wrist, and it loosened the grip on his knife. Alyonna snatched it out of midair and pressed it against Jack's throat.

"Thinking." She released him. "If I were demon, you would be dead."

"Thanks, I got that," Jack said, rubbing his wrist.

"Come back next week. If I don't see improvement, I'm revoking license."

Jack snatched his knife from her and put it back in place. "Understood."

He took a long shower, filling his head with more self-deprecating thoughts. When he returned to his desk, he sat for a long time and considered the shitstorm that was his life, and what part he should fix first.

The phone rang—the archive was calling.

"Are they going to revoke my library card, too?" Jack muttered, swiping the phone off the holder. "Grenard."

"Um… Agent Grenard?" came the squeaky voice on the other side. "This is Rupert, from the library. Calling to see if you were going to return that book I lent you? And also if you had a chance to ask your grandfather about funding?"

Jack closed his eyes; he'd forgotten all about that. "Yeah, I'll bring it down this afternoon."

"And the money?"

"Er… I sent an email."

Jack found the book of demon mythology where he'd left it the day before. Desperate for some kind of distraction, he casually flipped through the pages, stalling and hoping that it would provide answers to the life questions he was grappling with. But all it contained was information about demons.

Out of curiosity, he located Parras' maker in the back of the book. Xerxes was transitioned by Biloko, the original eloko demon, in the fifth century B.C. near Athens. That meant Parras was a third demon in the large eloko hierarchy. He was still fairly young; per Cam's notes, he'd been transitioned around 1945. Biloko himself looked more like a dwarf than a monster, but like most originals, had a list of famous deaths.

Nunzia's maker, Freyja, was the least scary monster in this book. The original lilin with flowing golden hair seemed nice until he read the litany of forced sexual conquests that more often than not resulted in human death.

Finally, Jack turned to the front of the book, where he found a long chapter devoted to Bael—after all, the King of the Underworld had been seen well-documented during his five thousand year reign.

Bael Hadad is one of the original five demons banished from the world. He reappeared in present-day Syria in a rift around 3,000 B.C., although more recent scripts have placed him in present-day Australia, Siberia, and New Guinea. The last known sighting was in 1886 in Charleston, South Carolina, the worst Demon Spring in modern history, alongside his most trusted athtars, including Lazlo, Gita, and, of course, Anat, the so-called Lady of Destruction.

Bael is the original Athtar demon. Athtars are magical creatures who can wield the void and alter time and space. On the whole, are the least understood demonic beings. Scripts describe them as fearsome warriors, with the ability to move faster than the human eye can track. This is widely believed to be due to their ability to slow time.

Jack had never quite understood the concept behind "void" magic. The ability to slow time and space—or speed it up—always seemed so far-fetched to him, even surrounded by demons and magic. Even Parras' magic was just coercive, bending the reality of a single person. To be able to slow *everything* was a little terrifying.

Athtar demons are known to be excessively proud. Bael, the original athtar, is described as handsome and charming, needing neither magic nor glamour to coerce humans to join his side. Many early accounts of him describe a human-like man with kindness and generosity until the villagers drew his ire. Then the villages would be destroyed.

Jack paused, recalling Parras' words about Bael rewarding loyalty. That certainly fit a man focused on pride. Keep the despot happy and all would be well. Piss him off…

Jack turned to his computer and searched the online archives for mention of Bael, not quite sure what he was looking for. Most of the results were from the Charleston Demon Spring in 1886. One of the first newspaper articles drew his attention.

Demon Lord Rosannah Killed By Demon King Bael

Jack sat back in his chair, rubbing the growing stubble on his chin, and then opened a new search window. He filtered the results for the records just preceding Charleston and did a parallel search in another tab for demons who'd died in the rampage. Utilizing his double screens, he put the records side by side, then grabbed his padfolio to jot down notes.

When Bael appeared, thousands more humans had died—but so had more demons. Rosannah, the kappa lord mentioned in the news article, had owned Atlanta before Nunzia. Before that, she'd been the second to the main lord in Raleigh, North Carolina. Atlanta had grown under her watch, and from the scattered articles Jack found, she took great pride in that fact. A quick search in a third tab on Nunzia's activity showed only a brief mention of her until around 1845, but no major demon lord activity until 1890—after Bael went back under and Rosannah was out of the way.

1886 was the last time he'd been seen, but from what Jack could find, there wasn't a pattern to his appearances. He'd shown up in Switzerland and China in two back-to-back Demon Springs, then disappeared for fifty years. The only thing that jumped out at Jack was Bael would kill whichever demon lord had laid claim to the city he was ravaging.

That still didn't answer why Parras was throwing in his lot with Bael. He seemed convinced, almost like a cult follower sipping poison. And if he was sacrificing a measly fifth to Nunzia, he was still placing his money on Bael returning. The question still remained: why would an eloko demon be taking sides with an athtar?

Jack flipped through images from Charleston in 1886, looking to see if—

There she was.

The mystery woman.

She wore strange clothes—demonic armor, if Jack had to guess. The sword she carried was bedecked in jewels, but she carried it as if it were feather-light. She also looked healthier, younger—*powerful.* But why was she there at all? To protect humans? Was that why she was running from Bael, because she'd defied him in 1886?

"Hello?"

He jumped at the sound of Cam's voice. "Shit, Cam, you scared me. When the hell did you get back?"

"Turns out Nunzia decided to retrieve her sacrificial lamb herself," she said with a shake of her head. "But I got photographic proof it was done, so I guess we're good to close out that case."

"O-oh, good," Jack said, nursing a feeling akin to being caught with his hand in the cookie jar.

"You finish our forms yet?"

"Uh, no," Jack said with a blush. "I got distracted. Librarian called to get his book back and I started doing a little research."

"On La Colibrí?" Cam said, nodding to his computer screen. "Back to that again, are we?"

"Not intentionally," Jack said. "I was actually looking up Parras and started doing some research on the Charleston Demon Spring. This…well, she kind of just appeared."

"She does that, apparently," Cam said. "So what did you find out?"

Jack briefly filled her in on Bael and his theories about why he appeared and what he was after.

"So this is her, huh? Are you sure?"

"Fairly sure. But that's the only photo I've found so far, and I don't know what to search for in the records. There's no mention of her anywhere. It's mostly about all the death and destruction Bael caused."

"Where's the original photo?" Cam asked.

Jack squinted at the screen, and his heart fell. "Charleston."

"Lucky for you," Cam said. "By the way, your mom can't wait to see you."

Jack could've asked why she was having conversations with his mother, but that would've been a dumb question. Even when Sara was alive, Cam and Karen had a special bond. Karen had considered the Macarro sisters the daughters she'd never had.

"I'll email the archivist there," Jack said, hoping he wouldn't have to tell Cam why he wasn't looking forward to the prospect of going home. "Maybe they can ship it here."

"Or you could just pick it up when we go in a few weeks," Cam said with a quirked brow. "Unless you don't want to go back to Charleston?"

"I didn't say that."

"You didn't not say that either." She tilted her head, as if trying to read him. "What's going on with you? Why don't you want to go home?"

"I want to go home," Jack said, focusing on his computer. "I just...who knows when Demon Spring is going to happen? I'd rather get the photo sooner than later, you know?"

Cam narrowed her eyes, but turned back to her computer. "Whatever you say, Jackie."

CHAPTER FOURTEEN

When Jack arrived home that night, he decided to finally start unpacking. He'd arrived at the conclusion that perhaps his issues stemmed from being unsettled at home. Once everything was in place in his apartment, he could get back to the business of being Jack.

His first goal was the kitchen, so at least he'd stop eating takeout every night. But when he opened the first box, the grief came back with a vengeance. The pots and pans had been her pride and joy, and he couldn't stop remembering the nights of watching her standing over the stove, trying out some new recipe she'd seen on Food Network on her lunch break. He stood in the center of the kitchen for almost half an hour, before deciding the kitchen was simply too difficult, and moving into the living room.

There, his confidence returned after unpacking one box, but

the second revealed his and Sara's wedding shadow box. Her bouquet of sunflowers and baby's breath was now dried and withered, hanging on top of her wedding veil. This had been Sara's pet project a month after their wedding, and she'd gotten so angry at Jack for suggesting she was framing garbage. Now, it was precious—and painful.

Having struck out twice, Jack settled for rearranging the half-open boxes against the wall to make some more space for himself. In the kitchen, he stuffed the rest into the cabinets, ignoring the fact that they didn't close all the way. That was enough for now, and he'd call out for Chinese food.

An hour later, Jack was full of lo mein and whiskey, and was sifting through the emails that had come in when the window squeaked open.

"What part of 'stop looking' don't you get?"

The mystery woman stood in his kitchen, bathed in darkness, her ashen skin even paler in the scant moonlight. She took two steps into his living room, then in one fluid movement, she pulled one of her two swords from the scabbard on her back and pointed it at Jack.

"I gave you a chance, human," she said. "I told you to leave it alone, and you continued to search. You continued to talk. And now—"

"This has nothing to do with you," Jack said quickly, holding his hands away from his laptop. "This is Nunzia's forced transition—"

"I'm not talking about that. I'm talking about the search

results. The photograph you sent to the library in Charleston, asking them to find more information about me. I was halfway to Jackson, Mississippi when I got an email that made me turn around."

So she still had tracers on his computer. Even after the Division IT staff scrubbed it clean. Either she was as brilliant as she was deadly or she had some high-priced hackers on her payroll.

"I told you, I haven't said a thing to anyone. I just sent the photo to Charleston. I didn't mention it had anything to do with you—"

"Do you not know how computers work? They *monitor* every key stroke. They know—"

"Okay, now who's paranoid?" Jack said with a laugh.

"Are you…drunk?" she asked. "I'm about to behead you and you're drunk." She glanced at the discarded Chinese food boxes. "You're pathetic."

"If I'd known you were going to behead me, I'd have cleaned up for you," Jack said, sitting back.

She licked her lips, an uncertainty in her eyes that hardened to fury in a second. "Do you dare question me? I can rip your limbs from their sockets. I can kill you slowly, until you're begging for death. I can—"

"You won't."

Her eyes flashed, and Jack's heart skipped a beat. "Excuse me?"

"You won't kill me. If you were going to, you would've done

it by now. I know you've been watching my apartment. So skip the theatrics. Tell me who you are and why you're killing demons and we can move on."

"I told you, I was cursed—"

"Tell me about the curse. Tell me why you were in Charleston."

"And why are you so interested?"

"Because I want to help you."

At that, she laughed. "You're a pathetic, mortal human. I am thousands of years old. As if *you* could help *me* with anything."

"The Division could protect you."

"The Division can't even protect themselves. Parras and Nunzia have you running from here to Alabama trying to broker peace between them. They do it for their own amusement."

"Nunzia was—"

"Nunzia's a weakling," she replied. "She grew her lordship on fear and illusion and the absence of another strong demon to challenge her. And when someone gets a little too close, she calls on her Division minions to solve the problem. From what I hear, she's about to get her comeuppance."

Jack couldn't deny that a lot of that sounded true. "So you'd rather have an all-out demon war?"

She sheathed her sword and sighed heavily. "The war is coming whether you humans like it or not. But it's not going to be between Nunzia and Parras. It'll be between those who swear fealty to him, and those who don't."

"Him being Bael?"

She nodded, a ghost of worry in her eyes. "As for me, I'm staying clear of anywhere he might be. It's imperative that he doesn't know where I am, do you get it? Just until after the Spring is over, and the danger has passed."

Jack swallowed. "Do you think he'll show?"

"I think…" Her shoulders dropped and she spun away from him. "I don't know what I think."

"But you've faced him before?"

Her indecision was gone when she looked back at him. "That isn't the issue here. This Demon Spring is going to be bad, so you and your Division friends should stop focusing on peons like Nunzia and start focusing on getting ready for another slaughter."

"Are you going to help us?"

She hesitated. "I need to be far away from here when the schism happens."

"But it's supposed to be on the west coast," Jack said. "You'd be safe here."

She shook her head. "Time and space mean nothing to him. It's not about the distance, it's that he doesn't know where to look. Here, my presence is on the lips of every Division operative. He would find me in seconds."

"So why are you still here?" Jack asked.

"Because some asshole won't stop investigating me." She opened the window. "An asshole who obviously needs a hobby. Or a girlfriend."

"I'm not going to stop doing my job," Jack replied. "But I'll try to be more careful about covering my tracks. In the meantime, you should—"

He looked up and realized he was talking to an open window.

Having now been visited three times by his mystery woman without decapitation, Jack was feeling much more confident about his ability to survive against her. But he also hoped he didn't see her again—especially if she thought Bael would come to Atlanta to find her.

Whether to tell Cam that she'd come to see him again, that was another story. There had been precious few secrets between them over the years. If he told her the mystery lady had broken into his apartment again, she might raise it up the flagpole—thus ensuring more attention.

However, when Jack arrived at the office the next morning, it wasn't very long before Cam realized something was up.

"All right, out with it. What did you do?"

"Hm?" Jack glanced up and hoped he was the epitome of innocence. But Cam's scowl told him she wasn't fooled.

"You're typing like a man with a secret."

"How does someone type—?"

"*God,*" Cam breathed. "Jack. Talk to me. What's up? I promise I won't get mad."

"Don't make promises you can't keep," Jack said, suddenly very interested in the PDF read-out of local demon activity.

"Jackson."

"I might have seen our mystery woman again."

"Oh my God, you slept with her."

Jack sat up, leaning around his computer to make a face at her. "What? No!"

But Cam had hitched her wagon to that thought and was gone. "Have you completely lost your mind? You can't *sleep* with a demon!"

"Will you knock it off?" Jack snapped, glancing out the open door to their office. "I didn't sleep with anyone! She just showed up. I swear."

Convinced, but not happy, Cam kept her scowl as she crossed her arms over her chest. "And what did La Colibrí want this time?"

"She just asked me to lay off the investigation until after Demon Spring, and that's what I'm going to do," Jack replied, conveniently leaving out that her appearance had been because of the photograph. And also that she was still monitoring his activity.

Cam clicked her tongue. "For once, she and I are in agreement. Seismologists are predicting Demon Spring will occur in the next two to three weeks. And the Charleston meeting has been bumped up."

"To when?"

"Thursday," Cam replied. "I already called your mom."

A jolt of dread zoomed down to Jack's stomach. "We don't have to stay there—"

"Are you kidding?" Cam said with a laugh. "In the first

place, your mom would kill both of us if we even mention the word 'hotel.' And in the second place, you've got thirteen rooms in that mansion of yours. I'm sure there's *plenty* of room for both of us."

Jack didn't argue, because he knew there was no point. He was growing tired of his own attitude, and Cam was most assuredly done listening to him complain.

"Ah, *shit*," she cursed. "You get that?"

Jack opened his email where five meeting invites awaited—all for that day with Navarro and others. Starting with an emergency all-hands in the large conference center.

"Well, I guess this is the unofficial start of Demon Spring," Cam replied, grabbing her padfolio and a pen.

"Demon behavior has been at an all-time high over the past few weeks, and ICDM HQ believes we're due for another appearance from Bael. I know, I know," Navarro said as murmuring began, "that's what they say every Demon Spring. But the signs are there, and we'd rather be safe than sorry."

Jack and Cam sat in the back of the auditorium during the first of several all-hands meetings. Kim and the rest of the deputy directors sat in the front row, and at least three hundred field agents and assorted support staff sat in the seats.

Navarro flipped to the next slide. "With the recent issues we've had with our local demon lord, we're asking our field agents to spend a little extra time talking with their contacts. If there's a problem, we want to fix it before the schism happens. If they know of any demons who plan on making an appearance, we want to know about it. And if they know where the schism is going to occur, we'd like to know that too."

A woman up front raised her hand. "Do we have an idea where it's going to happen?"

Navarro shook her head. "Out west is our latest projection, but there's no definitive answer. We don't have any indication that it would be along any *new* fault lines, which means Atlanta should be spared from the initial onslaught. We'll be looking for volunteers to travel to the front lines wherever it happens. The bottom line is we're standing by to help our ICDM brethren."

"Be kind of nice if it was Mexico," Cam replied. "My abuela's getting up there in age—"

"Cam, book a vacation. Don't wish for demonic hell to be unleashed near your family," Jack said with a shake of his head.

"Here's a list of assignments for each agent," Navarro said. "Those who have a contact should check in nightly and prepare a report for their demon's stated plans for Demon Spring."

Jack scanned the sheet for his name, but Cam's groan told him who they'd been assigned to.

"I told you, Kim wants me fired," she said. "Like Nunzia will even let me in the door after the Parras fiasco."

"I'll go see her, then," Jack replied.

"R-really?" Cam blinked. "Are you sure you're up for that?"

"Angela likes me, I think," he said with a shrug. "And maybe I need to do one of these on my own to build my confidence back." Cam opened her mouth to argue, but Jack placed a quieting hand over hers. "Honestly, having you looking over my shoulder freaks me out a little."

"Fair enough," she said.

CHAPTER FIFTEEN

Two days later, with an anti-lilin charm firmly pressed into his palm, Jack walked into the Belly of the Beast by himself. He'd just gotten off the phone with Cam, who'd reminded him to use his talismans about five times in the span of ten minutes. He also had marching orders to call her the moment he left the restaurant, and if he didn't within one hour, she'd barge in and rescue him.

He was torn between relief that his partner cared so much and embarrassment that she had such little faith in his abilities.

But he was determined to prove himself tonight. It wasn't unheard of for agents to conduct meetings alone, especially when there was a good working relationship. While the current status was a bit strained, perhaps the resolution of the Parras incident might have healed some of the divide.

The lilin magic wasn't nearly as thick as the first time he'd been there, but it still permeated the air and itched the skin around the charm. It was the end of dinner rush, but the restaurant was still packed with humans. Although he was sure the lilin magic was part of the draw, the food smelled pretty good too.

He walked up to the hostess and flashed a smile. She couldn't have been older than twenty, but Jack couldn't tell if she was demon or human.

"Is Angela in?"

"Uh…"

"I'm with the Division," Jack replied, flashing his badge. "Just a routine check-in."

A few moments later, Angela appeared, ravishing in a lilac business suit and black pumps.

"Agent Grenard," she said, shaking his hand briefly. Her hands were the softest he'd ever felt. "I hope you aren't here with more bad news."

"I don't believe so," he said. "Just doing a routine check-in and follow up on Parras."

"Oh excellent." She beckoned him to follow her back past the kitchens into her private office. Once inside the enclosed space, he got a whiff of expensive perfume mixed in with pheromones. The metal against his skin kept him focused, but his pulse had quickened.

"My apologies for the magic," she said, taking a seat. "I wish there was a bit more ventilation."

"It's fine," Jack replied, adjusting to the magic the longer he sat in it. Angela sure was pretty, but the charm against his hand reminded him of his purpose.

"Where's your partner?" she purred. "I didn't think she let you out of her sight."

"She's fairly protective," Jack replied, pressing his charm harder into his palm. "But she's conducting some other business today, so I'm here instead."

"Yes, you are." The pheromones were now pumping, and Jack's pants began to feel a little uncomfortable. "Maybe after we talk business, we could talk about you?"

"Um." Jack coughed into his hand to buy himself some time as he adjusted his seat. "No. Sorry."

"At the risk of getting too personal, is it a demon thing?"

Jack quirked a brow. "And the whole demon-transformation-thing."

"Oh." Angela giggled, and it drew blood into Jack's groin. "No. It doesn't always have to end like that. But if the Division told the humans they could sleep with lilins and *not* get transformed, well..." She gestured to the air around her, then leaned forward, the dip in her shirt revealing more of her breasts. "So how about it? You and me, on the desk. Promise I won't turn you." She winked. "Pinky promise."

Jack cleared his throat, the hard bulge now pressing uncomfortably at the seam of his pants. Angela's gaze dipped down to his crotch and lit with excitement. For the life of him, Jack couldn't remember how to block out the lust magic, so he blurted the only thing he could think of to kill the mood.

"My wife was killed by noxes three years ago."

"Oh."

It was like a vacuum had sucked up all the magic in the room. Jack's mind cleared and Angela's skin suddenly didn't look as perfect as it had a moment before. The bulge at his groin was more awkward than sultry now.

"I'm so, so sorry," she said, glancing down at her hands.

Jack had never seen a demon look repentant about anything, and Angela's complete reversal left him at a loss for words.

"Don't look so surprised," Angela said, tossing a lock of hair over her shoulder. "Not all of us are monsters."

Dull green eyes flashed across his mind, and he dismissed it as simply a reaction to the lilin magic. "No, Nunzia's little kingdom seems rather civilized." He adjusted himself once again and refocused. "Headquarters wanted us to start checking in with each of the demon lords before Demon Spring. Make sure you don't surprise us with anything. Offer assistance if you're getting bothered by anyone." He smiled. "Other than Parras."

"I believe the Parras issue has been resolved—for now." She tutted and shook her head. "Lord Nunzia seems pleased with the arrangement. As long as he keeps to his side of the interstate, I don't foresee us having any problems. Then again, there are always demons from down below who like to cause trouble."

"Do you hear much from down there?" Jack asked. "I mean, does Nunzia hear from her maker, or…?"

"Nunzia was created by Freyja herself," Angela said with a star-struck sigh. "The belu lilin."

"Belu?"

"It's what the demons call our originals. It means God-touched, because they were the ones God chose to bear the burden of original sin," Angela said. "Nunzia was one of the last turned by the belu lilin in the mid-fifteenth century."

"Why? Did she die?"

"No, she just tired of the world up here."

Jack inched forward, sensing there was something else Angela wasn't sharing. "So can Nunzia talk to Freyja?"

Angela bristled. "Lord Nunzia can speak with her, but hasn't in several centuries. The belu is busy keeping the lilins in the Underworld under her control. She can't possibly be in touch with all her spawn up here unless it's important. And Nunzia can handle her own domain."

"She grew her lordship on fear and illusion and the absence of another strong demon to challenge her. And when someone gets a little too close, she calls on her Division minions to solve the problem."

Jack cleared the mystery woman's words out of his mind. "My apologies for the questions. I've gone through Demon Springs before, but this one feels different. Like a volcano about to erupt."

Angela sat back in her chair. Her nails changed color from innocent pink to blood red before settling on a soft mauve—lilin glamour at work. "It's such a bother. Everyone gets their panties in a twist for three weeks then it all goes back to normal. None of the belus make an appearance, and everyone from below returns there before the schism closes. All this fuss for absolutely nothing."

"Well, I think the human casualties might beg to differ," Jack replied with a pointed look.

"Speaking of casualties, any word about the woman who killed Pueyo?" she asked, innocently examining her nails.

"I might ask you the same thing. Since I hear Nunzia is conducting her own investigation."

"I asked you first, Agent Grenard," she said with a coy smile. "Show me yours, and I'll show you mine."

He ignored the obvious innuendo and decided to lie. "Gone. As far as we can tell. There's been no sign of her."

"Oh really? Because my sources tell me she's been watching your apartment." Angela chuckled. "Seems like you've gotten sloppy. Or you're lying."

"It's an ongoing investigation," Jack said, although he began to worry. If Nunzia's people knew the mystery woman was staking out his apartment, so did the Division. And that meant whoever Colibrí was running from would know too. "What about you?"

"I believe I asked you to tell me what you have, and you didn't, so—"

"Fine," Jack said. "One thing I can tell you is she's trying to keep the investigation quiet. She thinks Bael is hunting her. And I don't know about you, but I don't want to give him any reason to visit Atlanta. Do you?"

Angela went quiet, and for a moment, Jack thought he'd

gotten nowhere. But then she sat back in her chair, flashing her deep cleavage. "If Bael is hunting her, there's nowhere for her to go. He's the belu athtar. Athtars in themselves are terrifying creatures. They can bend time and space—"

"Yeah, what does that mean exactly?"

Angela tapped her fingers again. "I've never understood it myself. I've only seen athtars during Demon Spring and they are... They move faster than light. It doesn't matter how strong you are or how quick you are, they're always quicker." She paused and looked at Jack. "How can you defeat someone who can stop time to slice your head off before you can even lift your sword?"

Jack hadn't thought about it that way before. No wonder everyone was terrified of Bael.

"Bael takes great care in choosing his spawn. Whereas elokos, kappas, lilins, and noxes number in the tens of thousands, there's maybe five hundred athtars. And even more, those spawn are not allowed to spawn themselves."

"Why?"

"The rest of us gain power from making more of us," she said. "That's why the more spawn a demon has, the more powerful they are. But athtars don't need to make spawn. They just *are* powerful."

"That explains why they all live in the Underworld." Jack was now extremely glad he'd spread the word in the Division that the woman had left town. The more he heard of Bael, the less he wanted to meet the guy. "If they aren't allowed to spawn, they can't make their own miasma to sustain themselves up here." That certainly explained the sickness.

"That's not even the scariest part. It's not just about their magic. They care very little for anyone other than themselves. That athtar I saw… She killed fifty humans in one breath." She sighed. "Merely the beginning of a slaughter that included a fair number of demons, too. And the demon lord. Gone in the swing of a sword."

"When was this?"

"A long time ago," she replied. "Luckily, the athtars usually only come when Bael does. We haven't had to deal with them in a while."

"So you understand why I'm eager to spread the word that she's not in this city, right?" Jack said. "Believe me, I'd love to bring her in for questioning, but—"

"No, I'll call off our investigation," Angela said with a nod. "But I can't understand why she would intervene with a transition. If she's athtar, she doesn't get involved in other demon business."

Why, indeed? If athtars were supposedly some deadly, careless creatures who killed without remorse, the curse must have been powerful to force her to do a complete U-turn, personality-wise.

"But…" Angela said, as Jack rose to leave. "Isn't there anything you could give me to offer Nunzia as a reason to let Pueyo's death go? Maybe the charges you've been considering against Jamal?"

"Is that one of Nunzia's seconds?"

She nodded. "You say it's a forced transition, but we maintain it was perfectly legal. Sadly, some people can't read the fine print."

As far as demon transgressions went, a forced transition was bad—but not the worst. If he did as Angela was suggesting and dropped the case, the innocent soul who'd been taken would be condemned to live as a demon forever. But if he didn't, and Nunzia somehow let Bael know Colibrí was in Atlanta, the millions of innocent humans in Atlanta would be in danger. He didn't think the Division was prepared for an army of time-stopping demons.

"Fine," he said. "I'll say you provided me with ample proof that the transition was not forced."

Angela smiled, and the lilin pheromones increased. "You know, when you feel up to it, I'd love you to come back and tell me more about yourself. I'd hate for someone as handsome as you to be alone for the rest of your life."

Jack shook his head and left, the charm pressed into his hand until he was free of the allure.

"Lust demons, whatcha you gonna do?" Cam said, pulling the paper off a plate and sticking it into his kitchen cabinet. She'd been waiting for him at his apartment, and he'd recounted the entire episode from start to finish while they ate takeout Thai and unpacked boxes.

"I feel sleazy for offering that deal," he admitted. "I know it's the greater good, but—"

"When you deal with demons, you deal in gray," Cam said. "I mean, look at Angela. When she found out about Sara, she sucked in her sex drive. That was awfully nice of her."

"Then she let it back out."

"Because she wanted to get in your pants." She glanced at him. "Did she really tell you transitions don't always happen when you sleep with a lilin?"

"Yep."

"And you believe her?"

Jack shrugged. "Who knows? She seems decent enough, but she's a demon. Maybe she wanted to coerce me, or maybe, as you say, she just wanted to get in my pants."

"She's not the only one," Cam said, as she put another plate on top of the stack in the cabinet. "At least five hot young things at the office have asked me to introduce them."

Jack turned, torn between surprise that he'd been the object of office gossip and admiration that Cam hadn't mentioned it once.

"So…why haven't you?"

"Because you told me you weren't ready, and I'm honoring that," Cam replied, taking the now-empty box and placing it next to the stack of others. "Unless you are ready. In which case, I have them ranked."

"By what?" he said with a laugh.

"Which of them I get along with the best. There's this one who always approves my expense reports, no matter how many times I've missed something," Cam said. "She's top of my list. Adorable girl. Then there are a few field agents. Bottom of the list is the bitch who always takes my treadmill at the gym. But if you like her the best, maybe I can put aside our differences."

Jack smiled as he added another empty box to the pile. He'd managed to get through three boxes of memorabilia without the pang of sadness. Maybe he was still weaning off the lilin magic, or maybe Cam was distracting him. Probably a little of both.

"And to be honest, if it didn't mean you'd transition to a demon, I'd say go for it with Angela," Cam said with a smirk. "I hear sex with a lilin is incredible."

"Well, yeah, they're pumping you full of their miasma," Jack said.

"Still."

"I'm just glad we've got a lilin lord here. I think they're the easiest to deal with," Jack said, pulling out a vase and sticking it on the dining room table for Cam to put somewhere later.

"Heard some interesting chatter from the Montgomery team," Cam said. "Parras' fifth-turned-second said he was proud to be giving his life to show Parras' loyalty to Bael. Made a big show about it before Nunzia's thugs decapitated him. According to him, elokos and athtars are pretty close."

"Speaking of Bael, Angela said he won't let the athtars spawn, so that means our mystery woman is probably a second to him."

Cam nodded. "So why's she so skittish about her boss? Granted, I'd be batshit scared of any original demon…"

"The more I find out about her, the more confused I get." He cracked open another box, revealing glassware. "Maybe it's this curse. I have a feeling that's going to explain everything."

"Thought you were done investigating," Cam said innocently.

"Well..." Jack grinned. "Maybe now it's just a personal curiosity."

"Like a dog with a bone," she muttered. "Well, we'll have plenty of time to investigate tomorrow."

"Tomorrow?"

"Yeah, we're going to Charleston?"

Jack groaned. "Already? The meeting doesn't start until Thursday." The dread he'd been pushing aside returned in full force.

"Well, I wanted to go a day early so we had time to meet with people," Cam said, avoiding his gaze.

"You mean so you could have face time with Frank," Jack said, shaking his head. "I don't have a choice, do I?"

"Unless you want your mother upset with both of us, no."

CHAPTER SIXTEEN

"When was the last time you were here?" Cam asked.

"Christmas," Jack said. "Just flew in for the day and flew back out."

Jack's stomach churned uncomfortably as they got closer to Charleston. It had been another early morning for them, with Cam rolling up to his apartment before the sun rose. While she had been all smiles and excitement as they passed the four hours between Atlanta and Charleston, Jack had been more reserved. Finally, with fifty miles to go, they'd settled into silence and listening to Cam's music. But Cam couldn't stay quiet for very long.

"I thought you stayed for longer," Cam said. "You really flew in Christmas day?"

He nodded. "And out a few hours later."

"Why?"

"Christmas is hard."

Every Christmas, Jack and Sara had packed up Sara's small blue car and driven down 95 from D.C. to Charleston, and every year had been a fiasco. The first winter, they'd gotten caught in a massive snowstorm, and Sara was stuck behind the wheel, too panicked to pull over and let Jack drive. The next, they'd woken up at three in the morning and driven to five different places in search of coffee, only to have Sara scream at the drive-through lady, and then fret that her coffee had been spat in, even after she'd apologized and given the lady a large tip. By their third Christmas, they'd finally begun to embrace the crazy.

Once they'd arrived, though, there was no room for anything but love. The city was alive with festive cheer and Jack hadn't been able to stop grinning as he took Sara all over town to see friends of the family who owned shops and businesses. Christmas morning, they'd woken up snuggled together to the smell of his mother's famous French toast, and presents overflowing for all of his distant young cousins who'd traveled in to spend the day. They'd watch the kids squeal and run around with their new toys, while dreaming about when they'd introduce their own kids to the tradition.

The first Christmas without her had been the easiest, because he hadn't quite remembered how to feel anything. Everyone walked on eggshells and he escaped the festivities relatively unscathed. Gradually, the kid gloves came off, and soon everyone was back to their normal cheer and revelry. They asked how he was doing without noticing the black cloud that had settled over him. And he resented them a little for being able to continue on with their lives and plans when his had so abruptly ended.

Cam placed her free hand over his and squeezed. "It's going to be okay. If you can't handle staying at your house, we can go to a hotel."

"How'd you know?" he asked.

"You get this look in your eye when you think about her," she said softly. "And your mom said you're moody and angry when you visit, so I can only assume that's why you didn't want to go."

He sighed. "Do you think it'll ever get easier?"

"You build up a tolerance. Subjecting yourself over and over to the grief lets you come to terms with it, so it doesn't hurt as bad." She removed her hand and placed it back on the wheel. "At least, that's how I deal with it."

"I'm sorry, Cam," Jack said. "I'm acting like an idiot."

Cam half-smiled. "It's okay. Men are babies. Remember that time you got the flu at the Academy and cried to me about how you weren't gonna make it?"

"I was admitted to the hospital."

"See? Baby."

The Charleston ICDM headquarters building was a beautiful glass and marble structure, housing both the US Division Charleston Office and the US offices for the larger ICDM organization. There was always tension between the two offices —one funded and operated by the US government, but policy-driven by the world headquarters, and the other serving as the world headquarters' liaison and staff to Jack's grandfather.

"I can't believe Kim sent us here with a request for a hundred new agents," Cam said as she parked in the garage.

"I think she's just worried about the Nunzia and Parras issue," Jack said. "And you know Navarro's the one who signed off on the final number."

"I'm happy hating on my boss. Please stop bursting my bubble." She popped the trunk and retrieved her briefcase. "So we don't have to be at the seminar until tomorrow…"

"Yeah, yeah. Let's go find him."

The parking garage fed into a carpeted hallway, which then opened into a large atrium adorned with all the world flags hanging from the ceiling. On the far wall, above the elevators, the symbol for the ICDM was displayed in prominent gold leaf. Another wall held no less than fifteen televisions, each showing a different channel. Clocks with different time zones circled the room above large glass windows.

The global ICDM offices were housed to the left of the atrium, and the US Division headquarters to the right. Although Jack and Cam could've gone into the Division side with their badges, they had to stop at the security desk and obtain visitor's badges for the ICDM side.

"You know we all work for the same people, right?" Cam replied as the guard took their IDs (both their Division badges and driver's licenses) and typed them into the system. "See? This is the kind of crap I want to fix. There's no reason we need two systems doing the same job in the same building."

The security guard glanced at Jack, who chuckled. "Where is consolidating security systems on your world domination checklist?"

"Twenty."

"Well, good to know you've got priorities."

Cam took her IDs from the guard and pinned her paper badge on her lapel. "Smartass."

They passed through the metal detectors and anti-magic sensors, entering into the fanciest offices in the US. Even the administrative assistants had the latest technology, with video-enabled telephones and giant screens that put Jack's old D.C. computer to shame.

The glass-enclosed elevator took them to the top floor, where they were greeted by yet another security guard, who demanded IDs and visitor request clearance—until he read Jack's identification card.

"Oh, I'll let Councilman Grenard know you're here," he said, handing their IDs back without another word.

"Name recognition," Cam said with a sigh. "Wonder when I'll get that."

"That should be number two on your world domination list."

"What's number one, then?"

"Dominate the world, of course."

The mahogany doors opened and Frank Grenard appeared, a smile on his face. The elder Grenard was in his mid-seventies, although he was still as spry as he'd been when Jack was a boy. The two resembled one another, although Frank's nose and ears were larger.

"Jackie! Camilla!" He crossed the room in three steps and wrapped them in a bear hug. "I thought I might be seeing the two of you for the session tomorrow."

"It's good to see you, Councilman," Cam said, as if she hadn't orchestrated this whole thing.

"Please, Camilla. I've asked you to call me Frank—or Grandfather."

He led the two of them back into his office, which stretched over nearly half the building. Floor-to-ceiling windows overlooked the pristine water and riverwalk below. The room was big enough to house a six-person conference center, complete with video screen, a seating area with a couch and two chairs, and kitchenette with a refrigerator and microwave. Frank headed to the kitchenette and retrieved two bottles of water, which he handed to Cam and Jack with a smile before joining them in the sitting area.

"So!" he said, slapping his knees. "Tell me everything. How's Atlanta treating you?"

"Okay," Cam answered, with a too-bright grin. "We recently resolved a conflict between the Atlanta and Montgomery lords."

"Ah, Nunzia, right? She's a fascinating one," Frank said.

"You know her?" Jack asked. It was rare for ICDM to get

involved with local demon spats. They were more concerned with the originals, and keeping them from reemerging.

"Only because she's been in charge of Atlanta since I was in the field," Frank replied. "She runs a decent ship over there—and have you been to her restaurant?"

"I have," Jack said, a phantom smell of Angela's perfume rising in his nose.

"I try to go if I have business in Atlanta. Best pork belly I've ever had," Frank said. "Now that the two of you are there, I'll stop in more. Who's the agent in command over there? Brown?"

"Navarro," Cam replied. "Anne Navarro."

"Hm. Never heard of her. But I suppose she does a good job, if she's listening to the ICDM," Frank said with a chuckle.

There was a rap at the door, and an older Indian woman appeared.

"Ah, excellent. Camilla, this is my dear friend Myra Sharma. She's the aide for demonic weaponry to Councilman Khouri. One of our top graduates from Shanghai, and a visiting professor there."

Cam let out a small "meep" then popped to her feet so fast she nearly toppled over. "It's so wonderful to meet you."

"Camilla is part of the García clan from Mexico," Frank said. "María is your great aunt, correct?"

"Yessir," Cam replied quietly.

"Cam is one of the brightest students out of the Academy, and has been making a name for herself in D.C. and Atlanta," Frank continued, looking to Myra. "Her graduate thesis was in demonic weaponry, and Myra is doing great work with testing new technology with our Southeast Asian and Middle Eastern counterparts. I thought you two would have a lot to talk about. Perhaps over lunch?"

"Frank has spoken very highly of you, Camilla," Myra said, shaking Cam's hand. "Shall we?"

Jack observed the interaction from his perch on the couch, knowing what was coming next. While Frank adored Cam, and the connection with Myra was for her benefit, it was also a clever ploy to get Jack alone. As predicted, as soon as the two women left, Frank closed the door to his office.

"I just love that Camilla," he said. "She might just take over my job one day."

Jack smiled, remembering the quip about her world domination checklist, but his dread increased as Frank sat down across from him. "So what's the real reason you asked me to come out to Charleston?"

"A man can't want to see his grandson?"

Jack quirked a brow.

"How do you like your new job? All settled in your new place?"

"I like it well enough, I guess. Just getting used to being back in the field instead of behind a desk."

"I confess I was a little surprised when you requested a transfer to accounting," Frank replied. "If you wanted a change of pace, I would've thought you'd come home."

Jack exhaled. "It's still hard to be here."

"I thought as much, and that's why I asked you to come as part of a work trip. Hopefully, you'll be so busy with meetings you won't have time to think about anything." He unscrewed the cap on his water bottle and took a sip. "But I do want to know: the office in Atlanta is doing well?"

"Yeah, I guess. Same old political bullshit as in D.C." He sighed and watched a sailboat make slow progression on the bay outside. "It's nice to be working with Cam again."

"You two have gotten into some trouble, haven't you?"

"Most of that's in the past. Just trying to keep my head down."

"Is that so?" Frank chuckled. "I'm hearing reports otherwise. Something about a demon vigilante?"

Jack coughed. "Ah, yeah. You heard about that over here?"

"I hear about everything. Especially demons causing trouble for other demons right before Demon Spring."

"Yeah." Jack shook his head. "She's…something else."

"She, huh? Any ideas about who *she* is?"

"A few, but nothing concrete. She might be an athtar demon. She's been pretty clear that she wants me to leave her alone and stop reporting my findings to Kim." He glanced at his grandfather. "Guess I won't mention that headquarters is aware of her. She seems to think Bael's got spies in here."

Frank cleared his throat. "She's not wrong."

"Seriously?" Jack furrowed his brow. "But he's been trapped underground for over a century…?"

"Bael is the King of the Underworld," Frank said. "He owns

all of them. Lilins, elokos, kappas, included."

"But don't they have their own original demons?"

Frank nodded. "Somehow, Bael has forced them to swear fealty to him. Which means he owns all the demons topside, except the noxes, who, as we understand it, are the only demons he doesn't control. Even Lilins like Nunzia have quotas on how many demons they can turn."

"Parras' sacrificial lamb said something about that," Jack said. "But how does he enforce that if he never shows up?"

Frank smiled. "Fear. Everyone knows Demon Spring occurs every four years. Bael doesn't return because he doesn't see a reason to."

"Until Colibrí."

"Colibrí?" Frank blinked. "She's calling herself Colibrí?"

"Well, no. Cam came up with that. I still don't have a name for her."

Frank placed a gentle hand on Jack's arm. "Careful, Jackie. Sounds like you're getting a bit attached. It's been three years since Sara died. Loneliness and guilt does a number on a man."

Jack nodded. His grandmother had died in the line of duty when Jack's father was a boy, and Frank had never remarried.

"How did you get over your wife?"

"Time. Work. A few new non-demonic girlfriends." He winked. "It's not easy, and it's not quick. You won't notice it happening, until one day, you turn around and realize it's been a while since you thought of her." His eyes grew sadder. "Never quite leaves you, though."

"So do you guys have any idea who she is?" Jack asked, eager to change the subject. "La Colibrí?"

"We have some theories, but nothing concrete until we can get hold of her. Ideally, the Council wants her dealt with before all hell breaks loose—literally. Otherwise, Bael might take care of the problem himself."

"It...kind of sounds like we work for Bael, doesn't it?" Jack asked.

"It does sound that way, doesn't it?" Frank said with a grimace. "I know you never had any love for the politics of this job, but I wonder if you'll reconsider now?"

"Reconsider what? Coming to work for you here?" Jack scoffed. "No thanks. I like field work." That wasn't entirely true lately, but without field work, what did he have? The idea of moving back to Charleston seemed suffocating.

"Camilla's been making a name for herself. She's going to get promoted to deputy director in the next two years, preferably in a mid-sized city where she can do some good without ruffling too many feathers. Pad her resume a bit before she comes here."

"You've got one in mind?"

"Indianapolis, I think. Might send her abroad if Myra wants to take her."

"Mm." Jack stared at the marble tiled floor. Cam might be thrilled that Frank was looking out for her career, but Jack hated it when others meddled in his life. He wanted to be master of his own destiny, not the project of a well-meaning grandfather. "And what's your plan for me? Come back to Charleston? Take an advisor position with a senior council member? Start a twenty-year campaign to take over your seat?"

Frank smiled. "Is that what you want?"

"Not at all."

"I figured as much." He patted Jack on the knee. "Field work is an honorable profession. It's easier to feel like you're getting something accomplished when you're down in the weeds. But you know Cam won't be there forever."

"Yeah."

"And you already had a taste of admin work, and it didn't suit you." He smiled. "I'm not trying to sway you one way or another. I just don't want you caught unaware when gears start moving. And I don't want..." He paused and his gaze softened. "I don't want Cam to forego a stellar career because you're dragging your feet."

There it is.

"I promise I'll force her to go to Indianapolis without me," he said, shrugging his shoulders. "Or maybe I'll transfer with her. Who knows..."

That seemed to satisfy Frank, because he clapped Jack on the shoulder. "Enough about work. Your mom invited me over for a low country boil this evening, and I'm not about to miss it."

CHAPTER SEVENTEEN

The route from ICDM HQ to the Grenard ancestral home was well-known to Jack, but the familiarity was painful. Or perhaps the uncomfortable feeling in his stomach was due to his conversation with Frank. He was happy for Cam, of course, but if she moved on to greater things, where did that leave him?

For her, he kept his worries to himself. She hadn't stopped talking about the afternoon meeting she'd had with the weapons lead.

"I can't even begin to tell you how relieved I felt," she said, coming to a stop at a red light. "You know, every time I mention the talismans to María, she acts like I'm batshit crazy. Myra says if I have evidence to back up my claim, and I can put together an empirically-based study, the Shanghai Weapons Institute will fund it. She even said I could request a transfer."

"Transfer, huh?" Jack said with a sad smile. "To Shanghai?"

"God, could you imagine?" Cam replied with a starry-eyed expression. "The world headquarters for weapons study. I think I'd die. All my cousins down in Mexico have been trying to get María to fund talisman research. And hah! The American cousin gets it done." She grinned at Jack, then her face fell. "What's up?"

"Nothing, nothing," he said. "Just happy for you. You deserve to be successful. More than I do."

"If you think I'm going to China without you, you've got another thing coming," she said confidently.

"Moving to Atlanta is a lot different than taking an assignment on the other side of the world, Cam," Jack replied. "Besides, you don't want to spend your entire career dragging me along, do you?"

Another glance, then her finger went to her mouth as she chewed her nail. "Maybe I won't go."

Frank's warning echoed in Jack's ears, and he reached across the car to remove her hand. "You can't make career decisions based on what I want to do. You've got to branch out on your own. Fly away. All those bird metaphors."

"I have to take care of you, too," she said quietly. "How about this? I'll go to China when you smile for real."

Jack furrowed his brow. "What's that supposed to mean?"

"You know exactly what it means," she replied. "So if you really want me to spread my wings and other bird metaphors, get back to the Jack you used to be. One I'm not afraid to leave alone for long periods of time."

Jack would've argued that he was fine, but they pulled into the expansive driveway of the Grenard estate. The Grenards had lived in South Carolina since its foundation. Frank's favorite story was how Sally Grenard had fought off both the British and a lilin demon using nothing but her frying pan in the front yard of the house—which, back then, had been no more than a one-room shack. But after 1886, after Bael appeared and destroyed the existing structure, the Grenards had built the current house.

It was one of the most beautiful homes in Charleston, featured on the covers of architectural and design magazines. Frank had moved out as soon as George and Karen had wed, and Karen had taken great care to restore the house to its full potential. It boasted thirteen rooms and bathrooms, a formal dining and living room, along with a kitchen that could've been featured on any cooking show. The showy house had been important for foreign dignitaries and congressmen who came to visit headquarters. Jack fondly remembered Christmas parties and formal dinners where he'd sat quietly while Frank and some old man or woman discussed the problems of the world.

The first time Sara had come home with him, he'd taken her through the front of the house first, showing her the antique tables and centuries-old oil paintings. He could still picture the frightened look on her face, perhaps questioning the sanity of dating a man who'd grown up in a museum.

But then Jack had taken her into the back of the house, where Karen had saved her best remodel. The private wing was really where Jack had grown up, amongst squishy couches in the living room and the craftsman table in the dining room where he'd done his homework. Karen had even made herself a smaller, non-photogenic kitchen where she'd perfected her recipes and fed Jack and his friends.

The house was surrounded by a brick wall, but the iron gates were open. Cam drove by the lush gardens that led up to the giant house as Jack fondly remembered climbing the massive oak trees and breaking his arm when he was seven. The back lawn where he and Sara had snuck out and had some awkward sex on a picnic blanket. The vegetable garden his mother started every year then lost interest when it got "too hot."

They pulled up to the back entrance, a cozy porch overlooking the gardens with two white wooden rocking chairs and a swing. Every evening when they'd visited, Jack and Sara would sit out there and watch the sun set, talking about nothing. Sara had been scheming with Jack's mother to move into the house when they were ready to have kids, and had already started thinking about decorating ideas.

"Maybe we could redo the kitchen? Your mom thinks we could blow out a wall. Could we do that?"

"Whatever you want, honey."

"I love it when you say that."

"You okay?" Cam asked, standing outside the car.

"Yeah." Jack pushed the memory out of his mind as his mother appeared on the front porch. Karen Grenard was in her mid-fifties, but still as beautiful and put-together as any pageant queen. She reached Cam first, pulling her into a hug much as

Frank had. Jack heard whispers of thanks for taking care of her Jackie before she let go and turned to Jack.

"Hi, baby."

"Hi, Mom." He hugged her quickly, not wanting to linger.

"Well, you two look starved," she said with a bright smile. "Why don't we get y'all inside and feed you some supper, hm?" She held open the door. "Your dad's already in the living room."

"Is that Jackie?" George Grenard was the aide to a close family friend, Shriver, who worked with the Council liaison from Europe. It was two steps away from a seat on the Council, and Shriver was looking to retire any day now. He was a younger version of Frank, and an older version of Jack.

"Good to see you!" George said, clapping his son on the shoulder. "You look good."

"Thanks, Dad."

"Come on in and I'll open the wine," Karen said, arm-in-arm with Cam, who paused only briefly to get a hug from his father before heading into the kitchen.

"Come on, son, let's have a seat," George said, clapping Jack on the shoulder. Jack followed him into the living room and sat down on the old couch, sinking into the leather and relaxing somewhat. George handed him a glass of whiskey and sat down in his recliner, moving some of the thick biographies out of the way.

"So, Jackie. How's Atlanta? Settling in nicely with your new job?"

"Yeah," Jack replied, hoping to keep it light. "Busy as ever."

"Heard about your little demon-killer problem. What's the latest on that?"

"Uh..." News traveled fast, it seemed. Perhaps Colibrí was onto something. "Still investigating. How'd you find out about it?"

"Oh, it was reported up the chain as soon as it happened. You don't kill the Atlanta lord's third and not make a name for yourself." He leaned forward with a somewhat familiar grin on his face. "Say, you don't know her name, do you? Or what kind of demon she is?"

"Are you going to share it with the Council?"

George looked taken aback. "Why wouldn't I share it with the Council?"

"When I have something concrete to report, I'll let you know," Jack replied, taking a sip. "How's Shriver?"

"Shriver's good, but I'd like to talk more about the demon woman. Why don't you want to share your investigation?"

Jack blew air out from between his lips. "Because I don't have much to say. She shows up, threatens me, then leaves. She stole my phone and hacked my laptop."

"And that's not concerning to you?" George replied, leaning forward. "If there's a demon in your house, you should see if the Division will spring for a hotel. Surely they have some kind of witness protection program."

"Dad, if she was going to kill me, she would have done it already," Jack replied, downing the rest of his drink. He walked into the dining room, if only to get away from his father's pressing questions. There was an annoyed itch in the back of his mind, something that had nestled in there when he'd arrived in Charleston. Everything in this city made him angry.

He stopped in the dining room. The table was set for a true low country boil—newspaper adorning an empty spot in the center for everyone to dig-in. But the place settings weren't exactly right. There was one for George and Frank at either end of the table, one for Karen, one for Cam, and one for Jack—but none for Sara.

Rage threatened to come to the surface. Sara was gone; of course they wouldn't have a seat for her. Gone and forgotten.

Jack wasn't even sure why he'd fixated on that particular fact, but suddenly he was noticing all the things missing from the house. His wedding photos had vanished, replaced on the fireplace mantle by Jack's Academy graduation photos and various other family members. It was as if she'd never existed at all, and Jack was the only one who noticed it.

"Something wrong, Jackie?" Karen asked while placing a basket of rolls on the table. "You look worried about something."

"Yeah, just…wondering where all the photos went," Jack said, clenching his fists. "Of Sara."

"Oh honey." Karen gripped her arms, looking unsure. "I'm sorry. But I can't bear to look at them."

Jack nodded. "But you still have them, right?"

"Of course I do." She took his face in her hands. "Are you all right?"

"Yeah, I am. Just hungry, I guess."

Their brief moment was interrupted when George carried a large pot into the dining room, tipping it over the center of the table. Out spilled bright yellow corn, steaming red potatoes, fresh pink shrimp, and plump sausages, all smelling of Old Bay and home. Jack sat down at the table next to Cam as his mother poured glasses of white wine.

Cam leaned over the offering and inhaled. "This smells amazing."

"Aren't you a sweetheart?" Karen cooed with a wink. "It was no big deal for my two favorite people coming into town."

"Ah, Karen, this is a feast!" Frank appeared in the doorway, pausing to shake his son's hand before embracing Karen. He clapped Jack and Cam on the shoulders, then took his seat at the head of the table.

After a brief grace, the family dug in, piling their plates high with all the fixings. Karen began the conversation by asking about work, and Jack let Cam take the reins. He shoveled potatoes and shrimp into his mouth and kept his head down while she filled them in on every detail of their case. When the conversation steered closer to Jack and settling in, he decided to take an active turn and change it back.

"Cam's got a new defensive strategy she's been working on," he said, winking at his partner. "Why don't you tell them about it?"

"I—uh..." Cam glanced at Frank, who smiled brightly.

"What's a family dinner without Camilla sharing her latest

brilliant plan? I had a feeling you and Myra had a lot to talk about."

"Absolutely," Cam said. "So, I've been thinking about Demon Spring and how our defenses aren't much better than what we had the last time Bael came. You know, the Garcías have been using these talismans for centuries, but nobody's really thought it more than superstition. And I mean, Jack and I know they work, but they're not foolproof. You have to remember to use them, and they lose effectiveness around more powerful demons. But my question is: what would happen if we put one of these talismans *inside* a demon?"

Frank put down his fork. "I'm listening."

Cam retrieved her set of talismans from her back pocket. "I'm thinking iron bullets with these symbols imprinted on them. Load 'em up in some assault rifles and see what happens."

"It certainly merits investigation," Frank replied with a grandfatherly smile. "Did you discuss it with Myra?"

"I did," Cam said with a hasty nod. "She agrees it would be a great offense, but the logistics would be difficult. Civilians could get caught in the crossfire, too. But we've never really had an effective weapon against Underworld demons. They don't listen to reason and politics like the topside ones."

"And those topside ones need a reminder every so often too," George said with a smile. "You know, I might have to have you chat with Shriver while you're both in town. We're still dealing with the Netherlands leaving ICDM, and the lilins think they own Europe now."

"Have you informed Agent Navarro about this idea, Cam?" Frank asked.

"Ah… Er…" Cam glanced at her plate, still full of food. "Not yet."

"I'd hate for the Atlanta agent-in-command to think I was overstepping her," Frank said. "Run it by her first. Then we'll talk about how we can get this socialized. Then, maybe, we can talk about Shanghai."

Cam nodded and thanked Frank, but Jack knew inside she was cursing. Going through Agent Navarro meant first going through Agent Kim, and there was little chance of anything getting past her. Perils of bureaucracy.

"So, you two have a busy day tomorrow?" Karen asked. "Lots of meetings?'

"Mm," Cam said. "Navarro wants us to wrangle an additional hundred bodies for Atlanta."

"You'll be lucky if you get fifty," George replied, and Frank nodded in agreement. "All the cities are beefing up operations."

"Do they think Bael's making an appearance?" Jack asked.

Frank put down his fork. "We honestly don't know. There's no concrete intelligence that suggests he will. But your Parras isn't the only lord who's been making moves against more established demons, claiming he's swearing fealty. And this new demon woman…"

"I don't think she has anything to do with that," Jack said.

George glanced at Cam, who'd pursed her lips in disagreement, then shook his head. "We can't rule out anything.

But I think it's clear we're not going to have a typical Demon Spring. Wherever the fissure happens."

"What do we do if Bael comes?" Cam asked quietly.

"Pray."

CHAPTER EIGHTEEN

The next morning, Jack awoke in his childhood bed, staring at the Spiderman stickers he put on the wall when he was ten. He spread out on the mattress, memories of sharing it with Sara creeping into the forefront of his mind.

He slid his fingers along the single pillow, wondering if any of her hair had been left on it. Any scrap of evidence that she'd been here, sleeping, breathing. Living. That she'd existed at all and wasn't some fantasy he'd created to torment himself.

He sat up and checked his phone. Frank had been right about one thing—he'd picked a good week to come back to Charleston. Cam had forwarded ten hours' worth of meeting invites for the day. By the end of it, Jack would probably be too exhausted to feel sorry for himself.

But first, he had somewhere to go.

He managed to get out of the house with only a cup of coffee and a muffin thrust at him by Karen, and then he was on his way to the Division in her car. Jack could've waited for Cam, but he wanted to get an early start on his research. And he also wanted a little time to himself.

When he got to the headquarters, he bypassed both the ICDM and Division wings. Jack instead took the elevator down to the basement, where the archives were housed.

"Good morning," said the librarian. "Can I help you with something?"

"Yeah, I'm Jack Grenard. I sent you a note about this woman." He pulled the photo from his back pocket and showed it to the librarian. "I was wondering if you were able to find the original photo"

"Oh, Mr. Grenard! So glad you came to visit." The librarian, Paul, went to retrieve a box from behind his desk. "I'm afraid I didn't find much that wasn't already digitized. Obviously, our records from the Demon Spring of 1886 are a bit…fuzzy. But I did find a few diaries that might be of interest."

He placed the box on the table, but when Jack went to take it, the librarian clamped a hand down on the box.

"Now, I'd be willing to part with these under two conditions," he said. "First, that when you've completed your research, you'll hand them over to Rupert so they'll make their way back to me."

"Of course." Anything to prevent another trip to Charleston.

"And second, that you'll put in a good word with your grandfather so he'll funnel some more money to us during the next budget exercise."

That was a bit more challenging. Jack was starting to lose count of how many people he'd promised money to. "I'll do what I can."

When Jack emerged from the basement and his cellphone got service again, he'd received a few texts from Cam. He stashed the box of journals in the trunk of his mother's car, then set out to join her.

He found her having a conversation with three other agents, each holding a small cup of coffee and wearing name badges.

"Ah, here's my partner, Jack," Cam said, putting her coffee down on a nearby table. "Jack, this is Charlie from the Orlando office, Abby from the Mobile office, and Eric from the Indianapolis office."

Jack shook all their hands, before taking the name tag Cam handed him.

"These guys have seen an uptick in demonic misbehavior over the past few weeks too," she said by way of introduction. "We were comparing notes to what I found with Parras."

Abby nodded. "We have a kappa demon lord near us, and he's been taking more demons. Twice as many as usual."

"We've got a nox lord, and they're doing the opposite," said Eric. "But what we hear is that nox demons are always the odd ones out. Sounds like Bael has the others under his thumb. So if he is returning, all the nox demons are trying to lay low."

"What about in Orlando?" Jack asked.

"We've got lilins, elokos, and kappas all over the place. There isn't one single lord down in central Florida," she explained. "But our lilin demon, she's one of Nunzia's. They've been rattling her cage for months now. Word on the street is Nunzia's pissed off Bael, and she's in for it."

"What's Nunzia done?" Cam asked.

"If you ask me," Abby replied with a furtive look, "it's not a matter of what she's done. Someone just has to take the fall for topside demons as a whole. When he used to appear every couple of years, Bael would pick a city to make an example of. Last time he showed, it was Charleston."

Jack thought about the journals in the back of his car and itched to dive into them. "So everyone's in agreement that Bael's going to make an appearance? Anyone know where?"

They shook their heads. "Nobody knows. Nobody even knows if he's *going* to show, really. This could just be a whole lot of nothing."

And they were back to square one. It was the same every Demon Spring. Everyone knew it was going to be bad, but no one knew exactly how bad, or where would be hit.

A chorus of bings on phones alerted them of the start time of the meeting, so they ditched their coffees and breakfasts in the trash and filed into the room. Before Jack could follow, Cam grabbed him by the arm.

"So why'd you take off this morning?" Cam asked. "Sick of me already?"

"No, just wanted to head down to the archives," Jack replied.

"Got a box of journals I want to sort through."

"You were pretty weird last night," she said. "Hope I didn't get under your skin with that comment about Shanghai."

"Nah," Jack said. "It's just hard to be back here. But I guess I need to suck it up, huh?"

"No, you don't," Cam said with a sigh. "I'm sorry. I'm still pushing you, and I shouldn't be doing that."

They'd had this conversation too many times lately, and it was starting to bother Jack. He couldn't help but feel they were growing more out of sync.

"Agent Macarro, it's nice to see you again." Myra strode up to them, looking awe-inspiring in a black suit and heels.

"Agent Sharma." Cam shook the other woman's hand. "This is my partner, Agent Grenard."

"Frank's grandson, hm?" She nodded approvingly, then turned back to Cam. "Listen, I've been thinking about what we talked about yesterday, your idea with the talismans on the iron bullets. We have a slot later today in one of the conferences about new technology. Three o'clock. I'd like you to present your idea."

Cam gaped in surprise. "I'm…not sure that's a good idea. I haven't really tested it or—"

Myra smiled. "That's why I want you to present it. I'll make sure the head of technology development is in attendance—he's an old friend of mine from school. If you play your cards right, you'll get a fellowship to join him in Shanghai."

"I'll…put something together then," Cam said, a little

breathlessly.

"I don't think you should," Jack said after Myra had left.

She spun on her heel, a rebellious glint in her eye. "Yeah? And why shouldn't I?"

"You haven't told your superior, or her superior, that's why," Jack said with a shake of his head. "You know you'll get your ass handed to you."

"So? Beg for forgiveness and all that."

Jack sighed. "I just started there. Please don't get me fired."

"At *most*, we'll get reprimanded. If that. Especially if it brings all those hundred bodies and a fellowship."

"It'll bring *you* a fellowship," Jack reminded her.

"Jealous?" she asked.

"Not at all, just trying to look out for you," Jack replied. "You know I'm right."

"No, you're wrong," Cam said after a moment of silence. "See you at three."

Cam had stormed off after that, but Jack knew better than to go after her. And to be honest, he wasn't sure he wanted to. She was digging her own grave, especially after both Frank *and* George had warned her against going over Navarro's head. She was going to get her promotion regardless, so why she was being so headstrong about it?

Instead of attending the larger seminars, Jack wandered around the different meeting rooms, listening to strategy and communication techniques for the upcoming Demon Spring.

Jack's experience with it had been more "go in, slice up what you can, try not to die." He'd never really spent much time dealing with coordination efforts.

He met with one of the financial officers, a guy he'd graduated the Academy with, and relayed Kim's request for more money. John had the same response as Jack's grandfather.

"Yeah, there's no money for a low priority city like Atlanta," he said. "So how are you, man? Still causing trouble with Macarro?"

"Ah, yeah," Jack said, with a pang of guilt.

"Didn't you date her sister?"

"Married, actually," Jack said. "She died a few years ago."

"Sorry to hear that," John said. "Oh, hey! There's Geoffrey. Come on, Grenard, we can have a lacrosse reunion."

Jack didn't follow his Academy friends, stuck in the very weird realization that the extreme pain of his wife's death merited a "Sorry to hear that." Not as if he'd expected much more from John—a quintessential jock who'd barely made it to the final year at the school.

John wasn't the only one from the Academy Jack ran into. Most of the seminar presenters were friends he hadn't seen since graduation. They'd all settled nicely into their careers as leaders within ICDM or the US Division. Jack and Cam were the only ones who'd chosen field agent work.

He hadn't seen Cam since their small fight, and he was missing her. Not just because he had no one to make snide comments with, but because they'd taken the same path. They had done everything together. And now Jack felt they were drifting farther apart.

At a quarter to three, Jack walked into the conference room, where Cam was nervously typing on her keyboard. She glanced at him, pursed her lips, then went back to her presentation.

"You don't have to watch."

"For the record, this is a terrible idea and you know it," Jack said. "But that doesn't mean I'm not going to show my support. We're in this together. Even when you're an idiot."

She stopped typing and looked up at him. "You know Kim's never going to let me past her."

"Then why not quit and take a job here? Frank will—"

"Yeah, *Frank* will. But I don't want *Frank* to pave my career for me," she said. "I want to get where I get on my own merits. My own ideas."

Jack could've pointed out that her meeting with Myra was only because Frank had arranged it, but he also saw her point. Maybe they really weren't so different.

"Don't get me wrong, I'm grateful for everything your grandfather's done for me," Cam said. "But—"

"I get it," he said. "You're going to rock it." He spun on his heel and took a seat in the front row. "Just like your thesis."

Cam chuckled. "If you make faces at me this time, I'll cut you."

The levity disappeared as the doors opened and people filed in. Cam stood and pulled at her jacket, looking like the eighteen-year-old girl who chewed her nails to the quick before her thesis presentation. But as soon as the room settled, she took a deep breath and smiled.

"Good afternoon," she said, only a hint of nerves in her voice. "Agent Sharma asked me to speak with you today about an idea I've been playing with for a few years." She held up her hand, letting the talismans dangle. "These are simple iron coins imprinted with a special writing and symbol, and my family has been using them to protect against demonic miasma for centuries.

"When I was a little girl, my abuela told me that the original noxes appeared in Mexico City. After a few years of suffering under Mot and Xo, the Aztec priests developed these talismans to fight against them and the other four demons. We haven't been able to replicate how or why they work because...well..." She chuckled. "Most demons aren't volunteering to be a part of a scientific experiment so we can get to the bottom of it.

"Even within my family, there's skepticism about whether these things really work, or if it's psychological. But I've been testing it in the field for years, and I know there's a difference." She flipped the slide and spoke about several investigations she'd gone on where the group had been taken in by lilin magic, but Cam had remained lucid. It was no wonder Cam was on Nunzia's radar; after all, how frustrating must it have been to take the entire Atlanta office except for one obnoxious agent?

The longer she spoke, the more confident she became, until she was grinning from ear to ear as she came to the last part of her presentation.

"So what I'm proposing is that we take these same defensive symbols and turn them into an offensive weapon. We could inscribe the symbols on some iron bullets and, well…see what happens. I think with proper research, we could revolutionize how we deal with demons during Demon Spring, or even in general." She paused, glancing at her slides once more before turning back to the audience. "Thank you for your time."

A smattering of polite applause followed her away from the podium, and Jack stood to congratulate her.

"Have I mentioned you're awe-inspiring?" he replied with a smile. "How you could've pulled that together in a day, I have no idea."

"I mean, it's been stewing for a few months," she demurred, pulling the cords out of her laptop.

"Cam, take the compliment. You're a preparedness badass."

"Thanks, partner." She play-punched him in the shoulder. "And thanks for coming to watch. I was a little nervous."

"This is impressive, Agent Macarro," Myra said, coming to the front of the room from her spot in the first row. She had an older Chinese man in tow, who shook Cam's hand. "I'd like you to meet the head of technology development, Wei Weng."

"Pleasure is all mine," Cam replied, a little breathlessly.

"Can I get a look at your bracelet?" Wei asked.

Cam unhooked the chain from her wrist and deposited it in the man's hand. He hmmed with delight as he examined the talismans closely.

"Aztec writing, you say?"

Cam nodded. "My ancestors were the ones who fought the noxes when they first breached this side."

"You mentioned that in your briefing," he said, sharing a look with Myra. "Do you have any data to back up your claim?"

"Other than what was in my briefing?" Cam said, with a nervous glance at Jack.

"Hard data, no," Jack said with an affirming smile. "But I can tell you there's a difference. We were meeting with an eloko demon and I forgot to use mine. If Cam hadn't been there to place it in my palm, I would've been a goner."

Cam beamed at him as Wei reached out to take his hand. "Jackie, look at you all grown up. Frank said you were in town."

"Just here to support my partner," Jack said. "Cam's the brains behind everything. Don't let her tell you anything different."

Wei handed Cam her bracelet back. "I think this idea is fascinating. Do you have time to come out to Shanghai and brief our directors? I'd love to start putting a funding proposal together. I'm sure the Mexican Councilwoman would be happy to throw in some money to help her great-niece."

Myra turned to Cam. "So what say you, Agent Macarro? Plan a trip to Shanghai after this Demon Spring mess is over?"

"S-sure," she said. "Sounds great."

The two senior agents left shortly after that, promising to email Cam with all the details about her trip. Cam, on the other hand, had taken on a sickly appearance.

"What's wrong?" Jack asked.

"Oh," she said with a nervous chuckle. "I just remembered that I gave a presentation to the top echelon of ICDM without going through my supervisor first." She winced. "This is going to suck."

CHAPTER NINETEEN

"Unbelievable. Completely unbelievable. What could have *possessed* you to present such a thing to the ICDM?"

As predicted, when they returned to Atlanta, Cam and Jack got called into Agent Navarro's office, courtesy of an irate Kim. There, she proceeded to lay into Cam for all the ways she'd broken protocol, with Navarro watching quietly.

Cam, of course, took the verbal beating like a champ. Her steely gaze conveyed none of the fury and frustration boiling underneath the surface. Jack had told her to prepare for the worst, and she was ready for it.

Until Kim dropped the bomb.

"I am sick and tired of you trying to undermine me. You're fired," Kim said.

"F-fired?" Cam sputtered. "You can't *fire* me!"

"Oh, can't I? You've been walking a thin line since you

started here. Engaging with a demon. Overstepping your bounds with Parras—"

"I *fixed* that problem," Cam said, rising to her feet. "In case you forgot, I staved off demon war—"

"And you went over the heads of the Montgomery bosses," Kim replied. "I got an earful from them about how you dragged fifty agents into Parras's stronghold without proper authorization."

"Bullshit," Cam said. "I'd be glad to show you all the forms and signatures. They're just pissed I showed them up."

"Enough," Navarro said. "Macarro, you aren't fired," she said with a stern look at Kim, "unless you continue this behavior. But you are suspended, effective immediately, for two weeks."

Cam clenched her jaw, her foot jiggling angrily as she stared laser beams into the carpet. Kim, too, was furious.

"I'm within my rights, Anne," she began.

"Patti, take a walk. Cool off," Navarro said. She glanced at Jack. "Grenard, unless you have anything to add, you're dismissed as well." She paused at his horrified expression. "I mean dismissed from the room. I want a word with Macarro."

He stood and shared a look with Cam, who was either on the verge of tears or ripping someone's head off. After pausing briefly to pat her on the shoulder, he followed Kim out of the office.

"I cannot believe her," Kim growled. "She's—"

"She's Cam. You knew who she was when you hired her,"

Jack replied. "And if I were you, I'd stand down and let her make you look good while you can. Because eventually, she's going to leapfrog over you, and everyone will realize you aren't as good at your job as you think. But what do I know? I've only been her partner for almost a decade."

Kim glared at him, muttering something about nepotism and egotistical agents. Jack felt somewhat better telling her off, but he was still uneasy about the whole thing.

Fifteen minutes later, Cam walked out of Navarro's office, looking less angry and more shocked. She passed Jack without stopping, so he followed beside her.

"So I'm suspended, and there's going to be a giant red flag on my file indicating my insubordination," Cam said quietly.

"It's not that bad," Jack said, trying to look on the bright side. "ICDM won't care."

"Yeah, and why the hell didn't you stand up for me in there?" Cam snarled.

"Whoa, this isn't my fault," Jack replied, holding up his hands. "You gave the presentation—"

"And you were right there with me!" Cam said. "So why aren't you suspended too?"

"I'm not suspended because my ass wasn't up on the stage, overstepping my pay grade," Jack shot back. "You can't pin this one on me. I told you not to give that presentation, but like always, you did whatever the hell you wanted to. So as far as I'm concerned..." He swallowed, as the anger rose in her eyes. Wisely, he decided against 'I told you so.' "I mean, Cam, you know how this works. You've been around long enough."

"You've changed, Jack," Cam said with a sad shake of her head. "You used to follow me on every stupid decision I made. And I did the same for you. It was how we worked—"

"Yeah, and it's how Sara ended up dead."

Cam recoiled as if she'd been slapped. "Jack, that *wasn't*—"

"If it helps you sleep at night to think that way, fine. But deep down, you know the truth. We pissed off the wrong demon and he took revenge." Jack sighed, feeling tired suddenly. "Cam, we aren't kids anymore. We can't just do whatever we want and get away with it."

"Who the hell *are* you?" Cam asked. "Because my partner isn't some wallflower bureaucrat who bends over for rules he knows are stupid." She leaned against the wall, shaking her head. "It's like you died with Sara. The only time you even show the slightest bit of life is when it comes to Colibrí, and we both know that's not healthy. I thought getting you down here would bring you back to life, but apparently not. You can't even manage yourself in the field anymore."

Jack cleared his throat, feeling her words deep in his heart. "What are you saying?"

"I'm saying…I don't know what I'm saying." She pushed off the wall. "I guess I just thought things would go back to normal. Things haven't been normal since…"

Jack waited for her to finish, but didn't expect her to.

"Cam, things will never be the way they were," he said after the silence drew out between them. "I'm never going to be the same. I can't be the same. You aren't the same. And the sooner you figure that out, the quicker we can figure out who we are again and get to work."

"Yeah, well, maybe I should find myself a new partner when I'm off suspension," Cam replied with a dangerous look. "See you later."

Cam didn't even return to her office to gather her things, and wouldn't answer the door when Jack stopped by to drop off her club and briefcase. He knew she was home—her lights were on—so he told her he was leaving them on the porch. Knowing his partner, she'd probably carry this grudge with her for the rest of her life. She was still harping on a B she'd received from a professor their second year at the Academy.

Still, while nothing Cam had said was a lie, it wasn't all bad either. So he wasn't as reckless as he used to be? So he didn't want to stick his neck out anymore? That just meant he was more mature, not that he'd lost himself. Perhaps this fight was simply revealing what had already been there. Like blowing dust off a table to reveal a giant crack in the wood.

With Cam gone, all her casework fell on Jack. As meticulous as she'd been, there was still a lot of background information that Jack didn't know.

The proper thing to do would've been to throw on his jacket and pound the pavement, talking to demons and trying to get to the bottom of things. That was his job, after all, his chosen career path. Instead of sitting in his ivory tower and making policy, he was supposed to go out and make things happen.

But the hours ticked on, and he busied himself with paperwork instead.

Cam's words echoed in his mind every time he looked at her empty desk. They'd made a lot of stupid decisions together. They'd been reprimanded more times than he could count for reckless behavior and countless other infractions. But they'd never been suspended.

Kim seemed to have a short fuse when it came to Cam, so maybe there was some truth in Cam getting the shaft over Jack. But it still wasn't fair that Cam expected Jack to cover for every decision she made. She needed to own up to her actions and suffer the consequences. After all, *she'd* made the presentation, not *them*.

But she was his partner. And that, at least to the two of them, meant they were there for each other, no matter what. They disagreed, they fought, and they needed time to cool off, but there was never a moment where Jack felt Cam would abandon him. Regardless of how she felt, she would be by his side, taking whatever punishment because that's what partners did.

There really was no getting around it—he'd fucked up.

He stood, dreading the conversation he was about to have, and marched down the hall to Navarro's office, knowing if he didn't do it right away, he'd lose his nerve. And Cam deserved better.

He knocked on the door. "Got a sec?"

"Agent Grenard, here to talk to me on your partner's behalf?" Navarro asked.

"Yeah," Jack said, sliding into the seat. "Just wondering why you decided to suspend her instead of reprimanding her."

"Macarro's been undermining me since the moment she set foot here. She walked in here with a chip on her shoulder, acting like we were all humble bureaucrats while she was enlightened." Navarro snorted. "Kim could've fired her for what she did. It's not as if she wouldn't get rehired somewhere else in a heartbeat."

"So why did you send her to Charleston?" Jack asked.

"I didn't send her. In fact, I told Kim I thought it was a bad idea, but we get our orders from the higher-ups." She glared pointedly at Jack. "Your grandfather asked for you specifically. And who am I to say no to government-sponsored family reunions?"

The accusation itched at him. "I didn't want to go there as much as you didn't want to send me. As I recall, you were perfectly fine with using my connections to secure more money for your department."

"Which you failed to do for me." Navarro sat back in her chair. "Grenard, I didn't want to suspend Macarro. She's one of my best agents, but she needs to understand her place. Unless she wants to transfer to ICDM headquarters, she's under my purview. And I don't tolerate insubordination."

"That presentation would've given her a free ride to Shanghai," Jack said, quietly. "I'm glad she took the chance."

"From what she tells me, she's not interested in Shanghai,"

Navarro said. "We had a good talk about her career. She wants to stay here in Atlanta. She'll serve her suspension, solve a big case or two, and it will be all but forgotten. Kim will get over it."

That didn't mesh with what she'd told Jack. "She told me she wanted to go to the weapons institute."

Navarro shrugged. "Maybe she was lying to me. Maybe she was lying to you. Either way, I don't want to lose her as an agent." She clasped her hands together. "Is there anything else you wanted to talk about?"

"No," Jack said, standing. "No, there isn't."

It had been two days since Jack had heard from Cam, but not for lack of trying on his part. He'd sent her a few texts, first with work-related things, then with some disparaging comments about Kim, and finally a plea to get coffee so he could apologize in person. All had gone unanswered.

He stared at his phone as the television blared the news and the ice melted in his whiskey glass, waiting for it to light up with her ringtone.

He couldn't understand Cam's sudden change of mind about Shanghai, except to pin it on himself. Cam wouldn't leave him if she thought he couldn't make it on his own. And maybe, *maybe* she was right to be concerned. After all, he'd been half-assing his job since he'd arrived. He'd fucked up the Colibrí investigation, he'd almost let Parras turn him, and he'd lacked a spine when it came to giving that presentation. Besides boosting Cam's career, her talismans might've revolutionized demon fighting, potentially saving hundreds of lives around the world. And Jack had been wishy-washy because of *protocol.*

Yet the idea of taking a risk exhausted him. Some part of him wanted to just go back to accounting, where he'd mope into work, sit quietly at a computer all day, and mope home and drink until he fell asleep. Or died.

His breath caught, and he stared at the empty apartment in horror. Even in the days and weeks after Sara's death, he'd never entertained the idea of suicide. Not so clearly, at least. But he'd been trudging toward it, like a bloodhound following an unknown scent.

The realization shook him to his core, and he swiped his phone off the table, popping a quick text to Cam and hoping she'd respond this time.

"You Goddamned human idiot."

The mystery woman stood in front of the bedroom, the window open behind her. Her swords were still stuck to her back, her green eyes steely with fury. But Jack was almost grateful for her appearance. At least she would distract him from the dark thoughts.

"To what do I owe this visit?" he asked, leaning back on the couch.

"I was halfway to Denver this time and I get wind that the Division agents are talking about me. Because their Councilman, Frank Grenard, has set up a task force to uncover my identity," she said, walking into the room. "Isn't that your grandfather? Didn't you just go visit him?"

"They already knew. I didn't tell him anything new," Jack replied with a shrug. "Besides that, I have a job to do."

She crossed the room, and he stood, wondering if he'd pushed her too far. But her swords remained at her back, her fists balled at her side.

"You are frustrating the hell out of me," she growled. "And I swear if you don't—"

Sick of indecisions—both his own and hers—Jack finally snapped. "You've been doing a lot of threatening, and not a lot of doing, so do something or get the fuck out of my apartment."

In a flash of athtar magic, her lips were suddenly against his.

CHAPTER TWENTY

Jack didn't move. He hadn't kissed another woman in years, and something about this felt wrong. She was probably only kissing him to try to manipulate him.

At the same time, the reckless voice in the back of his mind urged him to kiss her back. After all, he *hadn't* been with another woman in years, and although it *did* feel wrong, her lips were soft against his. The seductive lure of another human's touch—even if the touch wasn't exactly human—was inviting, as was the promise of what this kiss could lead to.

Fuck it. He was lonely, she was attractive, and he would've been lying if he said he hadn't thought about it after their tense back-and-forths. And maybe he wanted to prove to himself that he could still be the old Jack and take stupid, possibly career-ending risks.

He kissed her back.

She tasted human, she felt human, and soon he forgot she wasn't. She was a woman, and that's all he cared about. The swell of her breasts pressed against his chest, her hair was coarse and curly as he dug his fingers into it. He rested his other hand against her small but firm rear. She took the invitation and hopped onto his hips, pressing herself even harder against him. She weighed absolutely nothing, and he felt the bones of her ribs as his fingers rode up her shirt.

He carried her to the couch and tried to lay her down, but she broke the kiss and before he knew what was happening, she was straddling him, a coy, sexy glint in her eye.

"Wait..." Jack whispered before her hips on top of his swelling manhood drove him too crazy. Maybe he was rushing into something stupid...

"Ssh," she whispered against his lips. Her soft fingertips brushed the top of his waistband, then slid up his shirt. "Mm... They certainly keep you fit, don't you?"

Division. Jack blocked that out. He couldn't think about his job right now. Especially when she took hold of his nipples and toyed with them gently. He grabbed the back of her head and pushed her mouth to his again, drowning all other thoughts in the taste of her.

His shirt was nearly off, and with a gentle push and a brief separation of their mouths, it was on the floor. Cold air prickled his skin, and the rough fabric of her shirt brushed against him. He was surprised when she let him remove her shirt, revealing a white sports bra. She was even thinner than he'd thought, with her ribcage visible through her sallow skin.

"Are you sick?" Jack asked, running his fingers along her sides.

"That's rude."

Jack supposed it was, but she didn't seem too upset by it. She kissed a trail down his neck, slowly drawing lower and lower. With one glance at him, she unzipped his pants and found the bulge that had been growing painfully against his pants.

"Very nice, Altar Boy."

"Stop calling me that," Jack said with a shake of his head.

She slid her fingers up his shaft slowly, sending shoots of pleasure up his spine. "Doesn't seem to bother you too much."

"Uh, yeah, well…"

"Mm?" She pressed her lips to the head. "Problem?"

There probably should have been, but he didn't care anymore. "N-nope."

She grinned and then took him in her mouth. He exhaled loudly, closing his eyes to the sensations. She moved slow, then fast, and then slow again, teasing and tempting him. She sucked and licked and soon Jack forgot everything but her. He forgot his own name, teetering on the edge of climax, and hanging on for dear life.

"Did you enjoy that, Jack?" she whispered against his skin.

"Mm-hmm…"

Her breathy chuckle was now in his ear, as she took his lobe in her mouth and tugged gently. "This is fun."

"Mm-hmm…"

Something unfamiliar slid over his manhood, and he glanced down to see her rolling a condom onto him. A flitting thought crossed his mind about ulterior motives and her coming prepared, but it soon floated away.

She had risen to her feet and removed the rest of her clothes, revealing the whole of her small breasts, and a patch of black hair between her legs. She reached up to her bun and removed the band, sending black curly hair cascading down her front.

"Like what you see?" she asked.

"Uh-huh."

She stalked over to him, her breasts moving with each step, capturing his attention. He wanted to put them in his mouth, to kiss her all over, but she had other ideas. Taking his hands, she pinned them to the back of the couch and planted kisses all over his body while she took her position on top of him.

The moment she guided him inside her, he moaned loudly from the sensation. He hadn't felt this way in so long.

"Not bad, Altar Boy," she whispered.

"Stop calling me that," he growled, trying to free his hands from her grip. He wanted to take over this session, to carry her into the bedroom and do everything he could think of to her. The thought of taking control sent more blood to his groin, and he growled in frustration when she didn't free him.

Any thoughts about control went out the window when she curved her body into him, sliding herself up and down his shaft with excruciating slowness. Her gaze remained on his face, even as his eyes fluttered. She pressed a feather-light kiss to his jaw, taking his nipple again as electricity shot down to his toes.

"Tell me you love this," she whispered.

"I love this," he said. "I want you in the bedroom. I want to show you—"

"Ssh, this is perfect," she replied, increasing the speed. "Tell me this is perfect."

"This is perfect."

"Good boy," she said with a moan. "Tell me."

"P-perfect…"

There was nothing but her and movement and the sound of her panting breath and the increasing pleasure. The world exploded in a rush of release, the likes of which he hadn't felt in years. His body spasmed, and he was reintroduced to the world, to her breasts against his skin, her hair brushing his shoulder, and the feeling of her clenching around his shaft.

"That was good," she said, after a moment. "Well done, Altar Boy."

"Y-you did all the work," he replied with a bit of a stutter. Then, he frowned. "Wait, did you come?"

She snorted and dismounted, crawling off the couch with more dignity than he could've managed.

"Did you?"

"Don't worry about it." She glanced at him. "As long as you enjoyed it."

"I did, but…"

He'd never not brought a woman to orgasm before, except

for rare occasions with Sara. At least, he'd never failed *on purpose.* And the more he replayed their sexy encounter in his mind, the more he realized he'd contributed about nothing. More than his own pride, he had a very particular need to know what it sounded like to hear her moan.

"What's the rush?" he asked, as she picked up her sports bra. "Why don't you come back and we'll do round two."

She tossed another smirk over her shoulder. "I think you need a few days' rest after that."

Jack peeled himself off the couch. "Then let me focus on you. I'm very good. Or so I've been told."

"Hah," she said, stepping out of his reach. "That's not important."

"I'm serious," Jack replied, walking after her. "I kind of have a reputation to uphold. Can't have you leaving here unhappy."

"You're sweet, but it's really fine," she replied softly. But she let him put his arms around her, and even leaned into him. "Don't take it personally."

"I take it as a challenge."

"Then we'd be here all night," she replied. "No mortal can bring me to full pleasure."

Jack frowned.

"Quit pouting," she said with a laugh.

"No, it's not that," he said. It was the reminder that she wasn't human.

Suddenly, the full realization of what they'd just done slammed into him. He'd slept with a demon. Not a lilin, so there wasn't any danger of transformation. But a demon. An evil thing that killed humans. She had killed humans. And he'd let her seduce him because…

His paramour had stopped in the middle of the room. Her gaze had landed on the framed photo on Jack's bookshelf.

"Who the fuck is that?"

"Uh…" Guilt threatened to drown him. "My wife."

Her eyes flashed. "You're *married?*"

"Y-no—"

She turned to him fully. "I will ask again."

"She died," he spat out, wishing that the topic had never been broached at all. "You're the first person I've slept with since —"

Her black, lacy thong fell out of her hand as her eyes widened in fear. "Fuck."

"No, it's not—"

"Oh, *fuck!*" she cried, swiping her underwear off the ground and sliding it on. "Fuck, fuck, fuck. *Fuck!*" She punched the air in anger. "*Fuck!*"

"It's all right," Jack said, standing. "I mean—"

"No, you don't understand," she said, pulling on her pants. "I think…this might be one—or two…maybe *three* souls—"

"Souls?" Jack blinked as she walked to the window, hooking her bra as she went. "What are you talking about?"

She paused, her hand on the windowsill. "It's my curse. I can't…I have to be good. I can't go around breaking people's hearts—especially widowers."

Jack cleared his throat. "I mean, my heart's not *broken*, but... Tell me about this curse."

After a very long pause, she shook her head and went to the window. "I have to go."

"Wait...what *was* this?" Jack said.

She tossed him a catty look. "What do you think it was?"

"Honestly? I don't know. Normally, my one-night stands don't show up at my apartment first."

She unlatched the windowsill. "I just wanted you to stop trying to figure out who I was."

"By sleeping with me?"

"It wasn't my most brilliant plan," she said, glancing at him. "And maybe... I don't know. You were sending out some serious emotion."

"Emotion? Can athtar demons feed on emotions?"

Her jaw dropped, but only for a moment, replaced by something like guilt. "I mean, you just... Look at you. You're lonely. I guess I kind of pitied you while I thought I could... I don't know, manipulate you." She grimaced, turning away with a pained look on her face. "But you're just an innocent little altar boy with a dead wife." She tapped her fingernails on the windowsill. "And I just fucked you to try to get you to end your investigation. First girl you've fucked since your wife. Well, don't I just win a prize?"

"I don't understand," Jack said, hoping to keep her around a bit longer. "Why do you care so much how *I* feel about it? Which, for the record, I'm not... I mean, I don't..."

"I did a lot of bad stuff for a long time," she replied. "And the curse laid upon me states that I have to repent for every single soul I hurt over…over that time. And I'm pretty sure what we just did doesn't qualify. In fact, it might set me back a few."

Jack didn't know what to say to that, except to ask, "Can I at least have your name?"

"No," she said, glancing over her shoulder. "Just please, I *beg* of you. Stop looking into me. Demon Spring is coming. Please, I have to go."

He met her at the window. "I'll absolve you of your guilt for this…thing we just did if you tell me your name. Then it'll just be a one-night stand for both of us."

She licked her lips. "I don't think it works like that."

"I'm saying it does. Look, if it makes you feel any better, I've been trying to figure out how to break back into the dating world, and the sex was pretty damned good with you, so I'm okay with thinking of this as just two people who got laid." He took her hands in his. "Just your first name. Then we'll be square."

Her eyes, such a particular shade of muted green, danced for a moment, as she considered his bargain.

"An…Anya. You may call me Anya."

And with that, she slipped through the window and out into the darkness.

Jack stood in the center of the room, torn between post-sex bliss and wondering if he'd dreamed the entire thing. He hadn't had a one-night stand since…his time at the Academy. But this had felt different—she had been different. He'd known what it was when he'd decided to sleep with her, and he'd gone through with it anyway. The sex had been phenomenal, and it had been nice to be with someone again. He hadn't realized how starved for human touch he'd been until he'd had a living, breathing person in his arms.

Now, though, he wanted to know who she was more than ever, or at least, what kind of curse would force a demon to repent for every soul she'd killed. That was incredibly specific.

Glancing out the window and hoping she was long gone, he grabbed the box of old journals he'd picked up from Charleston. With all the excitement from Cam's presentation, he hadn't had a chance to leaf through them. They remained where he'd left them, on the floor next to the door. If she—Anya, if that was her real name—had been serious about trying to disrupt things, she would've taken the books. Something told Jack she hadn't slept with him purely for malevolent reasons. Maybe she was lonely, too.

Jack plopped down on the couch and pulled the box to him, switching on the nearby lamp and grabbing the first out of the set. The paper was thin and the words were hastily scribbled in dark ink. The date at the top of the first entry read August 1886, and the entry described an earthquake of epic proportions that had leveled half the city, followed by a swarm of demons escaping from the breach.

The first entry described the demons as simply monsters, but as the pages wore on, there was more detail. A group of eloko demons took over the French Quarter and drew countless unsuspecting humans to their deaths. Lilins had taken over the red-light district and transformed another fifty humans by the end of the first day. The kappas took the ports and were commandeering the local navy boats. Pandemonium didn't seem a strong enough word to describe it. A photo was stuck between the pages.

The man in the center of the rubble looked human. He wore a top hat and waistcoat, his black hair perfectly trimmed to muttonchops. In his hand, he carried only a cane, and Jack could see no weapons on him. It must've been Bael. No human would be able to smile amongst such devastation.

Bael has brought with him a woman—his lover, it is rumored. She is called Anat, the Lady of the Mountain and is as deadly as she is breathtakingly beautiful. She felled twenty human soldiers in under a minute with her bejeweled sword, then set her sights upon Bael's demon enemies. Rosannah, the demon lord of Atlanta, was brought before the demon lord and beheaded with a single blow. Then the evil creature set to behead all the spawn of the creature, whether still demon or returned to human form. She showed no remorse, no mercy. She is truly worthy of the moniker Goddess of Destruction.

He turned the page, pulling another photo—this one of the very woman Jack had just slept with, hanging off the arm of Bael with a smile on her face.

"Motherfucker."

CHAPTER TWENTY-ONE

"They called her Anat the Destroyer, Goddess of Vengeance. Lady of the Mountain," Jack said. "Otherwise known as Bael's right hand for three thousand years."

"No hyperbole there," Kim muttered.

"At her peak, she slaughtered hundreds of humans per year, sometimes entire villages. Our understanding is that she took orders from Bael, but he would give her the freedom to do what she pleased, as long as it involved torturing and killing humans."

"And you're sure?" Navarro asked. "You're absolutely sure the woman who killed Nunzia's third is this…athtar demon?"

Oh, he was sure, all right. After finding the mention of Anat in the book, information flowed like a waterfall. There were thousands of accounts through the centuries depicting her appearances along Bael—and her brutality.

Jack wouldn't have believed the woman he'd slept with could've been capable of such destruction, except for the ten photographs from Charleston and the three oil paintings that very clearly showed his mystery woman. Each painting was more grotesque than the last, featuring a woman standing in full battle armor atop a mountain of corpses, blood splattered across her face. The gleeful expression was the most horrific—artistic license perhaps, but most likely not too far from the truth, based on what he'd read so far.

But for some reason, he didn't feel like the mystery was solved. If anything, it had deepened. Anat killed humans without remorse; Anya had saved them.

Anat was Bael's right hand; Anya was running scared from him.

They couldn't possibly be the same woman, could they?

He'd called a meeting with Navarro, Kim, and his partner, but Cam's meeting invite had gone unanswered. As had texts, emails, phone calls, and voicemails. Although he hated to conduct a meeting without her, this couldn't wait.

"No one's heard from Anat since 1886. Why reappear now?" Kim asked.

"I think she's been topside since that Demon Spring," Jack replied. "From what I can gather, she believes she's been cursed, made to repent for, well…all this." He gestured to the painting. "I think she got involved with Nunzia's third because she's saving humans to undo that curse."

"How is that even possible?" Navarro asked. "I've never heard of a demon being cursed before."

"I have no idea," Jack said. "I don't even know if it's real or if she was lying or what. But I do know she's been on the run from Bael since Charleston, and I know she's definitely not working for him."

"But if she's Bael's most trusted general, why not go to him?" Kim asked. "He's the most powerful demon in existence. Surely, if such a thing existed, he could undo it?"

It's better if he doesn't find me. "I don't have any answers. Just more questions."

"Are you planning on seeing her again?" Kim asked. "You said she's shown up at your apartment a few times."

"I have no idea when she decides to show up, or why she keeps talking to me," Jack replied, hoping he didn't look like he was hiding something. "She's still linked into my computer, apparently. She knew the ICDM had set up a task force to find her."

"How long has *that* been going on?" Kim asked, a note of accusation in her voice.

"I just found out last night," Jack lied. "Apparently, it's how she's been keeping tabs on the investigation's progress. She showed up to convey her displeasure."

"We could use that to our advantage," Navarro replied. "She presumably already knows that you're sharing what you know. Do you believe she'll come back tonight?"

"It's…possible," Jack replied. He hoped she wouldn't, in any case. "But I don't think she will. It sounded like she was on her way out of here. She's pretty adamant about not being found by Bael."

"Do you think you need protection?" Navarro asked. "From her?"

"I…I honestly don't know," Jack said. "She acts like she wants to hurt me, but when it comes down to it, she hesitates. It's like she's physically incapable of hurting people anymore." He looked at the painting and shuddered. "That's why I think this curse is real. To her, anyway."

Navarro nodded. "Thank you for bringing this to our attention. I think it's best if we pass this case off to ICDM HQ. You said they've already got a task force assembled."

For once, Jack didn't object to getting this case off his hands. Knowing who Anat was, and what she was capable of, he was more than willing to let someone else take the lead. Whether she'd leave him alone was another story, but he'd cross that bridge when he came to it.

"I didn't get your report for Nunzia's Demon Spring plans," Navarro said. "Aren't you and Agent Macarro assigned to her?

"Yes, but with Agent Macarro's suspension," Jack said with a purposeful glare at Kim, "it's been a little hard to find the time."

"Well, then perhaps we might consider reducing her suspension," Navarro said, standing. "After all, we're about to enter Demon Spring, and she's one of the only agents who's seen an active uprising. Grenard, will you go fetch her?"

Jack smiled. "Sure thing. We'll have that report to you by the end of today."

<hr>

Even though Anat's case was officially getting transferred, Jack didn't want to take any chances. She most assuredly knew he'd briefed his superiors, and would most assuredly be pissed about it. Curse or no, with all he'd spilled, she might be more eager to decapitate him than give him another blowjob. So before he left the office, he strapped his knives to his waist and sent a silent prayer that he could hold his own should she make an appearance.

But first, he wanted his partner back. Groveling would presumably be involved, as would admission that he was the biggest moron on the face of the earth. He also knew he'd be on the hook for dinners for the next six months. As long as Cam was on the other side of the table, he wouldn't mind taking her for lobster every night.

His partner still hadn't responded to any of his texts, calls, or emails. That wasn't anything new. When they fought, they usually spent a few days not talking to each other. But with so much happening, he wouldn't be satisfied until he looked into her big brown eyes and apologized to her face.

Even if he had to pull her out of her house to do it.

When Jack knocked on her fancy townhouse door on the other side of Atlanta, there was no answer. He checked around back for her car and didn't see it. Not content, he climbed over her bushes and rapped on her window.

"Cam. *Camilla.* Open the damned door if you're in there."

Somehow, she had a key to his place, but he'd never asked for a key to hers. He banged on the window a few more times, until an angry old white lady came out and said Cam had left about an hour ago and that if he didn't stop peering in her windows, she'd call the cops.

So in lieu of jail time, Jack hopped back in his car and drove around the neighborhood, looking for places that Cam might frequent. When he didn't see her, he drove back toward downtown and the Division headquarters. That was the most logical place for her to go. Even suspended, she'd still hover around their offices, glaring at the building while she bided her suspension time.

He parked his car back in the garage and set out on the streets, checking in every cafe and coffee shop for his partner.

It took him about two blocks to get the feeling he was being followed.

His pursuer wasn't Cam, and it wasn't Anat, either. Two large men were strolling just far enough behind him to look innocent, but just close enough.

Deciding it was better to get it over with than draw it out, he turned down an alley and faced the two gargantuan men. An awful sensation of déjà vu struck him, only this time, he was alone and it wasn't Cam's stupidity that had gotten him in trouble.

"Parras sends his regards," said Leftie.

"Isn't he busy preparing for Demon Spring?" Jack felt a little more prepared than the last back-alley brawl he'd been engaged in, but not by much. He wasn't looking forward to having to relearn how to fight with real knives so quickly.

"There's about to be a new emperor in town," said Rightie. "Parras wanted us to make sure we brought you and Macarro to him to dispatch personally."

"I'm flattered," Jack replied, although he was beginning to worry. Was Cam's absence because she'd already been taken? No. Between the two of them, he was probably the easier mark. "But I'm not going anywhere."

They lunged for him together, but Jack was quicker, darting between them and slicing as he went. He got a good one on Rightie, but the scrape healed as quickly as it was made. A hand clamped down on Jack's throat and shoved him against the wall. Stars winked in front of him, and his knife dangled from his fingertips. Blackness enveloped his senses, although he remained conscious—they'd put a black bag over his head.

But the grip on his shirt loosened, then disappeared, followed by the sound of struggle. Jack yanked the bag off his head.

Anya—Anat—was facing the two demons, with a clear, cold look in her eye. Again, they came for her as a unit, but she was much faster. She wasn't even using her athtar magic, but glided through the air with her sword drawn in full view as she sliced through the demons' necks without stopping. She landed behind them, her swords dripping red as the bodies collapsed behind her.

"I didn't need you to save me," Jack replied, brushing the demon's blood off his cheek. "I—"

"*With me*," she snarled, grabbing him easily by the arm and pulling him out of the alley and away from the corpses. Jack scarcely believed that the same hand picking him clear off the ground had pleasured him so soundly the night before. But sex was the last thing on her mind, apparently.

She tossed him into another deserted alley and unsheathed her sword in a blur. Jack stared at the tip between his eyes, drawing his gaze along the steel shaft until he met hers.

"What the *fuck* do you think you're doing?" she snarled.

"You tell me, Anat."

The tip of the sword swayed slightly, but she drew it closer to his face, almost touching the bridge of his nose. "Who else knows? Your Division? Your ICDM? Bael? Everybody? I thought we had an agreement!"

"Do you really think sleeping with you would sway me that much? I know I said I hadn't gotten laid, but give me a little credit." He folded his arms across his chest. "I told you I have a job to do, and I did it. Now, tell me the truth: why are you saving humans instead of killing them with Bael?"

She narrowed her eyes at him and then, in another blur, pulled her sword away and resheathed it on her back. Jack was almost convinced she would turn and run, but instead, she pointed to the charm that hung around her neck.

"This. This stupid thing is the reason for everything. It's my curse."

"A necklace?" Jack said. "But you're...I mean, you're supposedly the most powerful athtar demon in existence, save for Bael. How could a talisman—"

"You'll have to ask the witch who bound me to it," she replied, letting the talisman fall to her chest. "It happened in 1886. I was well on my way to killing every human in my path from Charleston to the west coast when a bunch of witches caught me in New Orleans. She cursed me with this…thing."

"And what, exactly, is it?"

"I've never seen anything like it before, but the witch told me it was a talisman to ward off evil spirits. On a demon, it suppresses our demonic urges, leaving nothing but the human guilt." She sighed. "She said it would fall off when I'd atoned for every death I was responsible for."

"I don't understand," Jack said. "If that's what's cursing you, then just take it off."

"I *can't*," she said. "If I even *think* about removing it, or it gets hard to breathe. Like every human I killed is standing on my chest." She flicked it sadly. "So here I am. A hundred and thirty years later, trying to undo what I've done to lift this curse."

"How many lives do you have to atone for?"

"Ten thousand, seven hundred, and forty-two." She released a loud breath. "And in one hundred years, I've saved two thousand, two hundred, and four."

"Not making a big dent, are you?" Jack replied.

"I accumulated the first over three thousand years," she retorted with a glare. "I'm worried my time is running out. I've started…aging. Demons don't age. I think the curse is killing me."

"Maybe it's because you haven't been back to the Underworld," Jack replied. "Don't you need the miasma to survive?"

She nodded. "I can't. But not because of the curse, because of what…what he'll do. I'm dead either way. At least if I try to undo the damage, I have a chance at surviving afterward. But against Bael…"

"So that's your plan? Try to save as many humans as possible before the lack of demonic miasma kills you?" Jack asked. "How much longer do you have?"

She shrugged. "Fifty years. At most."

"Can I help you?"

She turned to him, surprise written on her face. "Why are you offering?"

"I don't know. Maybe I just want someone to save. Maybe I want to get laid again." He crossed his arms over his chest. "Or maybe I've been dead for a couple of years and for some reason, helping you is the only thing that gets me out of bed in the morning."

"Sounds like you need to find a good therapist," she replied. "I'm not a charity case, and I don't need help. What I need is for you to stop asking about me. Stop showing my Goddamn photo to everyone and their mother in Atlanta. Stop telling people that Anat the Destroyer is walking amongst them. How many times do I have to tell you: *the only way I survive is if Bael doesn't know where I am."*

"But he's down in the Underworld. He can't—"

The words died in his throat. The ground trembled, almost imperceptibly at first, but grew in ferocity until it seemed reality itself was breaking apart. Jack toppled to his knees to brace himself, while the shaking turned more violent. Glass shattered above, and pieces of the concrete wall crumbled and crashed into the street with loud *booms*. Jack gripped the ground, bracing himself for the shaking that seemed endless.

But eventually, it did end, leaving only the sound of car alarms echoing in the distance.

"What the hell was that?" Jack gasped, looking up at Anya, who'd grown pale.

"Hell is right," she whispered. "Demon Spring has begun."

CHAPTER TWENTY-TWO

"D-Demon Spring? *Here?*"

"That's what you humans call it, isn't it?" She walked over to the edge of the alley. "That was the start of it. A new fissure has been created."

"*Here?*" Jack repeated, still shaking. Earthquakes didn't happen in Atlanta. Not ones that powerful. Which meant the demons had created a brand new fissure.

"The damage doesn't look too bad yet," she said, walking back to him. "But it's only a matter of time before the city's overrun."

Crack!

Jack heard the concrete slab before he saw it, a fierce crack that sent dread down his spine. Before he could blink, the concrete split in half above his head, falling harmlessly to either side of him. Anya re-materialized as if she'd done nothing of importance.

"Are any of your mortal bones broken?" she asked as Jack stared at the pieces that most assuredly would've killed him.

"N-no," he said, placing a hand over his pounding heart. "Thanks."

"Don't thank me for anything," she said, walking to the edge of the alley. "This isn't a coincidence. He's coming. For me."

"Bael?" Jack said, his heart falling into his stomach. "Bael is here? How can you be sure?"

"I just am," she replied, squinting out into the distance. "He's not here yet, but he will be. And if I'm in the area, he'll find me. I have to go."

"God, I have to find Cam," Jack said, scrambling to his feet. "If she's out there in that mess—"

"Are you joking?" Anya said, grabbing his arm. "You need to get the fuck out of here. This city is about to become a war zone."

"W-what?"

"Only the belu athtar can create a new fissure point and Atlanta's a brand fucking new one," Anya said, her eyes filled with fear.

"You think—"

"I think I'm getting the fuck out of this city—maybe even this country—until Demon Spring subsides. And if you know what's good for you, you will too."

"Why?"

She sighed. "Because he'll know what we did. He'll know, and he'll punish us both for it. And unlike me, you're human."

"I'm not just human, I'm a member of the Division," Jack said, yet again second-guessing the brilliance of sleeping with a demon. "It's my job to run head-first into danger. That's what I signed up for. My partner is out there right now, risking her life, and I'm not with her." He paused. "And I'm not afraid of Bael."

"You should be." But she made no move to restrain him. "I'm leaving."

"Fine, be a coward," Jack replied as she walked away. "Although you could make a big dent in that soul count of yours if you stayed."

She paused, only briefly, then took off.

Based on the television screens blaring CNN as Jack ran past, the schism had happened in Centennial Park. But chaos had already flooded the city. Thousands of innocent humans ran past him, every age, every race, every size, each with identical looks of horror and panic on their faces. Demon Spring was supposed to happen in another city like Los Angeles, or even Charleston. Jack's office hadn't even prepared for the event that it would happen *in their backyard.*

It would take hours for ICDM to pivot and send all their best agents to Atlanta, and in the meantime, people would die. Thousands, potentially. There were maybe two hundred Division agents in the city limits. Most hadn't ever seen a Demon Spring up close. Most were investigators with basic defensive skills.

Desperation thudded at the back of Jack's mind as he pushed against the rush of people, headed to the very place they were fleeing from. He wished Anya hadn't deserted them; with her abilities, they might've had a fighting chance.

Anya quickly slipped from his mind as he rounded the corner. The gateway between the human realm and demonic one was right in the middle of the park, a gaping black void that seemed to have no end. It wasn't the first time he'd seen such a phenomenon, but normally, there were thousands of demons pouring out of it. To Jack's eyes, nothing had emerged yet. He'd never been around for Day One of Demon Spring, but he'd always assumed once the void was open, the demons came right out. This was worse—waiting and staring into the abyss. Hoping it would close before anything arrived, but knowing it wouldn't.

The Atlanta police had blockaded the area, and they stood far away with their guns drawn. Intermingled with them were Division agents, but based on the looks of fear on everyone's faces—they were about as prepared for this as the civilian police. Jack wished he'd tried a little harder to get more people. Then again, when Kim had asked for it, it had been ridiculous to suggest *Atlanta* would be the site of the schism.

Speaking of his boss, she and Navarro stood near an Atlanta PD car, talking with officers and doling out orders. Kim looked visibly relieved when Jack called her name and jogged over to report in.

"Grenard, good to see you here," Navarro said grimly, glancing at the weapons at his side. "We've got calls in to all the other major cities but I don't think they'll arrive until later tonight."

Jack nodded, understanding the unspoken end to her sentence.

"There's an evacuation order for the city," Kim said. "We've cleared out the surrounding areas, but it'll take some time to evacuate the entire city. Seismologists are still checking the data, but there hasn't been an earthquake this bad since—"

"Since 1886," Jack finished, remembering Anya's words. Suddenly, that void looked a lot more menacing. But next to it, Jack saw a familiar bun and Division windbreaker standing behind the first row of police cars, her macuahuitl sword ready with the sharp teeth exposed.

"Excuse me," he said, leaving Kim and Navarro behind and threading through the crowd of assembled enforcement officers.

"*Cam!*"

She jumped at the sound of her name and flashed Jack a relieved smile when she locked eyes with him. He jogged up beside her and they embraced briefly.

"Cam, I'm—"

"Don't bother. I forgot it," she said, with a wave of her hand. "I'm just so damned glad to see you."

"I was looking for you, but Parras' goons—"

"I know. They were staking out my house," she said with an annoyed shake of her head. "Son of a bitch must've known this was going to happen today."

"Yeah," Jack said with a glance at the void. Up close, he got a whiff of ionized air, and it made the hair on his arms stand up.

"I was on my way to the Division to get a protective guard, then this happened. I guess my suspension's been lifted because Kim practically kissed me when I showed up." She snorted. "Typical."

"I'm just glad you're okay," Jack said. "And I'm sorry I wasn't there for you."

She elbowed him gently. "You're here for me now. That's all I care about. I was starting to get worried that Parras' people had gotten to you."

"No, Anya showed up."

Cam blinked. "Anya? You mean La Colibrí?"

"That's her," Jack said with a nod. "I have a lot to fill you in on."

"Where is she?" Cam asked, looking around the crowd.

"Gone. She didn't want to be here when the shit hit the fan." Jack turned to the void again, wondering when the deluge would begin. "Can't say I blame her."

Cam nodded and twisted the handle on her weapon. "I wish I'd had more time to prepare for this. If I'd known the demons were going to come to Atlanta, I would've submitted my proposal to Frank months ago."

"Damn demons. No concern for anyone else's schedules."

Cam smiled. "God, I'm glad to see you."

"Me too. I—"

The air changed. Jack couldn't explain what it was exactly, but it killed the words on his tongue. There was some kind of energy channelling into the darkness, like water going down a drain. Pebbles and leaves flitted toward the void, disappearing into the darkness. The force multiplied, and Jack and Cam had to brace themselves against the cop car. Beside them, another car slid sideways across the ground, the two police officers clinging to it for dear life before all three disappeared into the void.

For a moment, nothing—then twin blood-curdling screams echoed from the darkness.

"Fuck," Cam whispered, as the car they were hiding behind creaked forward.

But just as quickly as it had started, the energy changed direction, pushing the car toward them so they had to dive out of the way to avoid getting pinned beneath it. It rolled without stopping until it crashed into another car.

"You okay, Cam?" Jack called, pushing himself up onto his hands. "Everybody okay?"

"What the hell is that?"

A creature hobbled out of the blackness. The grotesque turtle-like thing had black hair hanging around red, beady eyes, and its legs were more frog-like, webbed and green. It skipped along the ground, as if testing the gravity, before turning its red eyes on the humans facing them.

"Kappa," Cam called to the surrounding agents.

"That doesn't look like any kappa I've seen before," came the weary response from a nearby agent.

"Demons in the Underworld take on more of their original features, since they sit in that thick miasma all day," Cam replied, shifting her club from one hand to the other. "You're gonna see a lot more ugly things before today's out."

"You've been to a Demon Spring before?" another asked.

She nodded, sharing a glance with Jack. "Somehow, I have a feeling this one's gonna be a lot worse than usual."

No sooner had the words left her mouth than a loud rumbling began. It sounded like a train or a tornado. Then the demons came—first more kappas, each with different levels of disfigurement. The first band of eloko demons boasted green grass for hair and gnomish potbellies. Last to the party were true lilins, with long, gray hair, sharp teeth, and black eyes.

Demons flowed out of the void like revelers on Mardi Gras and the human force swarmed to stop them. Jack and Cam shared a glance, a prayer, and a tapping of weapons before they ran into the fray.

They worked as a team; Cam stunning the demons with her macauhuitl and Jack doing the killing blow with his knives. But before he could count to ten, there were more demons than humans—and they were getting past the boundary and into the city limits.

"*Retreat!*"

The call came from somewhere far away. If Jack and Cam didn't heed it, this would turn into a slaughter, and fast. He hacked away at the lilin clawing at his face and found his partner nearby.

"We need to regroup," Jack said, pushing away an eloko. "I don't plan on dying today."

"Me—" She grunted and sliced through another eloko's head "Neither. But where are we supposed to go? They're overrunning the city."

Jack paused, just for a second, then hacked off the hand of a lilin. "Fuck. I don't know. I don't even know how long until they—"

A loud zoom echoed overhead—two military jets dropped bombs into the void. Somewhere, far away, they exploded in loud booms.

"God, don't they know we're down here?" Cam growled.

"They gave the order to retreat," Jack replied as a plume of fire erupted from one of the fountains nearby. "Cam, we have to get the hell out of here!"

"*How*?" she cried, swinging wildly at whatever demonic body part was nearby.

"Cam! Look out!" Jack cried, running toward her as an eloko snuck up from behind with a sword in its hand. Jack was going to be too late—

The head of the eloko slid off its body like water over ice. In its place, looking neither scared nor winded, was Anya.

She was fury and beauty at once, her sword held aloft and dripping with blood. Another eloko came up behind her, she sliced off a leg, an arm, and then the head before turning to two others and cutting through them. The crowd of demons backed away, but kept a tight perimeter, as if wondering if they should test this new creature.

"What are you doing here?" Jack asked. "I thought you were leaving."

She glared at him, as if this were somehow his fault, then turned to fight off a pair of kappa demons who'd come closer.

"La Colibrí?" Cam said, wiping the blood off her face. "The actual Colibrí?"

"Anya's her name," Jack replied. "Or Anat, if you prefer."

"A…You're shitting me." Cam spun to watch the demon woman slice her way through the crowd of demons as if they were wisps of smoke. "As in Anat the Destroyer, Anat the Goddess of Destruction, the motherfucking right hand to Bael?"

"Yah."

"So…" Cam tilted her head. "Why is she on our side?"

"Long story." Jack whistled as she felled three elokos in a single move. "But I'm glad."

"Even—wow, she's gotta teach me that move—so, we need to get out of here. Maybe now we can slice a path to Division headquarters."

Anya glanced at Cam, surveying her for a moment. "You should return there. There's no stopping the tide—"

Another bomb zoomed over their heads and ballooned in a ploom of smoke.

"What the *fuck*?" Anya cried. "Don't you know those don't do anything except make them angrier? *Call it off!*"

Cam glared at her. "Yeah, let me just get right on that, Colibrí."

"What did you call me?" Anya ducked as another bomb dropped into the void. "*Shit*, isn't there anything you can do to stop it?"

"There!" Jack cried, pointing to the gaggle of cars about one hundred and fifty feet away. "There's a radio in there, I'm sure of it."

"Fine," Anya said, pulling her second sword from its scabbard. "I will make you a path."

And make a path she did. There was nothing but severed limbs and spattered blood in front of them as demons rushed forward to their deaths. Jack briefly wondered what could compel creatures to willingly submit themselves to such a slaughter, but Cam pulled him toward the vans. Luckily, one was still open, although the occupants had met the same fate as the demons.

Jack stared at the dull eyes of the men and women, memories of Sara pulling stomach acid up his throat, but Cam's clear voice snapped him out of it.

"Hey," she said, getting into his line of vision. "Don't freak out on me. We've got to get out of here alive then we'll freak out together. Got it?"

Jack nodded and tore his eyes away. "Got it."

Cam gently pushed the body of the radio operator to the floor and picked up the microphone.

"This is Agent Macarro and Grenard, is anyone out there?" she said. "Hello?"

"*Macarro? Grenard?*" Agent Kim's voice came through the

speaker. "*Thank God. What's your position? What's happening out there?*"

"We're right in the thick of this shit," Cam replied. "Tell the military to lay off. The bombs aren't working."

"*Macarro,*" Navarro's voice came through now, "*is there anyone else alive there with you?*"

"Besides Jack?" Cam glanced at the bodies on the ground. "I don't think so."

"*Get out of there if you can. Fall back to Division headquarters. We've blockaded the doors but we'll tell them to keep an eye out for you.*"

"What about all the civilians?" Cam replied.

"*The mayor has ordered them to stay in their homes with the doors locked. There's nothing we can do until ICDM resources arrive.*"

"She's right," Anya said, appearing in the open door of the van. Her face was streaked with blood, but her green eyes were clear. She didn't have a scratch on her. "Any humans out will be killed or turned. The best thing to do is to stay down until it's over with."

"Can you use some of that athtar magic and get us to the Division?" Cam asked.

Anya opened and closed her mouth. "It's been a while since I've been in the miasma, so my powers are limited. Some of it is coming back, but not enough to travel distances like that."

"When this is all over," Cam said with a curious glance, "you are going to have to tell me all about athtar magic and how it works."

"Let's get out of this alive, first," Jack said, poking his head out of the van. The demons had converged around them—lilins with long hair brandishing their razor-sharp nails, frog-like kappas with scythes and swords, grass-haired elokos with clubs and spears. "So, what's the plan?"

"Hack, slice, and run like hell?" Cam replied.

"Right." Jack glanced once more at the hordes and readied himself to fight with Anya. But the demons hadn't moved from their protective circle. In fact, it looked like they were waiting for something, and trapping the three of them together in the van.

The current of energy reversed course again, flowing back into the void. The van moved, so Cam and Jack jumped out. Anya stepped in front of them, ramming her sword into the ground, as they latched onto her arms.

The flow abruptly stopped, leaving an eerie silence. Anya helped Jack and Cam to their feet and pulled her sword from the ground, holding it ready for the demons to attack. But they didn't; rather, they backed away, their heads bowed in reverence.

A man stood in front of the void. He wore a black tailored suit with a white collared shirt and shiny black shoes. Black stubble lined his strong chin, giving him a ruggedly handsome look. As casually as any human, he left the void with his hands dangling by his side, ignoring the demons who gave him a wide berth.

"W-what's happening?" Cam asked.

"Back away," Anya barked at them.

Cam quirked a brow. "What?"

"This doesn't concern you," she said. "Take Jack and go."

Cam grabbed Jack by the arm and pulled him, but there was nowhere for them to go. Although the demons in front of them had made a path for the man, the demons behind them stood as still as a brick wall. They were trapped—getting a front-row seat for whatever new horror was about to happen.

As this new man drew closer, Jack got a better look at him. He was good-looking, and when he cracked a smile, white teeth glistened with an almost supernatural perfection. And this powerful, beautiful man paid no attention to Jack nor to Cam as he stopped in front of Anya.

Bael, master of the Underworld, Lord of the Mountain, emperor of all he surveyed, the original athtar demon, smiled.

"Anat, my love, my goddess, my beauty. It's so wonderful to see you."

CHAPTER TWENTY-THREE

"Damn," Cam breathed next to Jack. "I don't know whether to purr or piss myself."

For one of the original demons banished to the Underworld, Bael didn't seem all that terrifying. His smile was easy, his eyes bright and engaging, as they'd been in that old photo Jack had seen, and he carried no weapon. If Jack hadn't just seen hundreds of terrifying, powerful demons cowed by his presence, he might've guessed Bael was just a normal guy.

But one look at Anya and he was back on edge. This warrior of lore, the Bringer of Destruction, Lady of the Mountain was honest-to-God scared.

Bael rested his hands by his side and smiled curiously at the woman holding two bloody swords, who wouldn't look him in the eye.

The silence stretched out between them for an eternity before he spoke. "No words for your Lord of the Mountain?"

"I'm not sure I know what to say," she murmured.

He chuckled. "Hello, for starters."

She dipped her head. "'Lo."

He cocked his head, scanning her up and down. "My love, being topside doesn't suit you," he said with a shake of his head. He touched the hair at her temples. "Gray hairs? Surely the humans make dyes for it."

She turned her head away from him. "I needed the reminder."

"Of what?" he asked, amused.

"What I've done," she replied, glancing at him for a moment before looking away.

"And what have you done?" he asked, gently tucking a strand of hair behind her ear.

She flinched as if he'd struck her. "You know what I did."

"What? The humans?" He brushed a streak of blood off her cheek. "Since when do you care about the plight of humans?" His gaze left her for one moment as he surveyed the carnage she'd wrought. "Although I could've done without you killing so many demons just now."

"The curse is making me."

"Oh yes, this curse," Bael said. He slid one finger down her exposed collarbone to the talisman. He flinched when his finger touched the iron, but didn't pull away. "This puny thing. As if a simple human curse could bend my Lady of Destruction. Why would you let something so weak control you?"

"What're they talking about?" Cam whispered to Jack.

"I think she has a talisman," Jack replied quietly, lifting his wrist. "She says it's the reason she's been acting so weird."

"Huh," Cam said with a smirk.

Laughter echoed around them, interrupting their quiet conversation. Bael's levity was eerie next to the corpses of humans and demons.

"My love, you are confused. You've *done* nothing wrong. You are a warrior queen, exactly as I made you. The only thing you deserve is to come home. Have a good meal." He cupped her cheek, and again, she flinched. "I don't understand why you're acting like this."

"Because…" She swallowed, her voice hoarse. "Because this curse… and I thought if I came back, you…you'd…."

"I'd what?" he asked, tenderly. "Did you think I'd be angry?" When she nodded, he laughed as if it were the most ridiculous thing he'd ever heard. "You have no idea how much I've missed you. I thought you were dead, my love." He took her hands in his. "When I heard you were here, I knew I had to come for you. I could barely contain my excitement."

She licked her lips, but made no sound. Her face was a mask of indecision and confusion.

"This…this savior persona isn't you," he continued, closing the distance again. "You're my Lady of Destruction. And this?

Saving a pair of humans? I have..." Bael's gaze zeroed in on Jack as understanding dawned on his face. "Oh, I see."

"See what?" Jack replied, although dread was already blossoming in his stomach. He was pretty sure Anya and Bael had been "on a break," but Bael might not take kindly to Jack sleeping with his girlfriend.

"Bael," Anya said, taking him by the arm. "He's no one."

"No one, hm?" Bael broke away from her and in a blur of motion, appeared in front of Cam and Jack. "You must be the one who started the investigation. You have my thanks, human, for leading me back to my love."

Jack was nearly eye-to-eye with the demon, and even though he felt woefully inferior, he kept his gaze steady.

"So you *do* have spies in the Division," Jack said.

"Spies?" Bael chuckled. "Spies would indicate I am not in command of all I survey in the Underworld and here in the human realm." Bael's smile grew cruel. "And that, human, is most assuredly not the case."

"Yeah?" Cam said. "Prove it."

Bael turned his gaze to her, scrutinizing her for a little longer than Jack, then gave a little shrug. "While I'm not in the habit of taking orders from vermin, in this case, there is a bit of business I must attend to before I return to the Underworld with my lady."

Almost immediately, two humanoid demons appeared from the void, arriving in the now-familiar athtar blur. One was a younger white man with closely cropped brown hair, the other an Indonesian girl with a long black braid. Both wore identical looks of muted glee, resting on bended knee as they waited for their command.

"Lazlo, Gita. Bring them," Bael commanded, returning to Anya with a lazy drape of his arm around her shoulder. She still looked sickened, but didn't pull away.

The two kneeling demons nodded and disappeared.

"Do you know how they move so fast, humans?" Bael asked, licking his thumb and wiping more blood from Anya's face. "Athtars can slow time to slaughter our enemies, or bring farther distances close to us."

Almost as soon as he finished speaking, the blurs reappeared in front of him. But this time, they arrived with two guests.

Parras and Nunzia.

The lilin had lost all her glamor, and appeared much younger and frumpier than usual. Gone was her blood-red lipstick and fake eyelashes; she looked like she'd been in the process of running away when she was captured.

Parras, on the other hand, was dressed in his finest suit, which he ruined by throwing himself on the ground.

"My king, my emperor, my lord of the mountain." The words spilled from his mouth as he prostrated himself at Bael's feet.

"Quiet, eloko," Bael commanded softly. "You do not need to speak. Belu Athtar knows what you have done."

"M-my lord?" Parras glanced up once, then averted his eyes quickly.

"You, above all in this little kingdom, have listened well to your belu. You heeded the cry to show your fealty to me, and make war against those who have forgotten who allows them their serfdoms." Bael glanced at Nunzia, who sobbed out a breath. "For Bael owns this world and the next. He is the emperor of the five realms. The world lives because I allow it to. I am all things—"

And on and on Bael went, to the point where Jack got the impression that Bael spoke for his own ego and no other purpose. He chanced a look at Anya, who was frozen in place. She didn't look scared, but she didn't look happy either.

Finally, Bael's self-aggrandizing monologue ended and Parras flung himself at the athtar again.

"Yes, my lord, my savior, I have done what was asked. My fealty is to you and only you—"

"And you shall be rewarded," Bael said, kneeling to his level and taking him gently by the cheeks. "Rise, eloko."

Parras rose slowly, but kept his head bowed.

"What do you ask of your King of the Underworld?" Bael asked, cupping the other demon's face.

Parras trembled. "I-I wish to join my belu. I wish to live in the Underworld and experience the wonder of the Elonsi—the Eloko motherland. If it is good and well for the Ruler of the Five Kingdoms."

"Such a simple request," Bael replied, stroking Parras' face. "Is there not more you want? Perhaps this city?"

Nunzia made a noise, but the athtar nearby kicked her in the shoulder.

"M-my lord, I dare not ask such generosity from you," Parras said.

Bael smiled, as if hearing the eloko demon's groveling was giving him life. He gently released the demon and stood upright, with a proud smile on his face. "You do not ask, because you wisely know I am not to be asked. But I shall make you stronger than you ever imagined."

He released Parras and turned to one of the two athtars. "Lazlo, kill Xerxes and make sure the elokos under his command know that Lord Parras is to take his place. If they swear fealty to me, they swear fealty to him. Dispose of any who don't."

Parras fell to his knees, a loud sigh of anguish bubbling from his lips. "Sire, my king, my maker has not—"

"Your maker has become comfortable, and forgotten who is his king," Bael said. "Take care not to make the same mistake."

Parras made a strangled noise, but argued no further. He bowed his head and backed away. The athtar demon who had brought him took him by the shoulder, and in a blur, they were gone.

"Now, as for comfortable kings," Bael said, turning to Nunzia.

She visibly paled as Bael walked to her and threw herself on the ground, much as Parras had done. "M-my lord, I—"

"You wish to grovel now? In my presence? As if you think word of your treachery hasn't reached my ears?"

Her southern accent was gone. "My lord, I didn't—I don't know what I could've done to make you—"

"Oh?" Bael tapped his finger against his chin. "You have no idea what you could have done? Look around you. You claimed this city for your own. You told your spawn that it is theirs and yours when it was not yours to give."

"M-my apologies, my lord, Belu Athtar, it will never happen again. This city is yours."

"Oh, it never wasn't," Bael said. "Rise, lilin."

Nunzia stopped sniveling and looked up, the final bit of color draining from her face. While she'd been groveling, the athtars had summoned all her spawn. Even Angela stood in the crowd, pale and horrified.

"L-lord Nunzia!" she cried.

"It is good that you have instilled loyalty in your demons, Nunzia," Bael said. "Shame you didn't learn it for yourself."

"I am loyal. I have always sworn fealty to you and no one else." Her words dissolved into hysterical mumbling as Bael left her in the center of the square. Bael's target, it seemed, was Anya.

"My love," he said with a sad shake of his head. "Why do you look so pained? Did you not see the merciful justice I meted out to Parras?"

"I-I did."

"Do you not agree that Nunzia has been disloyal?"

She swallowed. "I do."

Bael's smile grew wider in relief. "That's wonderful to hear. I'm glad you don't hate me so much that it's discolored your perception."

"I don't..." Her voice was quiet and disjointed. "I don't hate you, Bael."

He took her free hand and kissed it. "I'm grateful to hear that."

"Are you going to make me kill her?" Anya asked.

"Make you?" Bael patted her hand. "My love, I've never made you do a thing in your life. It's clear this...curse has made you crazy. It's made you think I'm someone I'm not."

The corners of her mouth twitched; perhaps she wanted to argue with him, but she didn't. "Then what will you have me do?"

"I simply wanted to borrow your sword," Bael said.

In a blur of movement, Anya's sword disappeared from her hand, and Nunzia's head detached from her body. But instead of the soft sound of steel-through-flesh, a crack of power echoed through the square as the demonic energy Nunzia had gathered over hundreds of years dissipated.

A collective gasp rose from those gathered, and a whoosh of energy circled from Nunzia's body. The air smelled of flowers, sex, and charged electricity before a gust of wind blew it away.

"W-we're human!"

"He's killed Lord Nunzia!"

"*Run!*"

At once, the former demons scattered like rats into alleys and side streets.

"*Son of a bitch,*" Cam swore.

Jack, however, had been transfixed by Anya, who'd flinched

when the sword had severed the head. Her eyes remained closed and her fists clenched until Bael reappeared in front of her. He lifted her fist to his lips and pressed feather-light kisses to her knuckles.

"What is it that bothers you?" Bael asked.

"Will you kill them, too?" she asked. "Nunzia's spawn?"

"My love, do you think I am such a monster?" Bael said with a laugh. "They will die in fifty years or so. Theirs will be the slow, painful death of humans. I could not concoct a better punishment. It is fair, then. They were born human. They shall die human."

Anya released a breath, as if she were expecting some other outcome.

"Now that this unpleasantness is taken care of, I think it's time to go home." He extended his arm. "Shall we?"

When Anya took his arm, something within Jack snapped. Maybe it was her obvious discomfort. Maybe it was because he'd just seen Bael take out Nunzia, and he didn't want to know what Atlanta was going to be like without its lord. Or maybe it was because, despite all of Bael's platitudes, Anya had been terrified of him—and she didn't seem the kind to fear without good reason.

"Anya, you can't go with him!" he called. "Why the hell were you running for a hundred years if you're just going to give in?"

"What are you *doing*?" Cam rasped, grabbing him by the arm. "*Shut up!*"

Bael, however, found this exchange highly amusing. "My

dear Anat, it appears the mortal has fallen in love with you."

"I'm not in love with her," Jack said, although his cheeks had grown warm. "But I don't think she wants to go with you."

"Mortal, if I wanted to destroy this planet and everything in it, I have but to do it," Bael said. "It matters not what she wants or doesn't want. She will go with me. It is for her own good." He turned to her and stroked her cheek. "But I am not a monster."

The demons behind them parted, leaving an open path to freedom.

"Anat, if, as this mortal says, you don't want to come with me, if you find me repulsive and disgusting, then go." His expression grew somber. "But if you decide to stay here, it would destroy me."

And with that, he walked toward the void.

"Anya, come on," Jack called as she turned to follow Bael. "This is suicide! He's giving you a chance—"

She glanced over her shoulder, defeated. "You two should find a safe haven until Demon Spring is over. This war is unwinnable."

Her head bowed, she left her sword on the ground and stepped over Nunzia's headless corpse, passing by Bael without as much as a second glance before disappearing into the darkness.

"You can't go with him!" Jack called, a last-ditch attempt to get through to her.

"Oh, all right," Bael said, glancing over his shoulder. "If

you're that attached, you can come, too."

CHAPTER TWENTY-FOUR

The first thing that came to Jack's mind was the feeling of otherness, like stepping outside in the middle of a lightning storm. Goosebumps raised along his arms, and he couldn't quite inhale deep enough to catch his breath. And he was moving, although his body lay crumpled on the…floor? Hay, it smelled like. Was he in a barn?

"It's probably better if you stay asleep," came Anya's quiet, defeated whisper.

Jack opened his eyes, then sucked in a mouthful of the difficult air. Colors he'd never seen washed over him, and the very air was hard to breathe—like it was mixed in with something foreign. Demonic miasma, he realized. It was like stepping into a room filled with demons, only the room was stadium-sized and vacuum-sealed. His stomach churned uncomfortably as his awareness tilted from side to side, struggling to find a foothold.

"It takes a minute," Anya said. "Take a deep breath. And if you're going to vomit—"

The contents of Jack's stomach came roaring to the surface and he turned his head so he would spew out between the iron bars. He convulsed for a moment, forcing himself to focus on nothing but the inhalation and exhalation of air. After a moment of quiet meditation, the nausea dissipated, but the feeling of dread didn't.

"Where am I?" he rasped.

"Do you really have to ask?"

Jack sat up slowly, rubbing the ropes tied around his wrists, which made his hands numb. But that was be the least of his problems.

Sky blue palm trees with black leaves contrasted against a burnt orange, rocky terrain. The sky above was more purple than blue, with darker clouds that hung above the sky. The sun, at least, was the same bright ball of light, but nothing else looked real. The iron-barred carriage he was trapped inside rocked as it wheeled over the unpaved path.

"I don't remember anything," Jack replied. "How did we get here? How long was I out—God, what about Cam?"

"Your partner escaped as soon as Bael's men took you," Anya said. "She's fine, assuming she hasn't been killed by a demon during the uprising."

Jack was fairly sure nothing could kill Cam, but that begged another question. "So…why am I here?"

"To punish me, I'm sure," she said with a sardonic bark of laughter. "Or perhaps he found you interesting. Humans usually don't stand up to him the way you did."

"Lucky me."

Jack turned away from her to stare at the landscape and wrap his head around what was happening. He was probably the first human in the Underworld since the originals had been banished. If Bael had kept him alive, it was for a specific purpose, and as soon as Jack's usefulness had run out, so would his time.

"How do we get out of here?" he asked.

"We don't."

"You can stay. I have to get back to the human world," Jack said. "I'm not just going to let him kill me."

"You still don't get it, do you?" she said. "Bael is all things. He owns this world, and yours. If he wants you dead, it will be so. There is no escape. There is no fighting him. There's only…" She sighed. "There's only submission."

Jack opened his mouth to argue, but a large, rodent-like creature appeared on a nearby rock formation, hissing and baring sharp teeth as the carriage rolled by. Jack pulled his fingers inside the bars to protect them.

"The actual fuck is that thing?" he asked Anya.

"Ratatoskr," she replied. "Lilin magic."

"I don't know any lilin that looks like that," Jack said,

unable to tear his eyes away from the unusually large rodent.

"It's not a lilin demon, it's lilin magic," she said with a small sigh. "Demons are the humans who were trapped in this world. But they weren't the only ones." She pointed to the two horse-like creatures in front of them. "Kelpies are descended from horses. They've got kappa water magic."

"How long does it take for something to look like *that*?" Jack asked.

"Hundred years, maybe more," she said. "Down here, we have as much variety in animal life as you do. Ours is just improved with demonic miasma."

Although she wore a mask of indifference, Anya looked healthier than ever. Her skin had darkened to a brilliant bronze, and her green eyes had turned the color of emeralds, lined with long, black lashes. Her hair, previously frizzy and unkempt, was now in perfectly coiled ringlets cascading down her shoulder. Even her nails had grown longer and shinier.

"Why are you in here?" he blurted before he could stop himself. "Aren't you Bael's girlfriend?"

Her expression was grim and resigned to her fate. "Why couldn't you have just left me alone?"

"So this is my fault?"

"He never would've found me otherwise." Her gaze darkened. "I had a good track record of a hundred and thirty years until you came along and fucked it up."

"I'm sorry," Jack replied, and he was. "But that doesn't answer my question. Why are you in this prison with me? And where are we going anyway?"

She inhaled softly. "We're headed to Bael's palace, though we're taking the long way there." She glanced around at the demons gathering on the side of the pink road. "This is his victory parade."

"All this, for you?" Jack asked.

"All to prove to me that it's not worth it to fight him." She sighed as a small bird-like demon landed on a barren tree branch. The one-eyed crow opened his mouth, letting out a loud cackle, and then swung himself upside down on the branch as the caravan passed.

"What is—"

"Orev. One of ours."

"One of ours… Athtar, you mean?"

She nodded.

"So how does this demonic transformation work?" Jack asked. When Anya gave him a questioning look, he shrugged and added, "Obviously, we're just taught about the human-like demons. I had no idea there were all these other things here."

She sighed. "Magic—miasma—changes living things, the same way it changes humans into demons. When the first humans arrived in this netherworld, they were banished to the five regions. The regions were separated by mountains and water and distance, so each of their inhabitants developed differently." She glanced around. "This is Ath-kur. Athtar's land. Bael's domain."

"But there are kappas and lilins here, too? And elokos,

right?" Indeed, there were an assortment of demons surrounding the cart, all marching together like the world's ugliest parade.

She nodded. "Since Bael has taken the allegiances of other belus, their spawn are free to roam. Or be enslaved by him. The lilins and kappas are the lowest, and Bael makes them do the menial work. Elokos are free to come and go as they please. And athtars, of course, rule over everyone."

"And they just let him?"

"Well, he's Bael. The perfect mixture of seductive charm and ruthless power. When you're in his world, you're the most beloved creature. When you're out of it…"

"So that explains why you're in here," Jack replied. "You're on Bael's shitlist."

"I have no allies here."

"You have me."

She snorted and finally looked at him. "I wouldn't advertise that too loudly. I may have been Bael's favorite once, but I've defied him for too long. He's not a forgiving man."

"Is Anat your real name?" he asked.

"I don't remember my real name," she said quietly. "Bael named me Anat the Destroyer. Before Bael, I don't remember. It was too long ago."

"So long ago, my lady, my goddess, my bringer of destruction."

Anya froze. While they'd been talking, they'd stopped moving. The caravan was at the bottom of a deep valley, and the foot soldiers had made space for the group. Bael stood in front of the carriage, his clothes strangely unsullied by the dusty world, right down to his shiny black shoes.

"It pains me to see you in there, my love. Why don't you come out? Your human is awake, so there's no need to ride with him anymore. Unless," he cocked his head to the side, "you're simply avoiding me?"

Jack glanced at Anya; so it was her decision to ride in the carriage?

Two kappas rushed to the iron doors and held them open, each keeping their heads bowed revealing steel plates atop them. Anya shimmied to the edge of the carriage and stepped out, the apprehensive look still on her face.

"Why do you look so nervous?" Bael asked. "Come here. Let me look at you."

She walked closer, watching him as if he were a viper. But for some reason, Jack couldn't see the danger. Bael carried no tension behind his eyes, no anger in his gaze. In fact, he looked almost amused.

He held her tenderly, gazing into her eyes and scanning her face. "I'm happy to see some of your color has returned. You looked so ill before. It made me sad to see you that way."

She remained stiff, afraid to move.

"You still believe I'm angry with you?" he said after a moment. "My love, my *goddess*, my bringer of destruction, how could I ever be angry with you? I've never been angry with you —truly angry. Angry enough that you'd want to run away from me. That's just insane. This talisman is warping your mind, I'm now sure of it."

She nodded, but didn't meet his gaze.

In one motion, he ripped it off Anya's neck and threw it on the ground.

"There. Feel better?"

She stood absolutely still for a moment, stunned. But if there was something that signified the end of the curse, Jack didn't see it. She appeared as pale and scared as before.

"You just…"

"My love." He cradled her face. "Look at me."

And she finally did, gazing into his eyes as if for the first time. He stroked her cheek lovingly, and pressed his forehead to hers, closing his eyes.

"Please come back to me. *Please*, Anat. I can't live without you. I can't live while you hate me. I'm not the monster you've made me into. I love you."

Bael captured Anya's lips with a gentle passion, their intimacy making Jack's skin crawl. It wasn't jealousy, Jack hadn't grown attached enough for that, but there was something wrong about the way Bael held Anya.

Slowly, she raised her arms to embrace him back, and she deepened their kiss. Tears dripped down her cheeks, and a sinking feeling grew in his stomach. She pulled away, but her lips trembled with emotion even though she wore a smile. She looked younger, innocent. Like one hundred years of penance had disappeared with one kiss.

"My love," Bael whispered, a tear falling down his cheek.

"My love, is it really you?"

"Bael," she murmured. "Bael, I...I'm..."

She didn't finish, but she didn't have to. Bael cried out in joy and crushed her to him, tangling one hand in her hair and pressing the other into her back. She gripped his shirt, sobbing into his shoulder with happy tears, while the gathered assembly of demons cheered and whooped at their reunion.

None of that emotion reached Jack in the carriage. Only confusion and bewilderment.

Had it really just been the curse? Had it been so simple to remove it? Had all her fears about what he would or wouldn't do been completely unfounded? Bael gazed at her like a thirsty man at a river, holding her to his side with a gentle possession that reminded Jack of him and Sara. Maybe they'd just had the demon equivalent of a spat. Despite his treatment of humans and demons, Jack couldn't fathom the King of the Underworld *ever* lifting a finger to hurt Anya. He'd said it himself: she was his everything.

Anya, too, had begun to believe him. She seemed lighter—happier. Perhaps it was the talisman's magic leaving, or maybe because she was just back with her lover.

Jack heard his name and perked his ears up to listen.

"The human? Oh, my love, I brought him for you," Bael said, glancing in Jack's direction. "You're obviously a little fond of him. I thought he could make a pet for you. I could turn him, if you like."

She glanced back at Jack, disdain and disgust in her eyes.

"No, my love. He's a bother."

"Oh, you're so fickle," he said, squeezing her to him. "We shall dine and celebrate tonight and consider him in the morning. What about that?"

"I suppose."

Now Jack was pissed. That bitch.

"He looks angry," Bael said with a chuckle. "He's a strong human. Might make a good demon. Perhaps I'll turn him in the morrow."

"I doubt he'll turn," she said, toying with the lapel on Bael's jacket. "His family's been demon hunters for centuries."

"Oh? Is that so?" Bael said with an amused smile. "Those are the most fun to turn, don't you know? We can send them back to kill their families."

Bael and Anya—Anat, Jack had decided this flippant bitch was Anat—laughed as they strolled leisurely up the path. This was the cold-blooded killer Jack had read about, the woman who'd effortlessly killed ten thousand humans. Perhaps it had been the talisman after all.

Jack felt a bit duped and more than a little angry with her. Because he'd gotten himself in the middle of their lovers' quarrel, he was now doomed to spend the rest of his life in the Underworld—however long that would be.

He cursed himself for being so idiotic. Cam was going to have a field day.

If he ever saw her again.

No, fuck that. He was going to live, and he was going to get back topside, and he was going to never, *ever* listen to another demon woman for as long as he lived.

But first, he needed to figure a way out of this prison carriage, and then out of the demon world. Now that Anya was gone, he couldn't count on her, but maybe, *maybe* if he could find a lilin, they might take pity on him. Maybe he could make it back to the gateway before Demon Spring ended. They'd been traveling in this caravan for some measure of time; he'd had no idea how long he'd been unconscious. But if he followed this path, he might be able to find his way back.

"Ah!" Anat's cry of surprise drew Jack's attention, and had it not been for the wood floor beneath him, he might've fallen over. They—the entire group of demons—had somehow transported out of the plain and into a large valley. Lush, purple grass swayed in the breeze, and small, one-eyed crows danced in knobby trees.

"Yes, human," Bael said, his brown eyes boring into Jack's. "Your belu athtar can bend time and distance at his whim. We have crossed thousands of miles in the blink of an eye."

"You are most powerful, m'lord," Anya said, patting him on the chest, but Bael was still focused on Jack, who was wondering if the belu athtar could read minds. Or maybe Jack's escape plan had been written on his face.

"Is it not surprising to you, human?" Bael asked. "The magic I can wield? Or is it too complex for you to grasp?"

"Column B," Jack replied dully. He really couldn't have cared less about Bael's flashy show of magic, but he got the impression the demon would continue to do it unless Jack acknowledged his "greatness."

"Hmph," Bael said. "Well, if my magic is unimpressive, perhaps Mount Zephon will draw your admiration."

He gestured to the monster of a white castle before them. Jack hadn't noticed it at first, as the architecture blended into the mountain range it was nestled into. But now he saw the full measure of it—large towers with round tops, smaller turrets with black roofs, and levels upon levels that spilled out onto open verandas. It was part medieval castle, part Italian villa. Truly, a spectacle befitting the so-called Lord of the Mountain.

But Jack wasn't about to tell Bael that.

"Zephon has been a mere shell of itself without its lady present," Bael said to Anat, offering his arm. "Tonight, we feast in your honor. It shall be a celebration for the ages. But first… you and I shall celebrate."

CHAPTER TWENTY-FIVE

Before Jack could gag, Bael and Anya disappeared in a blur and he was left with a hundred leaderless demons.

Suddenly, he missed the demon king.

"Eh, don't you worry, human," croaked a nearby kappa. "We got special orders for you."

"Does it involve me on the menu?" Jack muttered as the caravan pushed forward without their leader. They paraded through a large iron gate—odd that the King of the Underworld would need such protections—and through a mostly empty town square before arriving at the base of the castle. It was much larger and grander up close, with intricate carvings and beautiful porticos Jack was sure he wasn't going to live long enough to enjoy.

The kappa demon who'd spoken to him also unlocked his cage and roughly pulled Jack out. Together with another kappa, they marched him inside the castle. Even through what Jack suspected were the servants' quarters, the interior was just as elegant as the exterior. Succulent smells reminded him that he hadn't eaten in some time (and he'd left the contents of his stomach back on the plains), but they walked him right by the kitchens, through a dark hallway, reaching a large staircase. Up, up, up they climbed, Jack's quads burning from the exertion, before finally stopping in front of a large, detailed door. The kappa unlocked it with a twirl of his finger, before shoving Jack inside the room and locking it.

On his hands and knees, Jack could scarcely believe *this* was where they'd put him. It didn't look much like a prison. There was a canopy bed with dark wood and a comfortable-looking mattress and bedding. A fireplace was already roaring in the corner with a sitting area and shelves of books. But most importantly—there was a window.

Pressing his face against the glass, Jack grimaced. The ground stretched out far below, so far that the people walking into the castle resembled ants. Even though they'd walked up stairs, he didn't think they'd gone *so* far—then realization dawned.

If this was Ath-kur, that meant the magic surrounding him was athtar magic—void magic. Perhaps the ground was five feet from him, perhaps it was ten thousand feet. Either way, he wasn't going to test it.

The door rattled, and Jack's heart began to race when one of his kappa guards appeared.

"Get dressed."

"I'm sorry?" Jack said.

"You're a guest of Belu Athtar tonight. You will need to be appropriately dressed." He pointed a thin, bony finger at a wardrobe against the wall.

Inside, Jack found a handsome suit, surprisingly fitted and modern. For someone who hadn't been topside in over a century, Bael had good taste.

Half an hour later, Jack was adjusting his cufflinks over his talisman bracelet and wondering what fresh new hell he was in for as he followed the kappa guards down a stairwell. They weren't manhandling him this time—perhaps to keep his fine tuxedo intact.

But his breath caught when he stepped out of a dark hallway and into what could only be described as a great hall. Huge tapestries depicting bloody battles hung from the walls, descending down from a ceiling—Jack gasped in surprise. The walls simply *disappeared* into a void, much like the gateway to the human world. But this void wasn't black, it was filled with stars, galaxies, planets.

"Is it not magnificent? The true power of an athtar demon."

Bael appeared beside Jack with his typical charming smile. His brown eyes sparkled with amusement and no small amount of hubris. "I can bring the entire universe to me with a single request. Is it not incredible?"

Despite every fiber in Jack's body telling him *not* to agree, he really couldn't argue. "It is."

"Excellent, excellent." The demon draped a friendly arm around his shoulder. "Come, pet. We will seat you at the table."

So Bael already considered Jack part of his domain—that explained the attitude. Perhaps he was hoping to charm Jack into transitioning.

The demon led Jack to a long table with chairs lining each of the sides. At the head were two chairs—the empty one, presumably, for Bael. Anat sat in the other, decked out in resplendent gold robes, trimmed with purple. Her curly hair was spilled over her shoulder with a golden clasp. Her throne was nearly as opulent as Bael's, although it was a little less decorative. Because no one, apparently, outshone the king.

Jack was surprised when Bael released him and pulled the chair out next to Anat. "Here, pet. I promise, the food isn't poisoned. And you'll be happy next to my dear Lady of the Mountain. She is growing healthier by the minute, is she not?"

Another thing Jack couldn't argue with, although she gave him a derisive snort as he took his seat. Bael patted Jack on the shoulder once and then strolled to his chair.

"Don't you see, my lady? Your human is fine," Bael replied as he sat.

"I wasn't worried," she said, toying with her wine glass. "I merely inquired. They do have to eat."

"I am so glad you're back, my precious lady," he purred. "You are the most beautiful, deadliest, the most perfect woman I have ever laid eyes on. I shall have you again on this table."

"My lord," she said with a coy expression, "mind your manners."

Anat's gentle chiding only served to make Bael more interested, but he thankfully resisted the urge to mount his woman. Jack tried in vain to erase the mental image of her and Bael re-consummating their relationship. It just made him angrier for getting involved. But Jack supposed that explained the whole "mortals can't make me come" comment. Sleeping with the King of the Underworld paled everyone else in response.

"The belus will be joining us, my love," Bael said, running his finger along her face.

"That would be wonderful," she replied with something of a tense smile.

"Are you familiar with the belus, human?" Bael asked, glancing to Jack. "Or has that education been lost in your schools?"

Jack thought it better to remain silent; Bael would probably delight in telling him whether he knew or not.

"The belus are the originals. The first humans cast into this world for our original sins. God-touched, they call us, for we looked upon the face of Him thousands of years ago. I, of course, am Belu Athtar." Again, he stroked Anya's face, drawing his finger down to her arm, before resting his hand over hers. "My lady Anat is the first demon. Aren't you, my lady? Do you remember the day I found you?"

"Yes m'lord. I remember very well."

"Tell me again." It wasn't a request.

"You found me by the sea, bruised and bloody from my father's hand. He was angry with me because I refused to marry the farmer to pay his debts. He struck me until I agreed."

"Yes, yes," Bael said. "You were a shivering thing when I found you. Terrified. What did I do when I found you?"

Anya spoke evenly, as if she'd been forced to relive the memory so many times it no longer burned her. "You took me to the mountain. You made me strong. You made me athtar. You returned me to the village."

"And what did you do then?" Bael asked breathlessly.

"I slaughtered every person there."

The original demon smiled, as if the story had been brand new to him. "They called you the destroyer. They said your robes were bathed in blood as you beheaded those who had hurt you, binding their severed heads to your waist and taking the hands as ornaments on your sash." He inhaled deeply. "It was beautiful."

"Yes, m'lord."

"You will never forget how your belu athtar made you strong."

"No, m'lord."

"And you won't leave me again?"

"No, m'lord. I'll never leave you again." She smiled. "I love you, my savior, my king. My Lord of the Mountain."

That seemed to placate him, because he clapped. "Bring in the belus!"

Loud groaning echoed in the stone chamber as two large doors, tall enough to disappear into the void at the ceiling, slowly opened. Bael placed his hand on top of Anat's and glanced to Jack in anticipation, as if this were the beginning of some great movie.

The kappa that hobbled in looked like a cross between a turtle and human, with a wide smile that stretched from cheek to cheek. Somehow, he looked even more kappa-ish than the creatures that had come through the void.

"Lord of the Mountain, King of the Demons, Emperor of all the Five Worlds, Belu Athtar," he said in a croaking, sniveling voice.

"Mizuchi, so great of you to come," Bael said lazily.

Jack nearly choked on his spit. Mizuchi—he was the *original* kappa demon. He'd pictured original demons to be something like Bael—human and deadly. But this monster was most assuredly subservient as he averted his eyes.

Bael stood and bowed from the hip, exposing the top of his head to the kappa. The other demon returned the gesture, but as Mizuchi dipped, water poured out from a cavity atop his head, landing in a puddle on the floor.

Bael picked up a gold goblet and poured it onto the belu's head, refilling what had been spilled. "You see, human, kappas are very polite demons. If you bow to them, they must bow in return. But they cannot survive long without water. Refill what has been lost, and they will swear fealty to you forever."

"Yes, Belu Athtar," the kappa demon whispered.

Jack doubted this spectacle was for his benefit. Although Anya had seemingly reverted to the Goddess of Destruction, Bael seemed focused on proving to her how very powerful he was, perhaps in case she was harboring any ideas about leaving him again. Or maybe the demon of pride simply enjoyed watching his power in action.

"It's a pleasure to see you so well, my lady," the kappa demon said to Anya.

She glanced at him once, then reached for her wine to take a long sip.

Bael found that amusing. He took a gold coin from his pocket and flipped it at the turtle demon. "The lady is still disgusted by your presence, kappa. Get out of her sight so you don't spoil her appetite."

The kappa dipped his head, although only a splash of water left his cavity this time, and bit on the gold coin as he retreated to the far end of the wide table.

"Bring on the next one," Bael ordered, resting his hand on top of Anya's.

The woman who walked into the room was the most beautiful creature Jack had ever seen. Long, silver hair flowed to the ground behind her. Lily white skin shimmered from beneath silken robes. Her pointed ears gave her away as a lilin demon.

"Overseer of All, King of the Demons, Lord of the Mountain, Grace upon Grace, Belu Athtar." She bowed low, revealing the full swell of her breasts right down to her pert nipples. She rose slowly, wearing a coy look on her face. Lust personified.

Her lust wasn't contained to Bael. She was eyeing Anya with the same hungry expression, and Jack's mind was filled with explicit scenes of what it might look like between the two of them, with him in the middle. And Bael, too. And maybe that kappa demon—he was suddenly not as grotesque as Jack had first thought.

Damn those lust demons, Cam's voice floated through Jack's mind, and he glanced at the shiny coins hanging from the string around his wrist. Dazed, he found the blue-rimmed one and pressed it against his skin. The feeling of desire subsided, although the original demon's magic was still potent.

"Oh." The belu lilin's gaze landed on Jack, and she clapped her hands in joy. "A human. May I have him?"

A crackle of energy echoed through the room, and Bael stood up angrily. "You do *not* request things of me, Belu Lilin. Things in this room are *mine*. *I* will give them as I see fit. And you do not deserve anything."

The original lust demon backtracked, covering her mouth and dropping to her knees. She begged forgiveness of the floor.

Bael's breathy chuckle broke the tension in the room and the lilin lifted her head. Jack suddenly wasn't so sure what he'd found attractive about the gray-skinned, wiry-haired creature with sharp teeth.

"Get out of my sight," Bael said, waving his hand.

She scampered toward the other empty chair beside the kappa demon, and Jack waited to see what other horrific creatures would appear. If they'd seen the kappa, lilin, and athtar demons, that left the eloko or…the nox.

The doors opened, and Jack released a breath. If the grass beard and hair hadn't tipped him off, the bell hanging from his hand would have. The belu eloko. Jack found the brown-rimmed coin and pressed it quickly, praying this one would work better than the lilin's had.

For this original demon, Bael stood and greeted him in the center of the room. "Biloko, my friend."

"Belu Athtar, my king." Friend apparently meant the eloko didn't have to kiss Bael's ass.

The demon's voice was earthen, grainy, and put Jack in a fine mood, so he released the pressure of the talisman against his hand. The more that bell rang, the more Jack thought the demon was rather cartoonish, almost like the little troll dolls he'd play with as a boy. The urge to go with this funny troll-man rose within Jack's mind, and he would've stood, if not for a firm hand on his shoulder.

"Sit, idiot human," muttered Anat as she forced him back down. "Belu Eloko, liege, if you'll reduce your magic so this human doesn't have a heart attack."

The dwarf looked at Jack, and the urge to go with the strange grass-haired man disappeared, leaving a headache in its place. No wonder humans didn't last long in this place; they were constantly being bombarded with magic.

"As customary, we leave two seats open for the dear belu noxes," Bael said, casting a glance at the open seats next to him.

The Eloko demon took the seat farther away, and looked pleased to be doing so. "Mot and Xo, who were vanquished by my love, the beautiful Goddess of Destruction."

Something cold slipped down Jack's back. Anya had killed *original* demons?

"Ah yes, human. She is the Bringer of Death to Death himself." Bael placed his hand over hers again as Anya gazed at the ground. "You look pained, my love. Is this story upsetting to you?"

"Yes, m'lord."

For once, Bael listened. "Very well, we shall save that story for another time, when you are stronger."

"Your grace is unending, m'lord."

"And now, we eat," Bael announced, and was answered by the clinking of silverware. Jack had seen enough to know that he should at least make like he was eating.

"My lady, my love, my goddess," Bael said in that singsong voice of his. The way Anya stiffened portended nothing good. "Perhaps we might talk about the nox prince?"

"We may discuss whatever you wish, my love," she replied evenly.

But now Jack was curious—did Bael mean literal son? He didn't realize demons could have children.

"Our fair Lotan continues to lay claim to this land, and our tussles haven't been the same without your sword," Bael continued.

"By your command, m'lord," Anat mumbled, although there

was something hidden behind her eyes. "Will you have me leave in the morning to the front lines?"

Bael chuckled. "You'd like that, wouldn't you? To leave again."

The fork paused halfway to her mouth. "That wasn't my intent. I will stay until you release me."

"Wasn't that what you promised me when you disappeared? You were off to slaughter the humans. And then Demon Spring ended and me without my lady."

She stared at her plate. "It wasn't my fault—"

"So why did you not return to me after four years?"

Anya didn't respond. The silence deepened the tension, which became so thick that Jack forgot to breathe. Bael stared at Anya, a smile on his face, but something sinister lurking beneath the surface.

"The curse…" she started.

"I removed it with no problems, as you'll remember."

She swallowed. "It prevented me from—"

"From nothing. You ran from me. After all the power I gave you. All the gifts. I don't understand why you'd run from me."

Jack could've offered a few reasons, but couldn't find the air to speak.

"Come," he said, standing. "I don't wish to discuss this in front of an audience."

Anya stood and followed without another word.

CHAPTER TWENTY-SIX

Dinner had continued in complete silence after that, with only the rare clicking of the kappa demon's beak. Jack, who hadn't touched a thing, somehow forced himself to eat, just so his stomach would stop rumbling. But the food sat uneasily in his belly, reminding him of how easily Jack had forgotten who Bael really was.

Once dessert had been served and taken away, the belus rose and left with much less fanfare than with which they'd arrived. The kappas returned to take Jack back to his room, but this time, they simply guided him, instead of marching him. Night had descended over the castle, and even though there was no moon, there was an eerie glow from the lamplights lining the hallway.

The castle almost seemed too quiet.

The kappas left Jack in the room as they had before, but this time, Jack was ready to take action. He changed back into his regular clothes, which had been laundered of the blood and gore from the day's battle and refolded in his absence.

The talismans clinked at his wrist, reminding him of their presence. They had been completely ineffective against the original demons. But maybe…

He located the gray-rimmed coin, the only one he'd never used. Supposedly, it was to combat athtar magic—although athtars didn't coerce (other than with fancy words and nice smiles), so he wasn't sure what would happen. Holding his breath, he pressed the coin to his skin.

At first, nothing seemed different. But when he walked to the window, the floor was merely ten stories below him, instead of ten thousand feet. Perhaps now he could see through the ways Bael had warped and manipulated things, and maybe find a path back to the void.

Jack poked his head out the window again, spying another open window just below his room. There was a chance, however slim, that room might not be locked and he could break out. He walked to the wardrobe and tied the ends of the shirt and pants he'd been wearing, as well as the sheets from the bed and the curtains on the wall. Everything he touched was soft and supple, but he felt no guilt in ruining the material.

He tied the ends of his makeshift escape route to the bed post and tested his weight against it. It wouldn't hold him for very long, but perhaps long enough to get to the window below. He fastened the sheets around his waist and walked to the window.

Click.

Jack froze, hanging out of the room and hoping his guards wouldn't be too pissed about him trying to escape, but the person who walked in wasn't a kappa.

It was Anya. She was bruised—the first he'd ever seen on her. They lined her arms and marred her swollen lips. Her eyes were red from crying, and her cheeks bore the tracks of tears.

"What the hell happened to you?" Jack gasped, all thoughts of escape gone as he scrambled to undo the bindings around his waist. Then, after a moment, he softened. "Did he do this?"

She said nothing, but walked to the bed and sat down on the edge. "I didn't know you were in here. This was…this used to be mine."

Well, that explained the finery. But why would Bael have put Jack in Anya's room? Unless… Jack swore silently to himself. It had all been another bit of manipulation. Bael knew he would hurt Anya, and he knew that she'd run to her sanctuary, where Jack would be waiting. For any other man, that would've seemed counterintuitive. But for Bael, this was another demonstration of his control. He wanted Jack to know that, even bruised and beaten, Anya was still his, even when she ran from him.

"Do you want me to…go?" Jack asked, pointing to the window. "I was on my way out."

"It's no use," she replied softly. "He would find you and

bring you back. He wants you here, so here you will stay."

Jack swallowed, scarcely believing that this ghost was the same woman responsible for killing tens of thousands—and an original demon, to boot. She seemed frail now, trembling like a small child as she stared into the distance at some unknown point.

Unsure how she might react if he got too close, Jack took a seat next to the fire and waited for her to speak.

"It wasn't that bad," she said after a moment. "At least he didn't kill me."

Jack remained quiet.

"He could have. I'm grateful he showed restraint."

More silence.

"He really does love me."

"You think so?" Jack asked.

"You heard him in there," she replied. "I'm his goddess. His lady. He was just upset that I'd been gone for so long. Worried, I mean."

"When I worried about Sara, I never hit her."

She quickly covered the bruises on her arms with her hands. "It's not that bad. I've had worse."

"From him?"

She reached for the talisman which no longer hung from her neck. She shook her head. "I thought I'd feel different after it was gone. Maybe I do. Maybe it was stupid not to go back to him in the first place. I mean, what was I so afraid of? I'm back home, and things are back to normal."

"So beating you is normal?"

Her eyes flashed. "No, of course not. As long as things remain peaceful, he's peaceful."

Jack could scarcely believe his ears. "So what? You're just going to live in fear for the rest of your life? Try not to piss him off so he'll never lay a finger on you?"

"This isn't how it normally is," she said, then screwed up her face in anger. "I don't have to justify anything to you, *human*. I am the Lady—"

"Yeah, yeah, Lady of Destruction, Anat the Destroyer, Goddess of War. Who's telling me that she's living in complete fear of her boyfriend—"

"And who could also kill you right now," she snarled, coming to her feet. "You do not *speak* to me as such. I am a queen in this castle—"

"Are you allowed to kill people without your boyfriend's permission?" Jack asked, sitting back in the chair. "Because he seems to like me, or thinks he can use me to manipulate you—"

She rose from the bed, fire dancing in her eyes as she approached Jack, cracking her knuckles. "Shall we find out?"

"If you're going to kill me, do it," Jack said with a lazy sigh.

"Are you offering yourself for slaughter?"

Jack shrugged. "Not really much left for me up there."

Anya lifted her brow. "That woman who's always with you, she's—"

"My sister-in-law. Partner. Friend. All those things."

"And you would rather die than see her again?"

"I'd like to see you try to kill me."

He'd never once feared Anya, not since that first night she'd killed Nunzia's demons. In his gut, he knew she had some measure of good in her, and that he had nothing to worry about from her. Even now, with the so-called curse removed, when there should've been nothing to prevent her from returning to the bloodthirsty warrior who dominated the legends.

And yet, there she stood.

"Well?" Jack said. "We're waiting."

"You aren't worth it," she snarled, turning away from him and stalking to the sheets still attached to the bed. "Besides, it's clear you're intent on killing yourself anyway. Have you not looked out the window? A fall like that would smash your frail little body."

"Uh-huh," Jack said, deciding *not* to tell her about the athtar pendant hanging from his bracelet. "I wasn't planning on falling."

"If you leave this room, you will be left in this realm," she said with an arched brow. "The belu athtar has decided we will be returning to the human one. Tomorrow."

Jack stared at her, sure he'd misheard. "We're…going back?"

"Bael wishes to show the world his power. The demon lords seem to have forgotten who is their leader," she said. "He wants me to remind them."

"Why do *you* have to remind them of *his* power?" Jack asked pointedly.

"Because I'm his lady."

"Sounds like you're doing his dirty work. Have you ever thought that *maybe* you're more powerful and don't have to listen to what he says?"

There was a flash of something in her gaze, and all the fire went out as quickly as it had arrived. "He is all things. There is no defeating him."

"Have you even *tried?*"

The anger returned. "I tried *plenty* and I have the scars to prove it."

"You didn't have to go with him in the first place. Bael didn't force you—"

"You don't get it do you?" she said weakly. "I'm here because I love him."

"You can't possibly..." Jack said, unable to wrap his mind around what she was saying. "I mean—"

"Bael *made* me. He took me from nothing and made me into something. And he's the only man who's ever truly loved me. I can't..." She slumped. "I didn't want to see him again because I knew I couldn't resist him. His power is nothing in comparison to my love for him."

"So..." Jack began, trying to wrap his head around what she was saying. "If you love him so much, why are you resisting him in the first place?"

She didn't answer, but she didn't have to. There was no logic here—at least, none Jack could see. Bael had poisoned her mind with lies and false equivalencies. In her warped mind, she'd equated those lies with love. Bael had made her believe he was the only man who would ever love her. The fear of being without him kept Bael alive.

That was why no matter how many times he hurt, beat, or manipulated her, Bael would always win.

Anya left after that, presumably for makeup sex with Bael. Despite his best efforts not to think about it, visions of them together plagued his thoughts as he lay awake in the bed he'd remade for himself. There was so much manipulation occurring within the walls of this castle, and none of it magical. If Anya was going to choose to stay in this hellhole, that was on her. Jack had never been witness to the mental gymnastics that went with someone staying in an unhealthy relationship before, and what he saw sickened him.

And now, Bael was taking Jack back to his realm. It had to be part of his larger strategy to break Anya, for everything Jack had seen so far had been in pursuit of that. He knew, even back in his world, he wouldn't be safe. But at least he'd be able to say his goodbyes to Cam.

When light began creeping along the floor, the kappa demon appeared and barked at Jack to get dressed promptly. Since he was already wearing his clothes, he rolled out of bed and followed the demon down the stairs. With the athtar talisman, the stairs seemed closer together, the ceilings not so high, but the artistry of the castle was still breathtaking.

This morning, Jack ate alone at the long table (which didn't look as long as it had the night before). The meal was simple—

fruit and cream—but Jack was starving so he ate his fill. Right as he swallowed the last bite, the doors swung open, and Bael and Anya sashayed into the large dining hall.

Anya was fastened to her lover's side with a cheerful smile on her face. The bruises had faded, as had, apparently, her memory of them. She freely kissed his neck, his cheek, and any other part of him she could put her lips on.

"My lady, your human is watching," Bael said. "Are you sure you don't want me to turn him?"

"My love, I don't wish to look upon him ever again," she purred, tossing a disgusted look at Jack.

Jack resisted the urge to flick her off.

"Then why don't I simply kill him, my lady?"

A flash of something crossed her face, but she hid it quickly. "Imagine the celebrations of the humans if you return their prodigal son unharmed? They would sing praises for centuries. Bael the Merciful, they would call you."

While Bael pondered, Jack caught her gaze.

Keep quiet and let me save you.

So this was how it was. Stroke Bael's ego and he would do what she wanted. She'd already proven herself to be a manipulator; maybe it worked both ways.

"I agree, my lady. We'll bring him with us." Bael released Anat and walked toward Jack. "Human, you have a choice. I shall make you my son, give you long life and the secrets of the universe. I shall even let you lie with my Lady of Destruction whenever she sees fit." He smiled. "But know that even as a demon, you will never unlock *all* her secrets, though I hear you've already had a taste."

Jack didn't look at Anya, but he knew enough to keep quiet. So he'd charmed that out of Anya, or beat it out of her.

"Or, you may return to your normal human life, to scurry amongst the outcasts and mortals like a bug under my shoe," Bael finished.

"I'd like to go home," Jack replied. He'd seen enough of this crazy place for one lifetime—he couldn't imagine staying there forever and watching Anya make terrible decisions with Bael.

"Ah, my lady! Apparently, you were not good enough for him," Bael said. "Did you even try?"

"Of course not, my love," Anya purred. "I told you. It was simply sex."

"And why, my love, did you sleep with him?" Bael asked. A flash of fear crossed her face, but melted as he chuckled. "I'm sorry. I told you I wouldn't bring it up again. I'm just hurt that you took another man instead of coming to me. Coming *with* me."

Jack swallowed so he wouldn't vomit the breakfast he'd eaten, but Anya replied, "Your lordship is the only one who knows me."

"Ah, I do. Your cries of pleasure echoed in my dream all night long."

What about her screams of terror when you beat her? Jack bit his tongue so he wouldn't speak, but it was getting harder and harder.

"You are the only light in my life," she said, although there was less effusing adoration than before. "My love. My Lord of the Mountain. I shall never leave your side again."

Bael smiled and placed a hand on her cheek. "Why would you entertain such a thought at all?"

"It would be lunacy. I am yours for eternity."

"You are, indeed," Bael replied, patting her. "Come, we shall return to the topside."

"Yes, m'lord."

A smile curled onto Bael's face as he turned to Jack once more. "Do you wish to see the true power of an Athtar? Do you wish to witness the great magnificence that you gave up?"

"Sure," Jack said with a half-hearted shrug.

Annoyance flashed on Bael's face, but he said nothing. Slowly, he walked to the center of the room and held up his hands.

The ground shook, as it had in Atlanta when Demon Spring had first begun, and a swirling black void appeared in the center of the room.

"Don't you see? I, the belu athtar, can create the transition between this world and the next," he exclaimed over the sound of the world breaking. "I decide when to release the demons into your world, and I decide when to call them back. You and the rest of your humans live at my pleasure."

Jack winced as two large sections of the wall broke off and slammed into each other. The winds grew more violent and he knelt to steady himself. A hand gripped his shoulder tightly. He glanced up at Anya, but her gaze was still on Bael, whose eyes had turned as black as the void.

The space between Jack's ears popped and the world expanded and contracted, roiling his stomach. The only thing anchoring him to reality was Anya's firm grip on his shoulder.

And then, as quickly as it began, it stopped.

CHAPTER TWENTY-SEVEN

Jack sucked in a huge gulp of clean air, filling his lungs for what felt like the first time in decades. Sound came back to his awareness first. A siren wail, the screaming of a nearby woman, rushing water. Then his sight returned, zeroing in on the fire hydrant spewing water into the air.

"Breathe, Jack," Anya whispered with the iron grip still on his shoulder.

With great effort, he lifted his other arm to place a hand over hers. "I'm good. Where are we?"

"Atlanta," she replied, releasing him.

"At…Atlanta?" Jack gaped, finally taking a real look around.

He recognized this place—the Centennial Park. But things

looked different—the giant statue in the center was gone. The trees burnt to a crisp. The sky was overcast with tints of red.

"How long have we been gone?"

She snorted. "A week at most."

"They destroyed all this in a week?" Jack gasped, standing up. The park was surrounded by old churches and tall buildings, all of them now mere shells of themselves. The city looked like a war zone.

"And more, I fear," Anya whispered. "Those who've allied themselves with Bael are spreading their reach, and those who haven't will find their comeuppance."

"Why are you still talking to me?" Jack asked. To her shocked expression, he added, "I mean, aren't you going off to kill thousands of innocents as a show of Bael's power?"

"Watch your tongue. I could send you back," she snapped. "I've been merciful so far. Don't make me regret it."

"Anat, my love," Bael called. "Come to me. And bring the human with you."

Jack wasn't in the mood to be manhandled, so he followed Anya across the decimated park to where Bael was apparently holding court. When Anya appeared beside him, he draped a lazy arm around her waist and kissed her cheek.

"What did you need?" Anya asked.

"Just to hold you," he replied, gently caressing her face.

Jack didn't miss the flick of attention Bael gave him, either.

"Now, as to the matter of these squabbles," Bael said, turning to the five demons assembled in front of him on bended knee. "I have heard your complaints, kappas. It is good that you came to me with your grievances. You shall be rewarded for your deference." He nodded at the first kappa. "You shall take the city of Tampa. Is that agreeable?"

"Yes, m'lord."

"And, you, Foriana, you will take Jacksonville."

"B-but my lord, Latricia is the lord of—"

"She is no more," Bael replied simply. "She was a spawn of Nunzia, and Nunzia did not show loyalty to her belu athtar. I suspect she is already reversed or dead."

The three demons shuddered together. "I shall make plans to relocate," Foriana replied.

"And you, lilin Angela."

Jack couldn't believe his eyes. Angela knelt before Bael, her gaze glued to the ground. He'd thought she'd reverted to human when Nunzia died, but he could still see her demonic form. She looked pale, petrified, but resolute. Jack would've guessed she'd be halfway to Canada by now.

"You come to me begging forgiveness on behalf of your brethren?" Bael asked softly.

"On behalf of my spawn," she said, her voice cracking. "I am the only second left. I have hundreds of…of children. They are in fear for their life. I humbly…" She closed her eyes. "I humbly beg you to spare them."

"You are no second," he said, bending down to take her face as gently as he had Parras. "You will be a first of your own demon clan. Your belu athtar is most generous, is he not?"

Angela burst into tears. "Y-y-your grace is unending. M-my spawn are m-my f-family."

"Ssh." Bael actually pulled the demon to her feet and into his arms, caressing her face softly. "You have nothing to fear from me, Lord Angela."

"T-thank you, thank you so much."

Bael stepped away from her and gave her hand to a redheaded man to his right who'd appeared out of nowhere. "You will go with Ekur to my castle where we will meet with your belu. Then, we will make your lordship official."

She nodded as Bael wiped her face, although his closeness was starting to verge on awkward. His gaze raked over her body as he cupped her rear. It was clear to Jack that Bael had only one reason for bringing Angela back to his castle.

"Bael." Anya's sharp voice broke through the square. She wore a look of annoyance on her face, one Bael didn't share.

"Oh, quiet yourself, my love. It's just business. Unless, of course, you'd like to join us?" He draped that same lazy arm around Angela, who looked uncomfortable to be in the middle of their quarrel.

Anya's eyes narrowed into a glare. "Shall we get on with our business?"

"I suppose, my goddess. I suppose."

An athtar appeared next to Bael and took Angela by the arm. But before she disappeared in a blur, Bael made sure Anya saw him squeeze the other demon's ass.

Anya gritted her teeth, apparently trying her hardest not to look angry with him, and Bael laughed. "My lady, after sleeping with the human, you cannot possibly be angry with me."

She blinked, the words seeming to make as much sense in her mind as in Jack's, but she didn't argue with him. She also didn't look happy when Bael pulled her into his arms and kissed her nose.

"Oh, don't be sour. It's just a bit of fun with a lilin. I know you like those. Shall I have Freyja—"

"Bael, enough," Anya said, breaking out of his grip. "Let's just get on with what you're here to do."

"We shall, my love." He pulled her to him, a bit rougher than before, and spun her around. "Will you look at our beautiful army?"

Jack turned and nearly jumped out of his skin. There were *thousands* of demons surrounding the park. Human-looking topside demons stood shoulder-to-shoulder with their uglier cousins, all waiting for the command from their belu athtar.

"What is this?" Anya asked quietly. "Why are they gathered?"

"Because it is as I wish," he replied, with a glance to Jack. Then, his smile widened. "Oh, look at that. The humans are joining us."

Jack spun around again, staring at the empty skyline. Somewhere in the distance, his ears picked up the sound of helicopters drawing nearer. Then, as if the cavalry itself were arriving, twenty military-grade helicopters appeared over the top of the nearest building. The first hovered over the edge of the park, releasing several black ropes to the ground. Ten humans dressed in black special operations gear rappelled down, scattering to defensive positions as soon as they hit the ground. They all carried rifles, but none took a shot.

"Oh, this shall be fun," Bael replied, grasping his hands behind his back and looking to Jack with glee.

Behind them, the demons continued gathering—now numbering in the tens of thousands by Jack's estimate. In front of them, the humans had grown to fifty. As the helicopters flew away, Jack almost wanted to tell them to come back.

"*Jack!*"

Cam's voice echoed across the square. One of the last black-clad figures to land in the square yanked off her helmet. She stood in the center of the demons, drinking in the sight of him as if he'd come back from the dead.

"Is it you?" she called. "Are you a demon? I'd hate to have to kill you."

Jack glared at her, and she sighed in relief.

"Oh? And who is this?" Bael asked, coming to stand beside Jack. "Dare I see another member to our romantic entanglement?"

"She's not your type," Jack replied dryly.

Bael actually seemed annoyed by the prospect. "*Everyone* is my type."

Jack rolled his eyes, but then jumped as the demon king placed a possessive arm around his shoulders.

"Welcome!" he said, squeezing Jack to his side as if they were best friends. "Welcome humans. Welcome, demons! Welcome, all of my faithful subjects. I am so grateful you're all here to welcome me, your Overseer of All, King of the Demons, Lord of the Mountain, Grace upon Grace, Belu Athtar!"

"We're not here to welcome you," Cam replied, leveling her weapon from behind an overturned car. "We're here to tell you and your demon friends to get the hell out of our world. And while you're at it, get your mitts off my partner."

"Such rancor," Bael said with a small tut to Jack. "After I, the Lord of the Mountain, King of the Demons, Emperor of all the Five Worlds, have brought back your prodigal son, unharmed. He lives, as do you all, *only* because I am gracious and merciful. I am the Lord of the Mountain, the King of Kings, the—"

"Save it, windbag," Cam barked. "I'm already tired of hearing you talk. Can we just shoot you and get it over—"

Whether it was Bael or one of his athtars, Jack didn't know, but someone knocked Cam across the square, where she landed in the gaggle of humans. Jack rushed toward her, but Cam waved him off, as she slowly got to her feet.

Instead, he looked at Anya. *Please, do something*, he mouthed.

"I do love human moxie. They have so few years to live, and they try to make such an impact," Bael said with a sad shake of his head. "Look at all these pathetic creatures. They fear me, but they still fight me. Why don't they submit, human? Why won't you submit? Am I not a benevolent emperor? Do I not allow the humans to live freely under my rule?" He sighed. "Tell me what I'm missing, human."

"Nobody lives freely if they live in fear," Jack replied. "I guess it's a human thing."

Bael chuckled. "Such loyalty to your species. Is that why you won't accept my gift to become an athtar?"

"Why are you so obsessed with making me an athtar?" Jack asked. "I'm no different from any other human out here."

"Because I want to own you," Bael replied softly with a cruel smile and a glance at Anya.

"No, you want to own her," Jack muttered.

"I do own her," Bael said firmly. "Never forget that, human. You are but an insignificant flash, a mild amusement to be toyed with. I am the one who owns her soul, and I will *never* relinquish it. Witness the strength of the belu athtar, and tremble at my feet."

He turned on his heel and walked toward a small carriage that had accompanied them from the demon world. Ten kappas stood guard around it, but they scattered in fear as he approached. Two brave souls returned, pulling a bejeweled box from inside the carriage and opening it. Bael removed a large sword, sparkling even in the dim sunlight. There was something otherworldly about it, and that made it all the more terrifying.

Anya had grown pale, but said nothing.

"You don't look pleased to see your sword again, my lady." He cradled the weapon in his hands as if it were his own child. "Your sword, the bringer of death and destruction, Sharur. It was strengthened with the blood of the belu noxes," he continued, raising it into the air to examine it. "It was sealed with the blood of ten thousand men."

He lowered the sword and crossed the open area, offering it to her. She took it, but after a moment's pause.

"That's better," Bael replied, brushing a stray curl from her face. "You are incomplete without your weapon, my goddess."

"Thank you," Anya said, grasping it tighter.

The deadly smile on his face sent Jack's heart racing. "I am most merciful, am I not?"

"You are, m'lord."

"It would make the humans tremble if I were to dole out punishments to those who were insolent," he continued, that same look in his eye. "But you, my lady, are Anat the Destroyer, Goddess of Vengeance. Lady of the Mountain. You will be the bringer of punishments."

She nodded, although a muscle tensed in her jaw. "Yes, m'lord."

"Now, my lady, my goddess, my bringer of destruction," he said, turning to gaze upon those gathered. "I shall give you your choice: slaughter a thousand humans this day," he paused and smiled at Jack. "Or kill your little human pet. I leave the choice up to you."

He walked away from her, leaving her speechless and stunned. If Jack had had any doubts that she wasn't the ruthless killer she'd been made out to be, they evaporated in that moment. Anya looked both sickened and unsurprised, as if this very disturbing order hadn't been the first she'd ever received. Jack wondered how many of these "choices" comprised the souls she was atoning for.

The moments passed slowly, but Bael was in no hurry. He breathed in her agony and reveled in her horror like it was the most delicious thing he'd ever tasted.

"I shall give Jackson his choice," Bael said, turning to Jack. "Although I believe he would choose his own life over—"

"Kill me," Jack said with a daring look.

Bael actually looked surprised. "You'd sacrifice yourself?"

"*No way!*" Cam barked, rushing forward from behind the car with her gun raised. She was bleeding from her forehead. "Jackson Grenard, I did *not* drag your ass down to Atlanta to have you sacrifice yourself to Colibrí. That is not how you're going out, do you understand me?"

"Oh, this is delightful," Bael said, standing to the side. "But sadly, human, you have no say. Jackson has given his preference, but Anat will make the final decision. Either he dies, or a thousand humans do."

"Or she could impale you with that fancy sword," Cam snarled. "I like that option the best."

Bael turned to look at Cam, amusement twitching the edges of his mouth. "You believe my goddess could kill *me*? I am Bael. I am the—"

"Yeah, yeah. King of the demons, emperor of your own ego." Cam adjusted the gun in her hand. "I still say we slice your head off and shut you up for good."

Bael chuckled and placed a possessive arm around Anya, who barely acknowledged it. "You're forgetting one thing: my lady and I are inseparable. She is the light of my life. Am I not the light of yours, my love?"

"Yes," Anya replied, but there was little feeling in it.

"You see? I made her. She would never leave me," he said. "Now my lady, you have one or a lot of humans to slaughter, and I don't plan on being here all day, so please, get on with it." He tossed a glance to Cam. "If you do choose to kill a thousand humans, please start with this mouthy one."

But as he walked away, Anya didn't move. She didn't raise her bejeweled sword. Her gaze remained on the ground, as if she were frozen solid.

Disgust flashed on his face. "Are you disobeying me?"

She shook her head, but her hand didn't move. "Please don't make me do this again."

"I don't want to do this. But this is what you've made me do. You ran away. You let yourself be tainted. You *slept* with this human."

Cam turned to Jack with her brows raised.

"This all happened because of *you*," Bael said. "You embarrassed me and threatened the order of this world. I have to show the humans that I am not to be trifled with. This is the only way."

She swallowed and tightened her grip on the sword. "It's not..."

"I don't understand why you're hesitating. The curse has

been lifted. Kill this human or a thousand or all of them and let's get on with our Demon Spring."

Anya gripped her sword and turned to Jack, seemingly making her decision. "This is your fault. If you hadn't led him right to me, none of this would've happened."

"Bullshit," Cam replied. "Bael is—"

"Cam," Jack said, wishing he could hug her one last time. "It's okay. You're better off without me anyway. Go to Shanghai."

"Like *hell* I will," Cam said, tears streaking down her face. "You aren't giving up that easily."

Jack tore his gaze away from Cam and faced Anya. "Just promise me one thing. Once I'm dead, you'll kill Bael."

Anya lifted her sword. "I won't kill him. I love him."

Bang.

CHAPTER TWENTY-EIGHT

Anya stopped, her sword still raised, but a confused and pained look on her face. The weapon fell from her hands with a loud clatter. She blinked once, twice, then her eyes fluttered as she toppled to the ground. A moan rumbled from her lips as she gripped her bloody shoulder.

"What is this?" Bael cried before laughing. "I told you, human weapons can't..."

Anya cried out, blood continuing to pour through her fingertips.

"I call it my talisman launcher," Cam said, aiming the gun at Bael. "See, we carry around these little iron talismans to ward off magic here. And I thought I'd test what happens if I inscribed the symbol onto an iron bullet and lodged it in your chest." She glanced at Anya. "Theory proven. Guess we can save all that government money."

Bael took a hesitant step back. "But you can't—"

"I've got this shotgun loaded with seven anti-athtar bullets," she said with a smug grin. "And my compatriots have thousands more with anti-eloko, anti-lilin, and anti-kappa magic. Even got a few anti-noxes in case one of those decide to show up." She gestured to the buildings behind them. "And there are even more waiting in the wings up there."

"You think you can defend yourselves against me?" Bael laughed, but it was clear Anya's pain had unnerved him. "I have hundreds of thousands of demons at my disposal." He raised his arm. "They care not for their deaths."

"Oh good," Cam said, pointing her gun. "Because we'll kill every last one."

It happened in a mix of bullet blasts and demonic roars. Bael disappeared almost immediately, and Cam tackled Jack to the ground as the humans behind discharged their weapons.

"What the hell, Cam?" Jack said, keeping his head low to avoid getting shot. "How'd you pull all this together?"

"It was you, actually," Cam said with a smile. "When you said La Colibrí's talisman was the same, it gave me the ammo I needed to push for all this. Frank and Myra helped, too."

"You got all this together in a week?" Jack asked. "All these people, all this coordination…"

"Grief's a powerful motivator," she said, not quite meeting

his eyes.

He softened and squeezed her arm. "I'm sorry I made you worry. I wished I'd never gotten involved."

"Yeah, and when were you going to tell me you slept with her?"

"As soon as we spoke again," Jack said. "Believe me, it's on the top of the list of things I wish I could change about the past few weeks. The *last* thing I want is to be the third wheel between them."

"Yeah, that seems like an incredibly healthy relationship." She nodded to Anya, still grasping her wound as bullets flew around them. "And look at that, he left her in the middle of the battlefield. Some boyfriend he is."

"We gotta get her," Jack said.

She blinked. "Are you serious?"

"Yes," he said, army crawling over to where she lay, staring at the sky with wide-eyed shock. He slid his hands under her armpits and dragged her. She cried out in pain.

"Why do I let you talk me into these things?" Cam said, taking Anya by the feet. Together, they carried the injured demon out of the line of fire.

"So…is she going to recover?" Jack asked, as they placed her on the ground.

"I haven't the faintest. She's the first person I ever did this to," Cam replied.

Anya spat out profanities and kicked weakly at Cam. "You fucking bitch. I should rip your fucking face off."

"Yeah, I'd like to see you—" Anya's foot landed hard in Cam's stomach at the same time her fist hit Jack's cheek. The two humans fell backward as the demon rolled onto her belly, pushing herself up with her good hand.

"Anat, my love!" Bael called over the din. "Come, we must retreat!"

But she didn't go to him. Clutching her shoulder, her gaze danced from Bael to Jack and Cam, then the humans firing bullets, and finally the demons, who were making their hasty retreat with their leader. She lifted her hand, staring at the blood, and then put the sword on the holster at her back.

And then, she spun on her heel and darted away.

"Hey—wait!" Jack said, turning to run after her.

"Don't you dare!" Cam said, grabbing the back of his shirt. "You've been dragged to hell and back—*literally*—for this chick! If she wants to go, let the bitch go!"

"Cam, she's dying," Jack said, yanking his shirt out of her grip. "And you don't know the whole story, either."

And with that, he dashed off after her.

Cam's shrieks of disapproval were quickly lost amongst the demons' cries of pain. Jack kept his focus on Anya's retreating back. She'd recovered some of her demon speed, so by the time he left the park limits, she'd disappeared from view. But she'd left a trail of red blood on the sidewalk.

He followed her south from the park, away from the scenes of battle, down the empty streets of Atlanta. She walked a long way—longer than he thought to be a random staggering of an injured person. She had a destination in mind.

The trail ended down an alleyway, in front of an unlocked metal door. Slowly, Jack pushed it open and peered inside, hoping she hadn't recovered enough to behead him.

But she had collapsed on the floor, her heavy breathing echoing in the space. She turned her head with effort, her unfocused gaze landing on him. She was as pale as the first time he'd seen her, and she didn't even move away from him as he knelt beside her.

"What…are you doing here…?"

"You needed help," he said, feeling along the wall for a light. When his fingers made contact, and light flooded the room, he took a step back, in awe. The room itself wasn't too surprising— a small air mattress, a few boxes serving as makeshift tables, a Chinese takeout box. But the wall in front of him was completely covered in small black marks.

"What's with the marks?"

"My tally," she replied with a grunt. "I like to keep track of all the souls I need to repent for."

"Used to repent for," Jack replied casually. "The curse is broken, isn't it?"

She sighed. "Should be. Guess it was more than just the talisman. I don't feel any different." She laughed and then winced. "What the *hell* was on that bullet? It burns."

"Do you have a small knife around here?"

She nodded to a bag on the floor against the wall, where Jack found an assortment of weapons. He retrieved the knife as she pushed herself up to sit and pulled off her shirt. The wound had turned her skin an ashen gray, and was pulsing out blood. The bullet was visible, but only barely.

"This may hurt," he said.

"Just do it, human."

To her credit, she didn't scream, but Jack still worked quickly to locate the bullet in her shoulder and remove it. She released a loud sigh of relief when it fell from her body, and slumped forward.

"Tell your girlfriend she's got a future in killing demons," Anya replied dryly.

"Partner," Jack corrected, placing a towel against the wound. "And I will. Are you going back to Bael?"

She stared at the floor, taking the towel from him and holding it against her shoulder. "I should. Maybe I deserve to."

"For what?"

"Who the hell knows?" She stood carefully, wincing as her shoulder moved, but not as much as before. Her demon healing was already kicking in.

"Is that your plan then? Just hide until you die?"

"If I go back to Bael, he's going to—"

"He's going to what? Beat you again?"

"He's not always like that," she muttered, but even she must've known it was a lie. "He can be good when he wants to be."

"So why do you keep running from him?"

"Because I'm confused, all right?" she barked. "I've been tearing myself apart at the seams. All I used to know was humans were chattel and I could kill a hundred men without a care in the world. And now…even without the talisman, I can't shake the feeling that if I kill another human, it will be the end of me."

She sank onto her futon, the gleaming sword lying on the table in front of her.

"Maybe I should just ask you to end me now with Sharur. It's the sword that killed the noxes. I know it could end my life with a single swing." She swallowed. "I already left once. Bael won't let me leave again. He'll kill me or beat me or…" She glanced at the bejeweled sword on the table. "He'll make me use that sword to kill people. And I don't know if I can stomach that anymore." She hissed and removed the towel, her wound now clotted. "Maybe I don't deserve to live. Maybe the only freedom is in death."

"You deserve forgiveness."

"Do I?"

"Hasn't that been what you've been doing all this time?" he asked. "The reason for those ten thousand marks on your wall?"

"I was doing it for self-preservation."

"I don't believe that."

"You don't know me."

"I don't think anyone knows you," he said, standing beside her. "And I think that's the problem. To me, you're Anya. To Bael, you're Anat the Death Goddess. You're whoever anyone wants you to be. Maybe it's about time you started telling us who you are."

She stared out the open door. "What if I don't like the person I am?"

"Sounds like a lonely life, not liking oneself."

"Which is why you should just behead me."

"I'm not going to behead you, not when you…" Sirens had begun blaring in the distance. The Division was following the same blood trail he had. "You've spent the last hundred years trying to make up for three thousand years under the thumb of an abusive manipulator. That's the worst kind of torture imaginable, and it would be unfair of me to take your life when you haven't had a chance to live it."

She closed her eyes. "It's fair enough. There's no solace for me, no matter where I turn."

"What if we look for the woman who cursed you?" Jack said. "See what exactly this curse is, find out if she'll remove it. Ask her—"

"What, exactly? She's dead. Probably been dead for a century," Anya said. Her shoulders slumped. "It's hopeless. I should just kill myself."

"Look at me," Jack said, grabbing her chin. "Your life is worth saving. And nothing's hopeless. I've got the resources of the Division, I'm sure we can find her."

"As if the Division will let me inside," she scoffed. "Bael would find me and—"

The sirens moved closer. Now or never. "Come with me. We'll get out of here and figure the rest out later. You've been hiding from Bael for a hundred years. You know what to do."

She licked her lips. "But—"

"No buts. You're doing this."

"Jack, if you go with me, the Division will...and Bael would..."

"Let me worry about that," Jack said. "Forget the Division. You've got connections and I've got...well, I've got some money. We'll find this witch, uncurse you, and see...see where we stand on everything else."

The sirens were almost on top of them.

"Why are you helping me?"

"I couldn't save my Sara," Jack replied. "But I'm damn sure going to save you."

To be continued in

REVIVAL

DEMON SPRING
TRILOGY
Book Two

AUTHOR'S NOTE

This book is many things, but Anya's continuing struggle with Bael is one that I took great care depicting. As perverse and ridiculous as he is, Bael is not unlike some very real abusive men that have touched my family. The gaslighting, the love-bombing, the alternate reality creation—it's all part and parcel of the narcissist's playbook. In Anya, I wanted to tell the story of how someone entrenched so deeply in this cycle of abuse can break free. Sadly, her journey is one so often taken alone. But it doesn't have to be.

If you or someone you love is in trouble, know there's help. The National Domestic Abuse Hotline (1-800-799-7233) is available 24/7 to talk confidentially with anyone experiencing domestic violence. Please know that help is out there, and you don't have to suffer alone.

This book is one hundred percent a work of fiction, but I wanted this story to represent mythologies from every corner of the globe, and to thread commonalities I found in each one. My goal was to use ancient folklore, taking care not to appropriate or use any currently practiced religious symbols.

Bael is based loosely on the Ba'al cycle, an ancient Canaanite tale that was used to describe the winter and summer seasons. Much of the names and plot come from this specific tale, including belu, athtar, Anat, Mot, Zephon, and more. Ba'al himself pops up throughout human history, eventually morphing into Baelzebub, one of the seven princes of hell in Peter Binsfeld's classifications of demons written in the sixteenth century. In researching Bael, I came across the idea of assigning him and each of the belus a so-called "original sin," although I only used five instead of seven. Baelzebub was the prince of gluttony; for my purposes here, I opted to go with pride.

In the Ba'al cycle, Anat was his wife or sister, depending on the translation, but she was the goddess of war. Much of Anya's mythology is inspired by her exploits. Athtar demons are wholly made-up, although their name is derived from Ba'al's son in the mythology.

Lilin demons are named for the early Mesopotamian name for succubus, or night spirits that attacked men, and it also has a place in ancient Jewish mythology. Freyja is based on the Norse goddess of love, sex, beauty, fertility.

Eloko demons are derived from an Mongo-Nkundo tale about a dwarf-like creature that lived in the jungles of the Congo. The tales say they lure unsuspecting hunters deeper into the forest with their bells. Hunters would carry a talisman or amulet to ward off the magic, which was the basis for this idea of an anti-demon talisman. Biloko is the alternate term for the demon.

Kappas might be the most well-known of the demons. A Japanese myth, they were said to draw unsuspecting women and children to the water and drag them under. I kept pretty close to the myth, especially around the plate full of water that keeps the kappa alive. Mizuchi is an alternate term for the demon as well.

For the nox demons, which we will see more of in Revival, I wanted to use South and Central American myths, but there are many cultures that still regularly practice older traditions. Therefore, I went with a wholly new creature based on hellhounds, fire, and fear. Lord Mot, the belu nox, comes from the Ba'al cycle, and is the God of Death that Ba'al fights. In the original story, Mot kills Ba'al and Anat kills Mot in revenge.

In this story? You'll have to read to find out...

ACKNOWLEGMENTS

Thanks to my parents, who continue to show faith and support for my work and my crazy schemes, and for letting me crash at their house between home purchases.

Thank you to my cover revealers, for helping me get this baby launched: Chelsea, Emily, MC, Alice, Alice W, Christina, Anna, Pavitra, and Elle.

Thanks to my bevy of beta readers:

Chelsea, for being the first to give me indications that the book wasn't a garbage fire.

To Liz, for being harsh.

To Josh, for being thorough.

To Gee and Mel, for helping me come up with the right names and making sure Cam's Spanish was grammatically correct.

To Emily and MC, whose flailing gave me a much-needed ego boost.

To Kristin, for being there since the beginning.

To Lilivette, RaeAnne, and Emily L., for giving me a final check.

Thanks to Dani, my incredible line editor, who always takes my book from good to great.

Thanks to my typo checkers: Lisa, MC, Mom.

Thank you to the S. Usher Evans Street Team for helping me get this book off the ground:

Alice, Emily from Emily Reads Everything, Lisa, Chelsea, Elizabeth F., Amanda, Katrina M., Jessica Stanton, Becca Stillo, Allen W. Shepherd, Taylor W., Thailor, Lady Kristin, Jordan from Heart of a Book Blogger, Alex D., Desi the Dragon Queen, Jay, Grace from DragonCon, and Kristin White.

ALSO BY S. USHER EVANS

THE MADION WAR TRILOGY

He's a prince, she's a pilot, they're at war. But when they are marooned on a deserted island hundreds of miles from either nation, they must set aside their differences and work together if they want to survive.

The Madion War Trilogy is available in eBook, paperback, and hardcover. Download the first book, The Island, for free on all eBookstores.

Empath

Lauren Dailey is in break-up hell, but if you ask her she's doing just great. She hears a mysterious voice promising an easy escape from her problems and finds herself in a brand new world where she has the power to feel what others are feeling. Just one problem—there's a dragon in the mountains that happens to eat Empaths. And it might be the source of the mysterious voice tempting her deeper into her own darkness.

Empath is a stand-alone fantasy that is available now in eBook, paperback, and hardcover.

ALSO BY S. USHER EVANS

The Razia Series

Lyssa Peate is living a double life as a planet discovering scientist and a space pirate bounty hunter. Unfortunately, neither life is going very well. She's the least wanted pirate in the universe and her brand new scientist intern is spying on her. Things get worse when her intern is mistaken for her hostage by the Universal Police.

The Razia Series is a four-book space opera series and is available now for eBook, paperback, audiobook, and hardcover. Download the first book, Double Life, for free on all eBookstores.

The Lexie Carrigan Chronicles

Lexie Carrigan thought she was weird enough until her family drops a bomb on her—she's magical. Now the girl who's never made waves is blowing up her nightstand and no one seems to want to help her. That is, until a kind gentleman shows up with all the answers. But Lexie finds out being magical is the least weird thing about her.

Spells and Sorcery is the first book in the Lexie Carrigan Chronicles, and is available now in eBook, paperback, audiobook, and hardcover.

ABOUT THE AUTHOR

S. Usher Evans was born and raised in Pensacola, Florida. After a decade of fighting bureaucratic battles as an IT consultant in Washington, D.C., she suffered a massive quarter-life-crisis. She decided fighting dragons was more fun than writing policy, so she moved back to Pensacola to write books full-time. She currently resides with her husband and two dogs, Zoe and Mr. Biscuit, and frequently can be found plotting on the beach.

Find her on the internet:

www.susherevans.com

www.facebook.com/susherevans
www.twitter.com/susherevans
www.instagram.com/susherevans

www.ingramcontent.com/pod-product-compliance
Lightning Source LLC
Chambersburg PA
CBHW030531190726
48283CB00006B/1860